Can You See Me?

Ruth Gilligan is 21, from Blackrock, Co. Dublin, and has just finished her BA in Cambridge University where she spent three amazing years. Now she is heading stateside to Yale for a year, before returning to the UK for a Creative Writing masters in UEA. Apart from being a perpetual student, Ruth writes articles for numerous publications such as The Sunday Times Style Magazine, hangs out with her friends (both English and Irish) and shouts at rugby matches a lot. This is her third novel.

Also by Ruth Gilligan

Forget
Somewhere in Between

Ruth Gilligan

Can You See Me?

HODDER &
STOUGHTON

First published in Great Britain in 2009 by Hachette Ireland
An Hachette UK company

First published in paperback in 2010

1

A CIP catalogue record for this title is available from the British Library

ISBN 978 0 340 97670 8

Typeset in Plantin Light by Ellipsis Books Limited, Glasgow

Printed and bound by CPI Mackays, Chatham, Kent

Hodder & Stoughton policy is to use papers that are natural,
renewable and recyclable products and made from wood grown
in sustainable forests. The logging and manufacturing processes
are expected to conform to the environmental regulations
of the country of origin.

Hodder & Stoughton Ltd
338 Euston Road
London NW1 3BH

A division of Hachette UK

www.hodder.co.uk

To Baby Niamh, for coming into the world
&
To Alex, for coming into mine

PROLOGUE

I opened my eyes. The room spun as his broad frame loomed over me like a cage. This was wrong, very wrong. This wasn't me. There was a fine line between letting go and betraying who I was, and I was damned if some horny third year was going to make me cross it. Who the hell did he think he was?

But now I wonder – who the hell am I?

*

I am just a girl telling a story – just a girl who finished school, went to university and hoped to have the time of her life. But now life is very different. Because the girl who spread her wings, kissed Dublin goodbye and was welcomed into Cambridge with open arms, is a very different girl to the one who writes this story.

Let's call me Alice. Let's give me a mum and a dad and two brothers and lots of friends – let's create for me a world, and then watch how it crumbled – how in one night, everything changed; everything broke.

Because now it is time for me to look back and tell the story I've been dreading to tell. The story of how this Alice lost her wonderland.

Because only then can I hope to find it again.

I

'This is the final boarding call for flight FR206 to London Stansted. Could all remaining passengers please come forward to Gate D67 with their boarding cards ready and their passports open on the photograph page.'

I closed the history book I'd been trying to make sense of while I waited and got up off my seat. The reading was incredibly dense, with any word below three syllables coming as a welcome relief amidst pages and pages of intellectual gibberish. But while before last term, that would have terrified me, it was strangely satisfying to know that in only eight weeks' time, when term two was over, it would all make sense. I smiled as I acknowledged that wow, Cambridge really *was* turning me into a geek!

'Passport please,' the air hostess broke through my train of thought.

I snapped back to reality, handing her a picture of a very different Alice. Although the passport was only a year and a half old, it felt like it belonged to another lifetime. It was a photo of the Alice who was going to do Medicine in UCD, become a surgeon, marry her amazing boyfriend Paddy, buy a house in south County Dublin, have kids and it was all going to be perfect. So what went wrong? Or maybe, what went right? Suddenly it was sixth year, and I was being handed the prospectus for Oxford and Cambridge and being told to seriously consider it. And then I was being told that there was no problem with doing History as my under-graduate degree; with embracing my favourite subject for a few more years before thinking about direction and careers and looking into the overwhelming future. And now look at me.

'Sorry, do you mind if I sit in there?' I asked a bulging businessman who had claimed the aisle seat in an otherwise empty row.

'Oh no, of course, love. Be my guest,' he bumbled in a thick country accent, undoing his vastly extended seatbelt and standing up in a flurry of flustered generosity. I sat down next to the window and strapped myself in, staring out at the grey day. This tiny vista would be my last vision of Dublin; a postcard image of farewell, until the sky ate me up and spat me back out again, into London's arms.

'Would you like one?' the hassled man offered, thrusting a crumpled pack of Triple X mints towards me that looked as if they'd been sitting in his pinstriped pocket for years, sweating their life away.

'No, thank you,' I found myself replying, even though I knew I had nothing else to chew on, and my ears would be popping like crazy within minutes. It was always the strangest sensation, being somewhere up amongst the clouds, with your hearing all muffled and wrong – it was as if you'd taken a step back from the world and were just floating in some kind of unknown limbo – no man's air.

Soon the engine started, and my middle-aged companion

blessed himself, out of habit more than worry I assumed, as I did the same. It was always a gesture I associated with flying out of Ireland: leaving England, the only thing the aircraft's ignition signified was time for all the mobile phones to be switched off and the laptops to be folded up, temporarily. But then we would be cruising and the typing would begin again – business as usual – not a moment to lose. However, there was no way this man was going to un-bless himself once we'd found a steady altitude. No, he had placed his trust in God for the whole flight, not just the scary bits, as we climbed ever closer to Him, and left Dublin, my Dublin, behind.

*

Christmas was already starting to fade in my mind, the neon glow not nearly as dazzling as it had been only two weeks ago, as we sat in a flock around the tree, its flashing lights like a string of car indicators, warning us that it was about to turn every which way. My younger brothers, Nick and Oisín, were making their way through the humble cluster of gaudy boxes, their corners glinting with foil smiles beneath the pine's foliage which bristled like toothbrushes. Mum and Dad watched on, calmly observing the manic scene, the boys almost in a race to see who could tear open their gifts the fastest, limbs and paper flailing in all joyous directions. I wanted to tell them to slow down – that it was all going to be over quickly anyway, given the modest number of parcels there were to get through. That was why we always delayed present opening till now – till after mass and after brunch

– to create a suspense which the meagre pile itself could not. For these were merely token gestures from the relatives who couldn't bear to abide completely by Mum and Dad's 'give the money to charity instead' policy, not to mention the dotty old woman next door who believed that my parents' approach to Christmas presents made even Scrooge look like a festive fanatic in comparison.

'In my day, we only had a few shillings to spare, but we would never *ever* be deprived of Christmas presents – and you lot up there with your big car and your big house, and the poor little rascals not even getting as much as the soot off a piece of coal?'

But Dotty had obviously missed the point. For indeed, we did have a nice house and a nice car, and plenty of fuel in the fire, which is exactly why Mum and Dad had decided that this time of year was about thinking of those who didn't – those with only a few shillings to spare, or even less. So instead of buying us presents, they would whisk us off to the toy shop just before the 25th, allow us to purchase as much as we could for the designated amount, and then deliver it to the St Vincent de Paul Society to give to those whose smiles and appreciation could never rival ours. That was what Christmas was about, and there was nothing dotty about it in the slightest.

*

Mum devoted most of her time and effort to the Society, while Dad was a doctor, making them the ultimate selfless superhero couple – double-handedly saving the world. They were inspirational, that was for sure, but it didn't stop the pang of knowing that as soon as Nick and Oisín had demolished their tokens entire, Mum would be off to serve Christmas lunch to Dublin's needy, while I was promoted, yet again, to head turkey chef. But it was only a couple of hours – she'd be back in time for the actual spread itself, and at least it meant she always did the wash-up! She kissed us goodbye one by one as Dad and the boys set up a film in the front room, and I donned my apron for my domestic goddess duties. But as the door slammed shut behind her, a new sound met my ears – the sound that could only mean one thing.

'Ah feck,' Dad cursed – a rare occurrence – as he glanced at his pager.

I headed back in for an explanation, though well able by now to guess what was about to come.

'There's been a horrendous crash on the M50 and they need me to head in to the hospital. Ah Jesus, God love them – on Christmas Day and everything.'

I knew the last bit referred to the people in the crash, but I couldn't help feeling, as Dad apologised profusely, grabbing his coat and slamming the door – the sound once more of a parent's departure – that it was them I should feel sorry for; giving up everything to help those in need, on Christmas Day and everything. But my pity swiftly relocated itself onto the boys as they gazed up at me, slightly lost and confused as to what had just happened; a shadow of their former over-zealous selves.

Luckily, my coping mechanism was well evolved for such scenarios.

'Just give me two seconds to stuff the bird and I'll join you for *Shrek*, OK? You guys can decide which one,' I announced, mustering all the enthusiasm I possibly could, praying it was infectious.

Thankfully, the joy swiftly returned to their eyes, now twinkling just as brightly as the tree's garish display. The relief was immense, for as long as they were happy – and as long as I could fulfil my role – then the day was a success. I had been Head Girl in school, and I was Head Girl at home – the strong, reliable, organised one who would sort your problems and wipe your tears. And my tears? I guess they weren't wiped. I guess they just never fell in the first place. I guess I was just . . . I was Alice.

★

'Any drinks or snacks, Miss?' the air steward asked in a vaguely Eastern European accent.

'No, I'm fine thanks.'

Out the window, the sun shone brighter than ever, as if calling me out from the greyness I'd left behind; liquid happiness I wished I could drink right up – to drink away the past which lumped in my throat.

★

'Alice Chesterton, I won't take no for an answer!'

'Paddy, stop it, seriously!'

'No, Alice, I don't care who hears me, I want absolutely everyone in the world to know that I am falling for you and

I want you to make it official and say you'll be my girl-friend.'

Sixteen-year-old Paddy had clearly been watching too much TV. He had always had this warped idea of teenage romance courtesy of Hollywood. I couldn't figure it out – surely he was just ridiculous – surely he was just the hand-some guy in my year that was the star of all the school plays but could never quite separate himself from all the crazy things he did on stage. But there was something about it that I liked. He lived in a dream world a million miles away from bustling Dublin, from bustling reality. Yet now it seemed that he was asking me to be a part of that; to follow him into his wonderland where he would make me happy. To this day I still didn't know why, but I did – I followed him. And I never looked back.

Until now.

*

'Do you remember the day I asked you out?' Paddy remi-nisced. We were lying in his huge double bed after sex, and he was stroking my hair with his long, firm fingers, untan-gling the knots his caresses had created only moments before.

'How could I forget?' I smiled, though I felt slightly weary at the prospect of yet another retelling of the story. I had been there, for goodness' sake! I had been there and nearly two years on I remembered it all. Yet he still insisted on telling me about it again and again, especially whenever I felt sad.

9

'Well, I climbed up on the scaffolding round the back of school when everyone was going home. And I was so nervous I was going to get caught – couldn't imagine Mrs Warren reacting too well to—'

'Paddy!'

'What?'

'I know the damn story, OK?'

I could feel his hand in my hair fall limp, his ego crushed. But it had nothing to do with his ego. It barely had anything to do with him at all.

All term, every time I met a new person in Cambridge or chatted to a new guy and I'd reveal that I had a boyfriend back in Ireland, they would just laugh, or give me that knowing look that said, 'Yeah, like that'll last.' But I would just shake my head and say to myself, 'They can think what they like, but they don't know me and Paddy.'

But suddenly I didn't know me and Paddy.

Was it a craving to be single? Did I want to explore the great unknown that was Cambridge men? English men in general? That well-dressed, well-spoken, ambitious plethora of forbidden fruit? Or was it something else? So many of my friends in England had purposely broken up with their boyfriends before coming to uni, claiming that they wanted it to be a new phase in their lives in every way possible, and that holding on to a guy from their old world just wouldn't do. But I didn't see it like that; I didn't see myself creating a new life and leaving an old one behind. I just saw two lives – one for term time, and one for holidays. And sure, it was hard while I had been in Cambridge last term and Paddy had been back in Ireland, and we didn't get to see each other. But he promised he would visit next term, and flights were so cheap and . . .

'You're going to tell me this is over, aren't you?' he whispered in the darkness.

I felt more naked than ever. He could see even that which I couldn't. Yet somehow, despite everything, I knew he was right. The clock struck three.

*

'Alice Chesterton, I won't ask you again – will you be my girlfriend? Will you make me the happiest guy in Dublin, in Ireland, in the world?' Paddy repeated.

Everyone had stopped, staring up at him – Paddy O'Leary, crazy, love-drunk fool – as I stood below in complete shock. I was desperate for him to come down – I hated that he was causing such a scene. Which was weird, because I never really minded attention – I loved debating, I was on the student committee – I just took stuff like that in my stride. But this time it was him making the speech, and it all just felt so immature; so clichéd.

But maybe, for once, it was time to let down my defences. To let him in.

'I'll only go out with you if you get your attention-seeking ass down from there and shut the hell up!' I answered at last as I tried to hide my smile.

I looked away, staring at the crowds of onlooking students. It was early spring, and the days were still short, dusk already tiptoeing in. The old, weary trees tried to squeeze out their buds, lifting their arms as they pleaded to the weakening sun for more.

I looked up at him again, ready for him to dismount and press his warmth against me in a kiss that I knew would be like no other kiss we'd ever had. Still I shivered in the fading day as time froze. My heart thumped. Paddy's hand slipped from the scaffold.

And that's when we fell.

★

'Have you been planning to do this for a while?' Paddy asked, clearly unable to quite process the reality of what was happening. 'I mean, I thought things were going pretty well. Obviously you being away last term was hard, bloody hard if we're being honest, but we've had a whole month back together now, and another week until you fly back to England again . . . so why now? Why today?'

He paused, his questions hovering with intent.

'I mean, we had sex five minutes ago, for God's sake, Alice – it's not like you had a problem with me then. So what was that? My goodbye fuck?'

'Paddy, don't be so . . .'

'So what? So harsh? So hurtful? That's a bit rich coming from the girl who's about to break my heart.'

'Paddy, please!' I pleaded.

He rolled back to face me, obviously wanting to look into my eyes and find whatever it was that was leaving me; to cling onto it for dear life. But I just stared at the ceiling; stared at the cracks. I didn't even blink. I couldn't.

'Paddy,' I finally began. 'Paddy, the past two years have been amazing, they really have. And last term, yeah – it was hard, but I honestly believe that if we really put our minds to it, if we really wanted to, we could stay together for the whole of uni. The distance isn't the issue . . .' I faded off, closing my eyes, taking myself even further from him.

A clock ticked painfully loud, stabbing us both with every second.

'I just don't think I *want* it enough anymore. I don't think I want *us* . . . I don't think I need it.'

'But, Alice, you've never really *needed* . . .'

'No, Paddy, I know – I've never been a needy kind of person, but I can't tell you that I haven't needed you over the past couple of years – you were such an important part of my life – I mean, I was completely and utterly head over heels in love with you!'

I could feel him wince in pain.

'But what's the point in that now, eh?' he spat. 'What's the point in reminding me how much you felt for me just as you're about to tell me you fucking don't anymore?'

I kept my eyes slammed tight. Hearing hurt enough. But the silence didn't last.

'So what? You've just . . . fallen . . .' He took a deep breath. My heart stopped. I knew what he was about to ask.

'. . . fallen . . .'

I wanted to tell him not to say those hideous words. But how could I? How the hell could I?

'. . . fallen out of love with me?'

They sounded even crueller than I'd expected. There was nothing I could say. The darkness held me tight, sealing me

13

in. But there must have been a crack, for suddenly I felt a single tear break free from the corner of my scrunched-up lid, falling to the pillowcase below, a river that led me all the way away from him.

'Yes, Paddy, I'm afraid that's it. I think I've fallen out of love with you, and I hate myself for it . . . but there's nothing I can do. I really am sorry.'

The seconds ticked as before. But I knew in that moment that he would never forgive me.

★

'Well that was grand, wasn't it? Very smooth. Not like last time I flew – there was rain, turbulence – the whole lot. I suppose that was . . . oh God, are you all right?' my neighbouring passenger asked in shock, having just seen the tear rolling down my face.

'I'm fine, thank you. Yes, very pleasant flight. Enjoy London,' I replied, wiping the tear away and hoping that hadn't sounded quite as fake out loud as it did in my head. I undid my seatbelt and stared out the window at Stansted's tarmac, swallowing furiously for the lump in my throat to go away. I was not going to arrive in England like this. Alice Chesterton doesn't cry; Alice Chesterton will get off this plane and onto the train to Cambridge and enjoy her second term and everything will be fine. I took three deep breaths before standing up, grabbing my hand luggage from the overhead locker and heading to the exit, thanking the air hostess as I passed, matching her plastic smile. Stepping out into the afternoon nip of new air, I promised myself once more that I had done the right thing and that, most of all, everything was going to be OK. Better than OK. And I really did believe it.

I shut my eyes. Almost.

2

Arriving in Cambridge is like arriving in another world. You get there, and everything else feels a million miles away. And it may as well be. For when you're in Cambridge, the outside world doesn't seem to matter. You don't have time for it to matter – Cambridge time is Cambridge time, and has a different pace from reality. The architecture mirrors this; there is no barrier between the new and the old, the ancient and the modern, giving the place a timelessness beyond compare. Stunning Gothic building looms next to Topshop which flashes next to kebab shop which whiffs next to a cathedral which harks next to the marketplace which heckles next to yet another stunning Gothic building. It is a blur. And yet it makes sense.

Gaggles of tourists wandered in awe, lenses pointed and necks craned to gasp at the towering splendour. On the river, those who could bear the biting nip of Siberian January winds sat huddled together in the wooden punts as their tour guide for the day manoeuvred the metal pole, pushing them through Cambridge's waters, regaling the passengers with stories and legends of the university's past. The River Cam didn't forget, only remembered summer days, when traffic jams of punts filled bank to well-trimmed bank. And this summer would be no different; the weak sunshine promised that, lighting up the postcard scene.

Dragging my suitcases out of the taxi, I headed towards my college – the centre of my Cambridge life. I once tried to explain the college system to my Irish friends and the only thing I could come up with to help them understand was to fall back on that book we had all read and loved. 'It's sort of like the houses in *Harry Potter*.'

They looked confused. 'So like, you live there?' they asked.

'Yes.'

'And like, you eat there?'

'Yes.'

'And you play sport for them?'

'Yes.'

'And like, everyone there does History like you?'

'No! I told you – it's nothing to do with your subject. All the History students from all the colleges come together for lectures and stuff in the History Faculty.'

I had watched as understanding hovered just within reach, but there was no denying that the college system was difficult to comprehend; I had struggled with it when first applying to Cambridge. And for my friends who couldn't experience it first hand, it must have seemed rather arcane, eccentric even. For some, it would click. 'Ohhhhh right.'

And then some would admit, 'Sorry . . . I'm lost.'

But I suppose in reality, aren't we all?

*

Thankfully, my suitcases and I found our way to my college

– the one I'd chosen, and more importantly, the one that had chosen me. I'd picked it for its stunning location and even more stunning aesthetics. Even the road it was on abounded in aged beauty as I clipped along the cobbles of Trinity Street before bundling into the most important building in any of the colleges: the Porters' Lodge. The Porters – the immaculately dressed, inconceivably helpful men that seemed to have about a million jobs rolled into one. You'd lost your key? Go to the Porters. Mummy had sent you a package? Collect it from the Porters. You needed to know where the nearest dry cleaners was? Ask the Porters. They put my school receptionist to absolute shame, and I had always had a major soft spot for that chain-smoking mother hen, so it really was saying something!

However, once I'd got my key and stepped into the first courtyard of my college, school suddenly felt very far away. Even though I'd walked through this courtyard countless times last term, I'd forgotten just how perfect it was. The bare branches of trees obscured the view of sixteenth-century turrets and towers which loomed above me. Every brick throbbed with memories, aching under the weight of carrying each other for over six hundred years.

I lugged my suitcases to the third court, into staircase C and up the stairs, until finally I was back in my room – back where I belonged. The bed looked smaller than I remem-bered, as did the window, but the framed glimpse of bustling Cambridge still sent tingles through me as I set up my laptop and played U2 on iTunes and began to unpack. I put the few books that I could sneak into my baggage allowance on the rows of empty shelves. I unfolded my Irish flag and pinned it to the wall. The Emerald Isle really did feel very far away. I wondered if my brothers missed me yet. Was I greedy to want them to? I knew my younger brothers hated me leaving, but the thought that my departure might mean that Mum would step up to the plate more eased my guilt. That was how it should be. Everything in its right place, like the order now slowly emerging in my room.

'Knocky knock,' an English accent distracted me from the momentary twinge that creaked in my heart. I spun around. It was Millie.

'Oh my God, hi!' I shrieked, so happy to see her. She threw her arms around me and the waft of Coco Chanel enclosed us.

'When on earth did you get back? You should have called me straight away, you bitch! I literally have so much to tell you. Oh my God, you've lost weight! You look great!'

I smiled. Only Millie would notice something like that – the girl hadn't so much as uttered the word 'carb' since she hit puberty and was an absolute beanpole. But still, I was impressed that she could tell that I had lost the grand total of three pounds during the holidays, owing mainly to the fact that over the festive period I consumed only a tiny fraction of the alcohol that had blurred my first term. Not that I was a big drinker. I was the one who looked out for everyone else. Sure, I'd drink, and sure, I'd get tipsy, but never to excess. In fact, touch wood, I had still never been sick from alcohol. The Brits informed me repeatedly that there was no way they would let that record last until the end of first year. I smiled. But I wouldn't give in.

'I only just arrived about an hour ago,' I answered one of

Millie's many questions. 'Just wanted to unpack and all first, you know?'

'Darling, I still simply do not know how you manage to drag all your stuff on an airplane. What did you say the baggage allowance was?'

'Fifteen kilograms. But I went over by five this time.'

'That is ridiculous!' Millie shrieked. 'How embarrassed do I feel that Daddy's four by four was literally *packed* with my stuff. And I didn't even bring my bean bags this term.'

I laughed. Millie was a scream. She was the epitome of how I had envisaged posh, rich English girls to be, but without the bitchy side I had assumed came with the territory. Don't get me wrong, Millie could bitch for Cambridge, but at the same time she was good to me, and although we were from totally different worlds, somehow we seemed to click.

'Are the lads back yet?' I asked, turning my mind to the rest of our group.

'Yeah, a few of them are floating about. Oh my God, you should see Henry's panda eyes from skiing – he looks like a complete twat!'

'Did you guys speak much over the holidays?' I asked tentatively, knowing that things had ended on a fairly awkward note between Millie and Henry at the end of last term. She had spent the whole term missing her ex, Louis, who was at university in Durham, and insisting that she was not going to pull anyone since she was still focusing on adjusting to being single in the first place. Of course, this disappointed most of the men in our year, since her long brown hair and legs up to her armpits left them all pining after her. But then, on the last night of term, she had spent the night with Henry, leaving us all with a million questions on our lips.

'Yeah, we spoke a bit. I don't know, to be honest I spent most of the holidays stressing out about Louis. It all got a bit messy . . .' she trailed off.

'Messy?' I prompted.

'Well, we slept together a few times, which was like, obviously fantastic as ever, but I don't know, we're still broken up. I mean, we'd always promised we'd go to university single, and I still think that's the right call. It was just so difficult saying goodbye again, you know? Oh darling, look at me rambling on about my silly problems – how were things with *your* man? Was it lovely being together again? I still don't know how you managed to stay faithful last term – I'm so impressed.'

'We broke up last week,' I admitted calmly.

'*What*? Are you serious? Babe, why didn't you tell me?'

I didn't really know what to say. I mean, it wasn't exactly the sort of thing you say in a text. And although I could feel myself growing close to Millie after only one term, it wasn't as if we had rang each other over the holidays. I was too busy catching up with my Irish friends and giving them my undivided attention – and it seemed like she had been too busy having catch-up sex with her ex. There had been a bit of Facebook contact, a couple of texts, but nothing that warranted news of my break-up. I'd barely even admitted it to my friends back home. It was something I could deal with myself without bothering other people about it. I was fine.

'So, who dumped whom?' Millie asked, her sparkling eyes still stretched wide with surprise.

'I broke up with him,' I replied, refusing to use the 'd' word. 'I think it had just run its course, you know? It wasn't great though. He was so upset.'

'I'm not surprised. Babe, you're gorgeous! But you've done the right thing,' Millie assured me, 'plus, just think of all those boys who were drooling over you last term – they'll be forming a queue as soon as word gets out!'

I smiled at how simple it all was in Millie's mind – how within a few excited sentences she was already considering who my new man would be. And though I appreciated her compliment, I doubted it was true. In fact, I'd really liked how all the boys I was getting friendly with over here honestly didn't seem to have another agenda – they had just accepted the fact that I'd had a boyfriend, and never tried anything. Maybe I was naïve. But I wasn't planning on putting myself back out there any time soon.

'Irish! You're back!' a voice bellowed out from over my shoulder.

Spinning around, I saw Henry standing in my doorway, looking like a total muppet.

'Jeez, Henry, Millie told me your tan was a bit dodgy but if you're not careful they'll ship you off back to China and feed you bamboo for the rest of your days.'

'Ah, Irish, good to see your sense of humour hasn't left you while you were back in the colony. Must've been all those spuds you were guzzling.'

'Actually, she's lost weight,' Millie interrupted, obviously missing the point entirely, but Henry and I barely noticed, giving each other a big bear hug, delighted to be reunited. How I'd missed his Irish stereotypes!

The three of us sat down on my bed, swapping stories of Christmas festivities and catching up. Their voices sounded more English than I remembered as I watched them both, flirting freely with one another. It was weird, since we'd only spent eight weeks together, and had been almost six weeks apart, yet already I could feel things effortlessly sliding back into place.

'Hall hasn't started yet so Joey and I were talking about going to Nando's, if you ladies fancied it?' Henry said.

'Sounds awesome!' I replied, delighted with this suggestion for two reasons. Firstly, by 'Hall' Henry was referring to dinner our college provided every night, charged to our college bill whether we ate it or not. I didn't mind it too much, because wherever I'd been all day or however hard I'd been working, every night at seven I could go to the dining hall and see a sea of familiar faces, without fail. Plus, being served three courses every night was hardly something you'd turn your nose up at. Unless the food wasn't great. Which, sadly, ours wasn't. People were forever up in arms about the whole situation, as most other colleges reserved serving dinner in their banquet halls for special occasions, or just once a week. But for me, such slightly ridiculous traditions were what made Cambridge so special.

The second reason Henry's Nando's suggestion had really hit the spot was because Joey was going to be there. Joey was another one of our circle of friends and probably, though I would never admit it to anyone, my favourite of the bunch. He was from Newcastle, studied History just like me, and we had hit it off from day one, laughing and joking like we'd known one another forever. For while Henry was a bit of a ladies' man and a tad too cool for school, Joey was the most down to earth guy I'd ever met and we'd been like brother and sister all last term. Of course, as members of the opposite sex, on more than one occasion last term I'd been asked whether there was something more going on. But there wasn't. Obviously I'd been with Paddy back then, but even so – it wasn't like that – it was just simple. Simple and wonderful and blissfully uncomplicated.

'Right, well, I need to have a shower before we go anywhere,' Henry announced, bringing me back to the present.

'Don't forget to moisturise, yeah? Otherwise you'll be peeling like a leper!' I joked.

'And yet somehow I'd still look hot,' he replied in his typical Henry way, leaving the room with a swagger and promising to meet us at the Porters' Lodge in half an hour.

I waited a moment before turning to Millie, wondering what she'd say. She practically glowed in the late-afternoon light, eyes following his departure.

'Oh my God, he's just so cocky, isn't he?' she blurted as soon as he'd gone, her perfectly cut-glass English accent making 'cock' ring out in all its glory.

I allowed a tiny smile to cross my lips and hers soon followed suit.

'But oh my God, he's just so gorgeous!' she finally admitted, both of us bursting out laughing like the schoolgirls we once had been.

'So, you think something's going to happen again?' I asked.

'Happen? Darling, let's just say I took a little trip to Brazil yesterday, and I did *not* go through that agony for nothing, yeah?' she grinned, skipping out of my room with a wicked twinkle in her eye.

And just as quickly as it had become a hive of babbling voices, my room was silent once more, but now the stillness was charged with the sparkle of rekindled friendship. I was so relieved. Part of me had been apprehensive that after so long apart, it would be like starting from scratch with my English crew, but it was as if we'd never been separated. The worries had been all in my head. But maybe *this* was all in my head. My mum still loved to tease me about the imaginary friend I'd had when I was younger – I used to call her Florence, after Florence Nightingale. Turns out I had been enamoured with the concept of this lady with the lamp so much so that I converted her into my very own best friend, whom no one else could see. 'Alice and Florence – best friends!' I used to write as soon as I could. Then I went to school, and my teachers used to ask me who Florence was and I would indignantly reply 'not telling'. I never even told my school friends about her, because she was my best friend and my secret. My best secret.

And then one day she just went away. Mum always jokes that that was the day I officially grew up; she makes it sound as if I left Florence. But I didn't. She left me. She didn't even say goodbye; not really. And I'll never quite know why.

3

January sunlight splashed through the college as a new day awoke. My own awakening, however, was less pleasant, as a banging at my door and that clear-cut voice I was growing to love broke through my sleep.

'Bloody hell! I'm coming, I'm coming,' I mumbled, stumbling out of bed.

As expected, Millie was standing at my door, grinning from ear to ear as she began her tirade about how she and Henry had got together, how it had happened, how many times, what positions . . .

I listened, and smiled, happy that she was happy, but I couldn't deny feeling slightly uncomfortable with what Millie was telling me. Half asleep or totally awake, this was certainly not my area of expertise. One of the major differences I'd noticed since coming to England was the fact that they were all just so open about sex. I just couldn't imagine one of my friends from home telling me any of the juicy details about their one-night stand. In fact, I couldn't imagine one of my friends from home having a one-night stand in the first place. Maybe growing up in south Dublin and going to a Catholic school meant that we had been bubble-wrapped from the sinful outside would. We weren't prudes exactly, but we all had an ever-present fear of doing anything remotely slutty that would deviate from what everyone else was up to. We were sheep. Tight sheep at that.

But was England's approach superior? I wasn't sure it was. When I found out the Pill was free over here, and that the morning-after Pill could be obtained over the counter, I couldn't believe it. The consequences of sex were apparently no big deal. Likewise for the act itself. When I told my Cambridge friends that abortion was still illegal in Ireland, they nearly fell off their bar stools.

'Yeah, and divorce was only made legal in 1998,' I added as their mouths gaped wider.

'Jesus, and you complain when we take the piss out of you for being a load of primitive potato farmers?' Henry teased.

Of course, I laughed in response. But it still made me wonder – was it primitive for sex to be taboo? Surely there was something far more base about having one-night stands with everyone and anyone, as seemed to be the case with so many people over here. Although I couldn't generalise too much either, because there were plenty who didn't engage in that sort of thing. But no one blinked an eye at those who did. It was just to each their own. And yet it was everyone's business if they were interested; any detail; you just had to ask. Sex with an ex, sex with a friend – this was minor compared to some of the stories that had already graced my embarrassed ears since arriving in Cambridge. But who was I to judge? I was just here to listen and give advice – that was one thing for sure that didn't change between the two countries – I was still good old Alice, the rock amidst the madness.

'So, did you, er . . . did you use a condom?' I asked, finally coming up with something to say.

Millie's rant came to a screeching halt as she looked at me with a mixture of pity and hilarity, grinning lovingly.

'Well, did you?' I repeated.

Another pause, before Millie finally said, 'Alice Chesterton, you are officially the cutest person I know!'

'What?'

'You're such a sweetie.'

Just as I was about to protest, Millie finally answered my question, still smiling as she did.

'No, *Mum*, we didn't use a condom. But it's all right, I'm on the Pill. Anyway, I'm going to go have a shower,' she added, clambering off the bed and heading out of the room. 'And listen, I love you, thank you so so much for listening to my mad ramblings.'

And just like that, she was gone. I sighed. Millie didn't need to hear what I had to say. She knew about the risks. And I didn't want to sound like my bloody sex-ed teacher. It was her business, her mad ramblings. And they would never be mine.

*

I supposed I had had it lucky in the past, since Paddy and I had been each other's first. That said, I still made him wait until I was on the Pill, made him wear Extra Safe condoms, and even went down to my local chemist in Ranelagh and asked for their finest tube of spermicide. It was one of the most embarrassing things I ever had to do, but I was taking no chances. Eventually the spermicide was phased out, and then, much to my anxiety, the condoms, but Paddy drilled me with statistics about how safe the Pill was and against my better judgement, eventually, I conceded. But I wondered now, would I phase out my Pill too? I didn't need it – I wasn't having sex anymore, and had no intention to in the foreseeable future. Then again, what if I got bitten by the casual sex bug? I laughed – pigs would sooner fly. But then I stopped – this magical place made it feel like anything could happen. I decided I'd keep the Pill up for now, just to be sure. Just to be Alice.

4

'Benedic, Domine, nobis et donis tuis quae ex largitate tua sumus sumpturi; et concede ut, ab iis salubriter enutriti, tibi debitum obsequium praestare valeamus, per Jesum Christum dominum nostrum; mensae caelestis nos participes facias, Rex aeternae gloriae.'

'Amen.' The voices of two hundred students echoed through the hall once the Latin grace was completed.

We sat back down on the wooden benches which ran alongside the long wooden tables in this glorious wood-panelled room. We were in a forest of wooden pomp, the candles dancing menacingly, reminding us of the havoc they could wreak. I was in between Joey and Millie, opposite Henry, each of us wearing our long, navy gowns, making us look like a group of extras from a Harry Potter movie. The night ached through the stained-glass windows, while the beams far above were sure to be concealing an owl or two, if not a ghost or some spectre of the past. Faces from the past stared down on us in the form of the portraits of the great fellows of our college, the names you read in science books, names that were the answers to questions on *University Challenge*; true academic greats. At the top table sat the current fellows – men and women who had lived and taught here for most of their lives – paying very little attention to us, the students, the next generation of greats, or so we hoped. The wine was flowing, and soon the waiters arrived with our first course, the buzz of conversation dancing in every aged corner, adding a new layer of tradition and experience; our part of a great legacy.

I still couldn't believe that every night, this was how I ate. Growing up, I'd heard all the clichés about beans on toast and macaroni and cheese being the staple diet of a university student. But as the waiter placed my warm chicken salad in front of me on a plate engraved with my college crest, Heinz felt part of a different world. But this *was* a different world – even some of the other colleges in Cambridge laughed at our nightly formal proceedings, priding themselves on being more modern and progressive in their approach. But my college was old and proud of its traditions. And I was delighted to have chosen a college so intoxicated by the past – for if you are to take the plunge and leave Ireland for Cambridge, you may as well go all out. I remembered hearing a story about how a clock in one of the rooms in my college stopped working, but no one would allow it to be removed. The students complained so much that eventually something was done, and what can now be found is a new clock, fully functional, hanging beside that same old clock, which will never be removed. One tells the time, while the other tells of a time gone by, but which has never really left.

There was shouting from across the dining hall, where a chant of 'easy, easy' had broken out, and a boy was standing up, downing his drink with rapid pace. The whole hall was watching. The fellows looked horrified. The head waiter sprinted over to tell him off, but it was too late – the lad had finished his pint, his friends were cheering loudly, and his masculinity was well and truly affirmed. His name was Danny, a third year, head of the infamous Peacocks, the college's male drinking society. Such societies were found throughout Cambridge, another one of the strange traditions which dominated this place, whereby groups of guys and girls respectively made up drinking societies within their colleges, and then once a week went for dinner with a drinking society of the opposite sex for 'banter', 'good chat' and all those other terms associated with the practice.

Often last term, I had seen the Peacocks entertaining a female drinking society in our dining hall: they would sit boy-girl-boy-girl, everyone would drink a bottle of wine, and they would get very rowdy and continue on to the bar for some raucous drinking games before heading on to a nightclub for what can only have been absolute drunken carnage.

'I just think the whole thing feels a bit seedy, that's all,' Joey had once said. 'I mean, twelve guys getting twelve girls drunk on a weekly basis can only mean one thing.'

But I had spoken to some of the girls in the Robin Red Breasts – our college's female drinking society – and they just saw it as a way of meeting people from different colleges and extending their network of friends. It seemed harmless. And anyway, if I did ever get involved in something like that, it didn't matter what other people's agendas were – I knew what mine was, and that was what mattered.

By the looks of things, the Peacocks weren't on a swap with any girls tonight, just a few of the lads having a quiet dinner, which couldn't pass without some display of just what 'lash monkeys' they were.

'God, they're such wankers, aren't they?' I heard someone a few seats down from us grumble as she returned to her meal.

'But Danny is so unbelievably fit,' someone said defensively.

'Yeah, I know. But I think Robbie is the hottest,' Millie insisted.

'Which one's Robbie?' I asked.

'The one with brown hair sitting beside Danny. He's kind of quiet but a total dark horse if you ask me,' said Millie, her eyes twinkling with delight. 'Still, Danny does have the advantage of being a Blue's rugby player!'

Playing sport for the university made you what was known as a 'Blue', and ever since the rugby team had managed a narrow victory over Oxford back in December, their popularity with the ladies had sky-rocketed.

'Oh my God, you're such Bluetac,' Joey teased.

Millie's lips smirked and her eyebrows twitched; evidently, she relished such a title. Henry looked jealous. I looked down, ensuring that I didn't catch Joey's glistening eye and burst out laughing. The main course couldn't have arrived at a better time; the Mad Hatter's tea party raged on.

After dinner we headed down to the college bar for a drink. Our bar was very much an old man-style pub, especially compared to many other colleges' flashy, modern drinking holes. But I liked the dusty booths, the wooden floor, the back room's dodgy carpet that looked as if it hadn't felt the caress of a hoover in over a decade, its pattern very similar to something my granny had had in her living room, only here, the layers of cat hair were replaced by layers of beer spills.

We stayed for one drink and then headed back to our rooms, pausing en route to check our pigeon holes, where the Porters place any post or flyers you receive. A white envelope with an Irish stamp was scrunched up in mine, informing me of upcoming events organised by my school's Past Pupils' Union.

I stared at the school crest. Only this time last year – though it seemed much longer – I was coming up to my mock examinations and working like a maniac. By this point I'd been accepted into Cambridge, but I needed five As in my Leaving Cert to secure my place. But I hadn't told a soul. Because if my results didn't work out, I didn't want to admit to them that I had had an interview, was accepted and then fail to get those five As. My friends would then feel like UCD was my second choice – my disappointment would tell them just how much I had wanted to escape. And for me, the fact that I would have to admit that I had had such an incredible opportunity in my grasp but had just let it slip away – that would hurt most of all. Because I never failed. Failure meant being weak, and I was strong. Always.

*

'Guys, there's something I want to say,' I announced on the last night of our sixth year holiday – the holiday that celebrated our last few weeks of freedom before college. We all gathered, sweating in our Greek apartment, getting ready for one last evening of drunken madness. We were wearing little and drinking lots. They half tuned in as they continued to apply make-up to their already melting faces.

'No, guys, seriously. This is big.' My tone warned them I was sincere. 'Look, I know I should have said something before now, but I just want to say firstly that I've had such an amazing week with you guys, and such an amazing six years, and even longer with some of you.'

'Alice, what the feck are you on about?' my best friend Róisín asked, the build-up making her nervous. 'Are you about to come out? Because if you're about to tell me I spent my youth sharing baths with a bloody lesbian I will not be a happy bunny,' she joked.

'Guys, just . . . just remember I love you all to pieces, and I'll always be there for you no matter what. Nothing changes, OK?'

'Now you're scaring me,' Róisín said.

'OK,' I braced myself, dreading their reaction. This was it. 'Remember when I told you back in January that I didn't apply to Cambridge? Well, the thing is, I did. But I needed five As and I didn't know if I was going to get them so I didn't tell anyone, but now that we have our results, and I did, so—'

A door slammed, echoing through the stunned silence and causing my throbbing heart to jump. Róisín had left the room. I didn't know whether to go after her or to finish my sentence or to just accept that I had said enough. The seconds sweated by. I felt like a mother betraying her kids; I had made a choice, and I knew deep down they would never fully forgive me. Everything had changed. The holiday was over, and so too was a period of my life; of our lives together.

5

Before I knew it, term had started, and I was sitting opposite my Director of Studies, being told about what lectures
I should go to, who my 'supervisors' – tutors – were, and
the absolute mountains of work that I was going to have to
surmount this term.

Even though I had known Cambridge was going to be
tough, it had still been a major shock to the system when I'd
arrived back in October. All my Dublin friends were so excited
about first year – about making new friends, destroying their
livers and having a well-earned chill-out year after the hell
that was the Leaving Cert. Obviously Cambridge was going
to be different, but they wouldn't want to scare us away and
set us a ridiculous amount of work on the very first day, would
they? Oh yes, you'd better believe it – that's exactly what they
did. I'd never worked so hard in my entire life. And it looked
as if this term was going to be no different.

'Well, we already have our first two essays set,' Millie
complained that night in the bar after another formal three-
course meal.

'Millie, you do English – it's hardly a real subject now, is
it?' Henry teased, winking as he sauntered off to get a fresh
round.

'Oh, he's being so fucking hot and cold,' she growled as soon as he was out of earshot. 'I mean, one minute I think I'm totally in there, then the next he's holding me at arm's reach. God, I hate men!' she concluded, making it impossible for me not to grin at the obvious untruth.

'Well, that's not good news considering what I'm about to ask you,' a new voice suddenly interjected as a curvaceous brunette from third year sleeked up to us and surveyed us with piercing blue eyes

Her name was Tina and she was every inch the alpha female. I'd only spoken to her a couple of times whenever Millie was flirting with the third year guys, but I knew that many girls in college were totally terrified of her. Personally, I didn't see what was so scary about her – judging by her over-brimming confidence she could probably be a complete bitch, but since I didn't have any intention of doing anything to piss her off I didn't think it was very likely she was going to turn on me. Millie looked star struck, as if some Hollywood diva had just sauntered into our conversation, oozing glamour and prestige from every perfectly preened pore. And in Millie's eyes, Tina was as prestigious as one could be in a college environment – she had slept with all the hot guys, had rejected all the not-so-hot ones and, most importantly, was head of the Robin Red Breasts – the girls' drinking society.

'So are we hating all men, or just one in particular?' Tina asked, her tongue curling over each syllable like a purring cat.

I'd never seen Millie lost for words before. It was time to save her.

'Oh, Millie's just having a rant about Henry – no big deal!' I answered casually, giving my friend a chance to regain her composure.

'Henry, eh?' Tina mused. 'Yeah, I've had my eye on him all right. Good conquest, Millie.'

Millie's eyes lit up with joy. 'Thanks,' she finally managed, relishing this compliment.

I rolled my eyes – this was ridiculous.

'And I hear you broke up with your boyfriend, Alice. I'd say there'll be a lot of chaps in college delighted to hear that.'

How the hell did she know that? I'd only been back in the country for less than a week. So how . . . ? I smiled. This girl really was the gossip queen, you had to give her that.

'Well, you'll both have plenty of chances to meet new men next Wednesday – the Red Breasts are doing a swap with a society called the Stallions and I was wondering if you two would like to come along?' she asked.

Millie leapt up from her stool in a flurry of excitement. 'Oh my God, that would be so totally wicked. Thank you so so much, Tina. We'd absolutely love to!' she cooed.

I smiled politely, until suddenly I realised what Millie had said. 'We'? Had she really said 'we'?

'Wonderful. I'll send you guys an email, but just get your beauty sleep before Wednesday, yeah?

And with that, she tossed her glorious mane and trotted out of the bar, probably off to have sex with some gorgeous guy who happened to be a male model when not achieving that all-elusive first in all his exams.

But there was no need for me to be bitter. I should have

been flattered really. And excited – I was going to meet a whole new group of people on Wednesday, have a few drinks, have a savage night out with Millie – what more could I want? Subconsciously, I slapped myself on the wrist and told myself to drop the cynicism. Luckily, Millie's excitement was infectious.

'Oh my God, how fab is this? Shit – what the hell are we going to wear? Oh my God, I cannot wait to tell Henry – he is going to be so totally jealous. Wow, this is so bloody cool, darling. I mean, I sort of knew it was coming, but still – yay for us!'

And she was right – yay for us indeed! When I came to Cambridge my two main aims were to work as hard as possible and make as many friends as possible, and if this was a way of fulfilling the latter, then brilliant. Plus, maybe Tina wasn't totally wrong – maybe I would meet a new boy. It wasn't long since I'd ended things with Paddy, but already he felt part of a different lifetime, part of a different me. A Cambridge boy was just what I needed. Or at least, wanted. I didn't need anything, remember? Just me. Just Alice.

*

'Millie, you look like you're about to wet yourself with excite-ment, and I'm sitting all the way over here,' Danny, the gorgeous third year, called from across the bar.

Millie couldn't believe her luck – an offer to go out with the Red Breasts and a chance to talk to Danny Lennard all in one night – I could tell she was in heaven.

'Well, are you girls going to join us or what?' he continued.

I turned to look at Millie; she was already on her way. I followed her, noticing out of the corner of my eye the pressing gazes of Joey and Henry from the bar, clearly feeling mildly territorial as we sat down beside the big boys.

'We just got asked to go out with the Red Breasts,' Millie said to Danny, batting her eyelids.

'We all saw that coming!' Danny replied. 'But still, congrats.'

'Thanks!'

'And how are you today, Irish?' he asked brightly.

'Ah sure, grand as always, you know?' I replied, equalling his brightness, resolving my momentary bad mood.

'I hear you broke up with your boyfriend,' a blond guy whose name I couldn't remember suddenly piped up.

'How the hell does everyone know this?' I laughed, though genuinely a tad perplexed about the amount of people who seemed aware of the fact.

'You know there are no secrets in college, Irish. Plus we've all been waiting for this moment, you know,' Danny teased.

I smiled politely.

'Literally counting down the days,' he continued.

I stared at the ground, not quite knowing what to say.

'Yeah, we've even got a bet on to see who'll be the first to sleep with you.'

I could feel myself stiffen. I didn't like this.

'Turns out I'm odds on favourite,' Robbie, Millie's 'dark horse', added, leaning back in the booth, so cool he was practically farting icicles.

I definitely didn't like this. But I wasn't going to let it show.

'Oh, I don't know. Good little Irish Catholic girl like me?'

I joked, hoping to fob them off with some innocence that wasn't entirely an act.

However, the lads seemed more intrigued than put off by this.

'Whatever, Catholic or not, I could have you any way I wanted, Irish,' Robbie insisted with narrowed eyes, causing the rest of the Peacocks to high-five and wolf whistle. Millie laughed along with them, of course she did – she was flirting her ass off as only Millie knew how. But suddenly I didn't want to be there anymore. I wanted to be back with Joey and Henry, not feeling somehow humiliated by these lads. Was I being a prude? I didn't care. There was something in Robbie's gaze that made my spine tingle, a kiss of fear.

'What's wrong, Irish, cat got your tongue?' Robbie persisted, obviously aware of my discomfort. He nudged Danny. They were both grinning gruesomely, like a sinister Tweedledum and Tweedledee.

But I wasn't going to let them get to me. Why the hell should they? And more importantly, why the hell was I getting so riled? I didn't need to get sucked in by their banter; I just needed to relax – they didn't mean any harm. Why on earth was I taking it so seriously?

'Well, the cat certainly hasn't got your tongue, Robbie,' I began, relaxing with every word, 'because we all know you're not exactly the most successful when it comes to pussy!' I retorted, sending the rest of the boys into convulsions, loving the sight of their friend being outdone by a first year. It was petty, it wasn't me, but at least I'd got my own back.

'Now, if you'll excuse me lads, I'm fecking parched, and

I've a feeling your banter will all be a hell of a lot funnier when I get a G and T down my neck.'

And with that I made my way towards the bar, the third year boys suitably amused and impressed. I heaved a sigh of relief as I stood beside Henry and Joey. I really did need that drink after all.

6

Work-filled day blurred into work-filled day as we hit the ground sprinting. It was hard, harder than I'd remembered, and there was a part of me which knew that I could pass the next eight weeks, the whole term, immersing myself into the current of intellectual effort, never once pausing for breath, drowning slowly. But I didn't come to Cambridge just to work – I came here because every day on the way to lectures, walking through King's College, gazing up at that sublime chapel, I realised how lucky I really was, and no amount of assignments or library-bound days was going to make me regret that fact. Even the library, the University Library, was staggering in itself – that endless maze of shelves stacked with every book ever published – the dark corners of dusty floors made me wonder how many weeks, months, years it had been since someone else traced this very shelf. Upon request, the Rare Books Room fetched manuscripts from centuries gone by, trusting little old undergraduate me with authentic documents from history. I placed them on the cushions provided, armed only with paper and a pencil – no ink allowed in here – and stared with wonder upon the dot of every ancient i: a tiny speck from the past, now here for my present; a gift from time.

A buzz in my pocket shook me back to the now. It was a text from Róisín.

Oi, Alice – wher d feck hav u disappeared to? Bcomin so bored in Dublin have considerd joinin a convent jus 4 shits + giggles (+ comfy shoes). Need spiritual guidance asap. Wb, Ró xx

I sighed – I really had been a bit rubbish at staying in touch. But it was hard. I'd spent the last couple of weeks trying to settle back in and reconnect with my new friends. But my old friends didn't understand that. All they understood was, since I was the one who had gone, and they were all still in Dublin, it was up to me to be in touch as much as possible. But it was so hard to strike a balance – in the rare instance of having a spare hour, should I sit down and phone Róisín, or should I pop downstairs and have a cup of tea with Joey? For me, the latter was preferable, because I was in Cambridge and had to make the most of every Cambridge moment. But Dublin wasn't content to just let me disappear for eight weeks, and I supposed at the end of the day, I just had to take that as a compliment. So last term I had taken to sending weekly emails to all the girls and boys back home, to fill them in on my various goings-on and to ask all about their lives. In fact, I'd sat down to one the other day, trying to capture it all – the magic of the dusty library, my first drinking society swap . . .

And we sat boy-girl-boy-girl and we all had a bottle of wine each. And the guys beside me were really nice, but they got me pretty drunk. And everyone here has this rule where if you put a penny in someone's glass they have to like, down their drinks – apparently it's something to do with the Queen drowning or something ridiculous, and . . .

But I had stopped typing. It was no use. I just sounded silly. Or at least, it did – not just my first drinking society swap, but everything; Cambridge. Words didn't do it justice, didn't share the sparkle. And yet, over the Christmas holidays, Róisín had complained that the emails sparkled *too* much.

'They're just always . . . oh, I don't know, this is going to sound all wrong, but like . . . they're just so . . . so . . . so bloody happy, you know?'

'OK . . . and what's wrong with that?' I enquired, clearly missing the point.

'Because it just seems . . .' Róisín was struggling. I thought her nail was going to bleed she was going at it so viciously. 'It just seems like you went over there, and the minute you arrived, everything was just like, perfect and rosy and fan-fucking-tastic, and like, how do you think that made us feel?' she pleaded, her voice starting to crack as she finally lifted her head, locking me with welling eyes.

'Ah, Róisín, that's not fair. It's not that I didn't miss you guys . . .'

'Well, that's what it felt like,' she snapped, her sadness turning to anger.

'But pet, I'm hardly going to start moaning on about how I have so much work and how part of me wishes I could still go clubbing with you guys and how I barely have time to breathe, not to mind go shopping or call Paddy or any of the things I love to do,' I explained.

'But why not? Why don't you tell us those things?' Róisín demanded.

'Because I don't . . . you don't want to hear any of that stuff,' I pointed out.

The truth was that it was me who didn't want to hear it. I wasn't going to admit to myself that at times I had struggled; that at times I found it all bloody hard. No, instead, I had just convinced myself I could focus on the positives and then I would be fine. Why would I write home and tell them the pitfalls of my big adventure?

'Alice, you don't always have to be perfect.' Róisín's voice was much quieter. 'You're not Mary-bloody-Poppins, you know? You don't always have to be strong.'

I smiled. She was right – I didn't have to be perfect – I wasn't perfect; nobody was. But I did have to be strong. I had always been strong; Róisín knew that. And now I needed to be stronger than ever – and for the first time in my life, not strong for other people, not strong for my friends or my brothers, or anyone else – but strong for me. It seemed they had loved me being a rock while I was around, but now that Mary Poppins was elsewhere, they almost resented me for it, almost wished that I would break, to show that I needed them. But how could they wish that on me? I knew deep down they didn't; I knew Róisín just missed me and for that I was touched. But no touch would ever make me crack.

*

February was almost upon us, coaxing the world with the promise of springtime, despite the constant shudder which racked Cambridge's streets. And then, as if by magic, it snowed and the city became even more glorious. Vast expanses of untainted white covered the courtyards and lawns. As we were not allowed to tread on the grass, no footsteps, snowmen or sludgy snow angels marred the effervescent sheen. It was pure perfection.

I sent Joey a text.

OMG its feckin wel snowin! Lets go play! xx

Within minutes he was knocking on my door, dressed like he had just stepped from a GaP advert, grinning from ear to ear and jumping up and down like an excited puppy. I quickly threw on the warmest clothes I could find, grabbed my camera, and the two of us rushed, hand in hand, out into our winter wonderland.

My foot wasn't even out the door when a snowball hit me square in the face. Third-year Danny was seen giggling from across the courtyard.

'Wanker!' I shouted, ready to get my revenge, before another one hit me, this time from Joey. Now this was just bullying! Shrieks of laughter echoed off the looming towers as the gargoyles watched on, bemused, with their little snowy hats.

'Some of us are trying to get our beauty sleep,' my favourite cut-glass accent called out from a window above.

'And God knows you need it, Millie,' Joey jeered, launching a snowball up at her and surprisingly whacking her right in the chest, leaving her unimpressed, slamming the window shut and wrenching the curtains closed again.

It was a snowball fight like none I'd ever had – not out in my back garden with my brothers, where dollops of wet Irish snow slopped unconvincingly on Mum's attempt at potted plants, or up in the Wicklow Mountains, where sleighs and plastic bags whizzed their passengers along in all directions. No, this was far more picture perfect. At the end of the courtyard, the stone arch framed an image of the next court down, a threshold to another world. I wondered if it could possibly get any better than this, whether I'd ever see details again like the icicles that hung from the end of the stained-glass windows of our chapel, their different lengths creating a frozen xylophone, calling out for a cantata to be clinked on their glassy points, to play them while we could.

*

We played for what seemed like hours, until all the footpaths were completely clear, and all of us looked longingly at the smooth white of the forbidden grass – what a tease. However, it made for some great photographs, the sunlight glinting off every flaky inch. But my hands soon went blue. It was time for tea. We headed back to the heat inside, where minutes later I was being handed a giant mug of Earl Grey by my darling Joey, the warmth wafting my circulation back to life.

'I hope it stays,' Joey remarked, nodding towards the window where flake after silent flake drifted ever downwards. 'Still, at least the theme for the bop this Saturday is appropriate,' he added ironically.

'Bop' was the word given to the college discos held three times a term. It was a chance for everyone in the college, and no one else, to come together and get very drunk on shitty alcohol and listen to shitty music and have a savage night. This weekend's fancy dress theme was 'Surfing USA'. The thought of wearing a hula skirt in these conditions made me feel physically ill.

'So, will you be on the prowl at the bop then, Irish? Any men on the horizon?' he quizzed, sipping his brew.

I shook my head. 'It's still too soon after Paddy, you know. Plus there's no one I'm really interested in, to be honest,' I replied.

The latter was the truth. The former I said just for form. With every day I pondered how heartless I must be to be over Paddy so quickly, but I really was. I supposed what made it easier was that I hadn't heard from him since I'd come back to Cambridge. Which was strange, because I'd kind of assumed that he'd plague me with phone calls and texts and pleas to reconsider. But I supposed his pride wouldn't let him, and I admired him for that. Or maybe he realised that our relationship hadn't ended a few weeks ago, but months ago, as we slowly drifted apart in our separate worlds. It was sad, but that's the way things go, I supposed. And the fact that I didn't miss him spoke volumes. I really had moved on. And I loved where I was now – here in this snowy wonderland – and I supposed ultimately, that was what mattered.

*

'Oh my God, darling, I'm like, so excited. I mean, I know the bops are shit, but like, I just have a really good feeling about this one, you know?' Millie squealed as she ran a GHD through her glossy mane. 'Oh Ally, please please kiss someone – come on, it would be so much fun – why don't you kiss Joey? It doesn't have to be a big thing, just a stupid drunken mistake, and in the morning we can all laugh about it and no one will give a hoot!'

I smiled, wondering if she actually believed it was that easy.

'Do my armpits smell funny to you?' she continued, shoving one in my face.

I laughed – our couple of 'getting ready drinks' had gone straight to her head.

'No, you smell lovely, my dear. But shove your pit in my face again and you'll get a major smack.'

Millie giggled, placed the GHD down on the bed and headed back to the bottle of gin we were steadily making our way through. I turned the straighteners off, just in case.

'Thanks, *Mum*,' Millie remarked over her shoulder with a grin while pouring us both fairly hefty measures.

My tummy felt odd – almost like butterflies, but that didn't make sense. It must have been the strange terrine Hall had offered for dinner tonight, which Millie, of course, had refused to touch. That probably accounted for her level of tipsiness, despite the fact that it was only just gone ten o'clock. 'My stomach feels funny,' I told Millie. 'I haven't a clue why.'

'Neither do I, darling. But gin will sort you out,' she promised. 'It's medicinable, you know. Wait, is that a word?'

I chuckled, clinked glasses with her and took a large gulp

of the quenching bubbles, letting them dance in my mouth, pricking my tongue with stinging delight.

*

An hour later, and it was time to hit the bop. My head felt fuzzy and my tummy still resembled something of a butterfly sanctuary, but with the rest of the crew in the highest of spirits, I knew the evening was going to be a success. We headed to the last court of our college, where the Junior Common Room was located, the venue for all the bops. The minute we entered, I was hit by a wall of heat. The lighting was so low you could barely make out who anyone was, but the smattering of coloured beams from glow sticks made the anonymity all worthwhile, as people raved in time with the thumping beats.

'Drink?' Millie shouted in my ear.

We secured even more gin and then joined the sweaty masses on the dance floor, just as everyone's favourite nineties dance classic 'Set You Free' blared out from the faux DJ box. I closed my eyes for a moment, lost in the euphoric heave, my bare shoulders rubbing against the unfamiliar limbs of those who swayed beside me. Glow sticks beamed from all directions, leaving coloured trails behind them as they were thrust vigorously through the heaving mass. I was in fluorescent paradise. This felt so good.

'Oh sorry,' I was snapped back to reality as someone whacked into my drink.

They barely noticed; drunken muppet! But I did realise it was a bit stupid to try and shake my thing while clutching a plastic cup. I downed my drink in one, wincing as I swallowed and wondering if that had indeed been the best idea. Oh well. Back to dancing. Back to closing my eyes. Back to being happier and freer than ever. At home I never danced like this – I never let go. But right now I was on top of this brand-new world, where I could be me, and free, and in glow-stick paradise. I opened my eyes. Millie was gone. But suddenly Joey was there, limbs flailing like a maniac, spinning around. And now my head was spinning, the neon was blurring, lines crossing, burning, crossing . . .

'I need some water,' I shouted, and Joey nodded in response before taking my hand and leading me off the dance floor.

'Are you OK?' he asked.

'Yeah, I'm fine, don't worry. Just a bit hot.'

'Right, well you sit there and I'll get us some water.'

'Thank you, my dear.'

So down I sat, sweaty but happy, watching the drunken chaos which whirlpooled around the tropical room. There were people kissing, people grinding on the dance floor, even some of the Peacocks with a giant funnel, pouring beer down each other's throats. I squeezed my eyes shut and opened them again. I was drunk. But it didn't matter. Nothing did. I was alive.

'Don't kill me, but I got tequila!' Joey declared, breaking the moment with a wicked smile.

'So what are we toasting to?' I asked, ignoring the fact that I'd wanted water and instead got three shots of my least favourite liquor.

'To getting fucked!' Joey shouted.

I laughed, clinked glasses, and downed one. It burned.

'And the next one?' I asked, my face still scrunched up with distaste.

'To our shitty hangovers tomorrow!' Joey bellowed, louder than before.

I laughed even harder and downed even faster. I felt better already, though the tequila still tasted foul.

'Jesus, that stuff is minging!' I screeched. 'Come on, let's get the last one over with.'

'OK,' Joey agreed, though pausing a moment, his breath heavy. Suddenly something changed, and his tone became lower than I'd heard all night, more intimate, binding us together in our own world. 'Let us drink . . . to how amazingly gorgeous you look tonight,' he said, looking straight into my eyes. The butterflies were off again.

I didn't laugh this time, just clinked and drank, never once breaking his gaze. A million feelings were dancing through me all at once, but the tequila forbade me from putting my finger on any single one. But I didn't need to; amidst the confusion, one single thing was clear – I was happy. Punch drunk joy. It was time to dance again.

7

'A toast,' Paddy had announced last September, raising his glass of champagne to mine as we sat in the bar of the Shelbourne Hotel, 'to my stunning girlfriend.'

I blushed; he could be so cheesy. But I loved it.

'And to being in love,' he continued, 'and most importantly, to an amazing future together, no matter what.'

'I'll drink to that,' I replied.

We clinked our glasses together and sipped the sweet bubbles. I had seen how much these two drinks had cost, and when I had told Paddy that we could just as easily go to one of the pubs round the corner, he had insisted. 'Ally, you're off to Cambridge in three days, where they drink champagne instead of water. I'm just trying to introduce you to your new lifestyle,' he joked.

I had told him repeatedly that it wasn't going to be all fancy smancy, and even if it was, there was no need for him to try and compete with that – I loved him, not champagne! But this was just his way of dealing with it – to wine and dine me one last time, as if to prove that he, and Dublin, could be just as lavish and amazing as my new university.

'We'll be fine,' I reassured him countless times, 'I'll be

home in eight weeks for Christmas, and everything will be better than ever. Like I said, baby, if it's meant to be, it will be.'

'And we are,' he insisted.

'I know,' I replied. And I'm pretty sure I really did believe it at the time.

Turned out fate had other ideas.

*

'That was a fucking wicked bop!' Joey declared, stumbling out into the night with the rest of the tired but merry students once the final tune had been played.

'Back to mine for more vodka?' Henry offered.

'Hells yes!' Millie replied with drunken enthusiasm, the biting breeze drying out her matted chocolate locks. Though the snow had thawed, winter was not giving up just yet.

'Henners, did I hear you saying you were having a bit of an after party?' It was Danny, whose question came from out of the blue.

I could see Henry was in the horns of a dilemma – he wanted to impress the third years, most of all the head of the Peacocks, but this Peacock had an eye on *his* bird, so inviting him back slashed his chances with Millie quicker than you could say 'but I got there first'.

'There's only a few of us, don't be a twat,' Robbie said roughly.

I rolled my eyes. Maybe I'd just go to bed. But it was a shame to go home and end what had been such a brilliant night so soon.

'You're looking happy, Irish,' Danny remarked as we all wandered back towards the indoors. 'Good night, then?'

'Very much so,' I replied.

'Kiss any boys?' he asked, nudging my side.

''Fraid not, Danny. No boys for me.'

'Ah, Irish – you've got to put at least someone out of their misery!' he laughed. 'Otherwise I'm going to have to just take one for the team.'

I smirked – I liked Danny, he was cheeky, but he meant well. I think.

'Piss off, mate,' Robbie suddenly joined in, 'she's mine, remember?' he said, putting his arm around me.

I thought back to the comment he'd made in the bar that other day which had made me so uncomfortable, and my resulting dislike for him. But maybe I had just been too cynical. I couldn't deny it felt kind of nice to have this handsome, older boy draped protectively around my shoulders. I smiled to myself, the butterflies alive again, and the twinkling sky full of glow sticks of its own.

★

Henry's room was filled with welcome warmth as I plonked myself down on the ground beside Robbie, only to be handed a dubious concoction of brown liquid.

'It's vodka and Coke,' Henry informed me.

I frowned and smiled all at once, unsure as to whether this was a good idea. But the buzz of friendship kept me there as everyone's smiles and stories hung sweetly in the air.

'Is it possible to break a rib from like . . . like . . . dancing too hard?' Millie slurred as she slumped on Henry's bed, clutching her side with dramatic conviction.

'If you want to know about broken ribs, I think Danny's your man!' Robbie joked, winking at his best friend.

'Oi, fuck off!' Danny shouted back.

'What's that about then?' I asked, turning to face Robbie.

'Oh, nothing,' he lied unconvincingly, luring me in.

'Tell me!' I shrieked, hiccupping as I did so.

'Only if you finish that drink.'

'But I only just . . .'

'Fine, no story for you.'

'You're so mean,' I accused, slapping him on the arm.

Wait, was I flirting? This felt very strange.

'Down it,' he demanded, giving me no time to think.

Staring at the brown liquid, the tiny shred of sense that was left in me told me not to do it. But before I knew it, the cup was at my lips, and I was gulping down every vile drop.

'Good girl,' he commended. 'Well, to cut a long story short . . .'

'Mate, if you dare . . .' Danny protested.

'Ssh,' I hissed, trying to place my finger to my lips, but managing to poke myself in my left eye.

I poured myself another drink from a nearby bottle, trying to cover up my clumsiness, but Danny had seen. While he laughed, Robbie explained his comment. 'On New Year's Eve, Danny fucked a girl so hard that he broke her rib,' he said.

His final word came just as I was taking a sip and my shock made me explode with surprise, sending a spray of liquid all over his face. I was mortified.

'Oh my God, I'm so sorry.'

But luckily, Robbie was laughing. Which made me laugh. And then I realised the whole room had seen the whole thing and were pissing themselves laughing too. I was such a mess!

'Let me get you a towel,' I insisted, my maternal instinct kicking in despite everything.

'Alice, honestly – it's fine,' Robbie assured me.

'No, it's not fine,' I shushed.

'No, really – I'm fine. But that poor girl still has a broken rib,' he added, increasing the giggles once more.

'Danny, don't break my rib, OK?' a moan was just audible from where Millie lay.

'Don't worry, love, I wouldn't dream of it,' Danny soothed, though clearly delighted by the implications of the request.

I tried to see Henry's reaction, but I couldn't really see properly. Poor Henry. And Millie was totally pissed – she didn't know what she was doing. I knew she thought Danny was hot, but that was just silly. She should go to bed, I thought. I should put her to bed. That's my job. Right, Alice, up you get.

Standing up straight with such determination was a bad idea, and my head had no problem in letting me know this. But dizzy as feck or not, I was a woman with a mission. Stepping in between the various people who sat chatting on the floor, I somehow made my way, without falling, to where Millie lay.

'Millie,' I whispered, not wanting to draw attention to what I was doing, 'Millie-poo, wakey-uppy,' I tried, shaking her slightly.

'What,' she groaned. 'I'm fine.'

'Come on, beddy-time methinks.'

'No.'

'Millie, come on, I'll take you . . .'

'Ally, I'm fine. Honestly,' she slurred. 'I'm just sleepy.'

I sighed. She was being annoying.

'If you're sleepy you should go to bed. Come on, I'm going now too.'

'I'll be up in five minutes,' Millie pouted, wrinkling her brow.

'Alice, she'll be grand. I'll look after her,' Henry told me, having come over to see what was going on.

I looked at him, hoping that he didn't have another agenda. But he was my friend – why would I jump to such conclusions? And she was a big girl now, after all.

'OK, well, just take care of her, OK? No funny business.'

I wasn't trying to imply anything, I just wanted to make sure she was OK. And she would be. I should have known that. Oh, I was nattering. It was time for bed.

I bid the group farewell 'Night, guys.'

'Ah, Irish, you're not going to bed, are you?' Danny was displeased.

'I'm about to pass out! Enjoy the vodka,' I added, shuddering at the thought of even one more drop.

'Don't I even get a kiss after getting your spit all over my face?' Robbie asked.

'Good night!' I repeated, my head dancing faster and faster, commanding me to lie down.

I stumbled out of the room and up the stairs, the stone cold against my soles as I tripped and stumbled up the winding steps, my eyes sagging with pure exhaustion, the left still weeping from when I had drunkenly poked myself.

I tried to fit my key in the door. I jabbed and missed and jabbed and missed. The key etched the wood, engraving it with haphazard scratches. A memory struggled to surface – Paddy was there, and there was wood, and we were carving our names . . . Focus, Alice, focus. You're almost in your nice cosy bed. I shut my left eye, cutting off its blur, and willed my right to do the job. Finally, with a turn of my wrist, I fell straight into my room.

'Home sweet home,' I announced much louder than I'd meant to. 'Ssh,' I chided myself. I looked around. The light was brighter than I remembered as I squinted to focus. 'Water,' I gasped, like a man lost in a desert – a dry, alcoholic desert.

Grabbing the glass on my desk, I filled it to the brim from my sink and gulped down every last precious drop. It felt good. Very good. Three glasses later and finally I was starting to feel alive.

I undressed slowly, running over the events of the night in my head – it really had been a cracker. I wasn't sure when was the last time I'd got this drunk. Had I ever been this drunk? Usually I was the one who kept an eye out for everyone else. But tonight felt like for the very first time, I was allowed to be off duty, to just kick back, let loose, and go a bit wild. It felt good. And it was weird, because it wasn't like anyone ever asked me to stay sensible; it was just my natural instinct. So what was different tonight? Why had I let go?

I put on a T-shirt and my pale pink knickers dotted with roses, and began to remove the remains of my make-up that the sweat hadn't already melted away. Staring in the mirror, I looked hard at the girl before me – the woman. I was quite pretty, I supposed. Nothing extraordinary, but definitely pretty. I thought of what Joey had said earlier; there was no need for that to make things weird, he was just being a sweetheart like he always was. And I liked the compliment. And then when Robbie had had his arm around me – that was nice too. He was a bit of a twat, but very handsome all the same. And Danny was handsome. And Henry. And Joey – I had some very handsome friends. And they were good to me. I was drifting off to sleep as I tried to brush my teeth, the bristles grazing my lips, my hand jolting this way and that by my latest eruption of vodka hiccups.

Three more glasses of water later, a trip to the loo, and finally it was time to crawl between my sheets, close my weary lids and bask in slumber's embrace. I had so much work to do tomorrow . . . but it would be fine . . . I was almost asleep already . . . almost . . . almost . . .

Moments later, it seemed, I awoke with a start, as if from a hideous nightmare. But I hadn't been dreaming of anything, so why . . . ? That's when I realised my door was open and a shape was outlined in the doorway: Robbie.

'Sorry, I didn't mean to startle you,' he said. 'I didn't think you'd be asleep already.'

I sighed with relief, his familiar voice expelling all fears of crazy axe murderers that my groggy head had conjured.

'Downstairs was getting pretty dull. Do you mind if I come in?' he walked in without waiting for my answer and sat down at the foot of my bed. My mattress sagged under his weight. I noticed how tall he was, even when he was sitting down. All I wanted to do was go to sleep.

'Is Millie OK?' I asked. He was here now, so I supposed I would chat with him for five minutes, but no more. Definitely no more.

'Yeah, she's fine. Completely out for the count.'

'And is Danny still in Henry's room too?'

'Yeah.'

'Hmm,' I grumbled, hoping that some kind of stand-off wasn't going on, waiting to see who could be the one to put her to bed.

Robbie stared around at my walls, and on the back of his neck a single drop of sweat wound its way down the nape like a waxy river escaping from a candle's burn.

'Did you have a good night then?' Robbie inquired, pulling his right leg up under him as he turned to face me. He hadn't turned on the light, but I was thankful for it, not sure my eyes would have been able to cope. Besides, the moon provided ample glow for our conversation, my curtainless window letting her light glide in.

'Yeah, it was awesome, thanks. You?' I tried to be as cheery as possible, but exhaustion weighed heavy on me. My head started to spin again, the vodka still lurking, thinning my pulsing blood.

'Pretty wicked, yeah.' He paused, looking at me through the darkness. 'You looked so fucking fit, you know.'

My butterflies awakened now, and a shadow of tingles crept on my neck. The venom of his 'fucking' resounded through the silence. I hoped he wasn't going to try anything, because I really did just want to go to sleep. It was time for him to go.

'Listen, Robbie, I am literally knackered, so I think . . .'

'Why can't you just take the compliment?' he questioned loudly. 'Why can't you just accept that you're fucking hot, Alice, and that maybe I actually fancy you?' he bellowed.

My shoulders tensed, frozen in uncertainty.

'Sorry, I didn't mean to snap,' he apologised, his voice much softer again. 'It's just hard, you know, because I've liked you for ages now, and it seems like you're just not interested.'

He stared at the floor, looking sadder than I'd ever seen him. Maybe I'd misjudged him. Maybe he wasn't just a Peacock who just cared about getting laid and getting lashed. Maybe there was a sensitive side to him that people never got to see. And who was I to judge him?

'Robbie, I'm sorry. I guess I'm just still in a weird place after breaking up with my ex, and I'm not really ready to get with anyone yet, you know?' I said tentatively.

His eyes were still fixed downwards, and I could tell that he was finding this hard. The wind outside howled to the winter skies in shivering agony. I felt more awake than I had before, though still drunk. It was all very strange.

The silence stretched longer and longer. I wished that I could see Robbie properly. He was frowning, that was for sure, but once or twice I could have sworn the ghost of a smile tensed his lips. It must have just been a trick of the shadows.

'Look, I just wanted to tell you how I feel,' he finally spoke, shifting his position up the bed so that now he was only a couple of feet from the pillow. A stench of beer wafted forth with his movement. I winced. I didn't want him to be so close.

'I just think you're really amazing, you know?' he continued, staring into me.

Why was my heart throbbing at such a rapid pace? Perhaps it wasn't discomfort – perhaps what I was feeling was excitement. He was a very hot boy. A very hot third-year boy. And he was in my room, wanting me, and that was nice; a compliment if nothing else. But deep down I knew I didn't want him. I barely knew him. It really was time for him to leave.

'Look, Robbie. I think you're a really lovely guy too. And maybe in the future something will happen. But right now . . .'

But I couldn't finish my sentence, because suddenly his lips were on mine. I didn't know what to do. My head felt suddenly fuzzier than it had been all night and as much as I willed it to come clear and tell me what to do, I couldn't make it work. His tongue crept in, tasting distinctly of alcohol. What should I do? I didn't want to kiss him. I didn't know him that well and my chest was pounding and my mind was full of fuzz. I wondered was the moon watching now, or was she diverting her face from this shadowy kiss? I began to panic, but then again, I reasoned it was only a kiss. And he was a good kisser too. Maybe I should just enjoy it. Maybe I should just go with it for a minute and then send him on his merry way. Because we were both a bit merry, and it had been such a wonderful night, so why not have a cheeky kiss at the end of it? And this kiss really was nice.

My heart began to thud louder than ever. I took a deep breath and told my mind to stop. I began to melt, unable to believe how easily it did. And as the tension flowed out of my body, I realised that now he wasn't just kissing me, but I was kissing him too. Slowly and gently and sensually. His lips cushioned mine with such tenderness. Maybe it was right after all.

A minute later and we were still kissing, but something changed. Robbie placed his hands on my face, holding it firm as his tongue moved quicker and quicker. My intoxicated mind began to think again. It told me to stop, though its conviction was wavering: one second I wanted this to end, the next I was kissing back passionately, my hands clenched on his back, giving in for just that instant. I thought and thought and kissed and kissed and finally, drawing from something buried deep within me, made my lips stop, and pushed him away, my breath heavy from the intensity of it all.

Robbie looked at me, his eyes a mixture of confusion and desire, inhaling and exhaling as rapidly as I was. So what did I say? 'I want you to go'? Was that too harsh? How about 'I think it's best you left'? Agh! This was hard. But I had to say something. The tick of an unknown clock boomed through the twilight, pressuring me into action.

'Look, Robbie, I think . . .'

But it was too late; he was on me again, sucking me into him as I gave in and resisted in equal measure. I felt his position begin to change until I was fairly sure he was moving onto my bed. My body stiffened. He was on top of me, the duvet the only thing separating us as the kisses grew ever deeper. Right – now I really needed to work out how to say this. I didn't want to make things awkward – I'd probably see him tomorrow in the bar and I didn't want things to be weird between us. Suddenly I thought of Millie – God, she was going to be delighted when she heard about this – finally I would give her some gossip to squeal about and spread as she wished. I wondered how people would react. I wondered if Joey would be jealous. Stupid thought; he would be fine. Everyone else would just talk. But I didn't really like being talked about. So now I needed to stop making there be anything to talk about. Robbie needed to go. The last thing I wanted to do was give him the wrong impression as to where this was going, because this stopped at kissing. In fact, this had to stop now. I took a deep breath amidst our lip-locked embrace, certain now of what to do.

I almost jumped with shock as Robbie's right hand moved inside of my T-shirt, grazing upwards towards my breast, reaching it sooner than my mind could process, my whole body a blur of sensations. I loathed it and loved it all at the same time; wanting him not to be there but part of me hoping he'd get there before I could tell him to stop. And the minute his fingers were on my nipple, the tingles all surged to between my legs and just for a moment I was completely lost in desire.

That's when I opened my eyes. My room spun around me as Robbie's broad frame loomed over me like a cage. This was wrong, so very wrong. This wasn't me. There was a very fine line between letting go and betraying who I was, and I was damned if some horny third year was going to make me cross it. Who the hell did he think he was?

'Robbie, I think you need to go,' I announced when our mouths parted for the first time in what seemed like an age.

But they were reunited almost instantly, his kissing more

vigorous than ever, as if trying to erase the fact that I'd just spoken. But I wasn't giving up.

'Robbie, I'm serious,' I said, calmly but firmly. 'I'd like you to leave.'

But once again, he muffled my words with his caresses. My head spun. What the hell was going on? Why wouldn't he just listen to me?

But all sense was momentarily paused again as tension shot through every inch of my frame, alerted to the fact that his hand was now heading south. 'Robbie—'

'You know you want this, Irish,' he declared, kissing me again as I lay in disbelief.

His words echoed through my cloudy brain. I'd obviously given him the wrong impression – I mean, I'd let him put his arm around me after the bop, I'd flirted with him back in Henry's room, I'd let him come into my bedroom – maybe he wasn't doing anything wrong. I'd just misled him. Maybe he thought my complaints now were just me being coy – if he really did fancy me, then he must have convinced himself that my flirting earlier was a sign that I fancied him back. I'd given off the wrong signals. I'd told him that I wasn't over Paddy but that maybe in the future something would happen with us. This was the future. I was only doing what I'd said might happen. Shit. I was such an idiot.

I didn't want him to be here at all. But maybe if I just let him do this, he'd stop. I'd given the wrong signs, I'd made him think I wanted him to come up here and kiss me, and put his hand in my knickers, so maybe I should just let him, and then he'd go and this whole horrible thing would be over. His fingers played and I could feel that I was wet, furious with my body for making it out like I wanted this, like I was enjoying it. Because I wasn't. But soon it would be over. I didn't think I'd tell Millie about this bit – I'd tell her we kissed, but not that I'd let him do this. She didn't need to know; no one did. Very soon it would end and I could just pretend it hadn't happened. Why not?

As if answering my hopes, his fingers stopped moving, and my body sighed with relief. The kissing stopped too. I opened my eyes, ready to say goodbye. But I couldn't see Robbie's face. His T-shirt masked him from my view as he pulled it up over his head. He dropped it on the ground beside my bed, his perfectly toned chest now in view as he leaned forward and let his hand resume its position. I was scared. But I knew what I was doing; just a few more minutes and he'd go away. I was in control. I didn't want it, but it was only his hand in my knickers – it was only the sort of stuff fourteen-year-olds got up to in the corner of teenage discos – it was nothing really. Nothing at all.

Suddenly I thought of the last person I'd kissed; I thought of Paddy. They were very different kissers – Paddy always so timid and slow, feathering me with soft pecks and longer, more sensual smooches that sent my pulse racing. But Robbie was far too swift for my liking, almost biting me as his tongue took over every corner of my obedient mouth. Our lips were both dry, chafing against each other with uncomfortable repetition. Surely this was enough – surely he had to go now. I needed him to go.

For the second time, his hand left my vagina, and relief took over again. We were still kissing, but I knew that things were phasing out; my plan had worked. The silence calmed me down; things were coming to a close. But a new noise came to my ears. A clink, and then a zip. I froze tighter than ever, gasping inwardly, and fearing the worse.

'You liked that, eh?' Robbie growled, making me feel sick. 'Well, how will you like this?' he asked, taking out his penis, fully erect.

Every inch of me was paralysed. I wanted to scream but it was stuck in my throat.

'Touch it,' he said, his voice a whisper, but the distaste of each syllable still abundantly resonant.

'Robbie, I want you to go,' I replied, my voice cracking and shaking with complete terror.

Despite my body's rigidity, my left leg began to shake, twitching with fear, its thud almost as swift as my heaving pulse.

'Touch it,' he repeated, louder than before.

I didn't want people to hear – I couldn't bear for anyone to know what was going on.

'Robbie, keep your voice down.'

'Touch it!' he shouted, grabbing my right hand and placing it on his penis.

What if someone heard? I was so ashamed, but right now there were only two people who knew what was happening. I could hide my shame. But not if someone heard – not if someone knew. And what if he told people? I'd just deny it – I'd say that we kissed but that nothing else had gone on and whatever embellishments he had added were just bullshit to massage his ego. I just needed to do this and then he'd stop – he was horny and he wanted me to give him a hand job to satisfy him, and though the very idea was rank, if it would make him go away, then I had left myself with no choice.

I clasped him, and in turn, he clasped my hand, beginning to move it backwards and forwards over his penis. I could feel it throb beneath my fingers. Robbie began to groan, the sound more painful than anything all night. I felt like a whore.

'Oh, Irish, that feels so fucking good,' he groaned again, the words spitting on my crumbling soul.

Why was I doing this? Why on earth was I here, massaging the dick of some guy I didn't even like? I began to panic. But it was OK – I wasn't doing this – not really; he was the one moving my hand, he was the one in charge. But that scared me most of all: he was in control. My heart went into overdrive, beating like the wings of a frenzied bird, wanting release from this torturous cage.

Then the cage began to move as Robbie lifted himself up, so as to remove the duvet from in between us. Oh my God, what the hell was going on? Still I held his disgusting penis, but his hands were now pulling down my knickers and the lump in my throat swelled to agonising proportion. I wanted to scream. Why didn't I scream? Surely this wasn't actually happening. He wasn't going to . . . He removed my hand from its filthy position and pinned down my arms with surprising force. I've made him think I want this. I don't want this. Well unless you say something, Alice, you're going to fucking do it.

'Robbie, don't,' I commanded, suddenly realising that it was almost too late.

He didn't reply, only leered over me like a heaving beast.

'Robbie, I'm serious, you have to stop,' I repeated, louder than before. But I didn't care who heard now. Because it was either that, or something far worse, something that didn't even bear imagining.

But in the blink of a terrified eye, I didn't have to imagine – because with one thrust, he was inside me, my disloyal body helping him glide right in as disbelief gnawed at my insides.

'No,' I gasped, my eyes starting to well up. This wasn't happening.

But he penetrated even further.

'No,' I said once more, my voice breathy and thin, hollow like my soul.

'You like that?'

'Robbie, stop,' I begged, wanting to shout it out but unable.

'I told you I would have you,' he snarled.

I felt physically sick. His eyes burned through the darkness and a hideous grin ripped across his face. The Cheshire Cat, that foul smile glowing out through the choking shadows. He thrust harder and deeper, hurting me in every way imaginable, stabbing me. The momentum built. It was fast and sore and I couldn't believe it – this couldn't be real. Panic consumed me. I had to do something. If I end it now it hasn't really happened – we haven't really had sex. The last word made me retch. I had to break free. I broke my arms and pressed them against his bare chest, feeling his hair and his sweat beneath my quivering palms.

'Stop it,' I tried.

'Shut the fuck up!' he bellowed, shocking me to my core. I was like a tiny child, more vulnerable than ever. And I was never vulnerable. Never. But here I was, lying in a heap, my eyes stinging with tears as Robbie fucked me with all his strength, breaking me slowly.

'I told you I'd have you, Irish,' he repeated.

I closed my eyes tighter than ever. This wasn't happening. It was a dream, a drunken dream. The very worst of nightmares. There was no way this was real. I was Alice Chesterton, I was on my big adventure in Cambridge and loving every minute. Loving my life.

'I told you I'd have your tight little Catholic pussy.'

I wanted Paddy. I needed Paddy. Where was he? What was he doing now? Now, as I was lying here, failing my adventure, becoming a disgrace.

Harder and harder Robbie pounded.

And why had I thought of him tonight? Amidst all the madness, why had I been sucked into thinking about the past?

Deeper and deeper, he made me ache within.

I hope Millie's OK. I hope she didn't do anything she regretted tonight. I hope the boys looked after her.

My thighs hurt with every angry thrust. My eyes were tightly closed, not wanting to look on his disgusting face. Each tear burned as it trailed down my skin. 'I'm going to come. I'm going to fucking come,' he growled.

I bit my lip. This couldn't be. His breathing quickened and quickened and I bit harder and harder to stifle the wailing that wanted to escape. It wasn't real. It wasn't fucking real.

It was over just as the blood poured from my lip, my teeth breaking the skin. The hot blood oozed out until it met my tongue, neither nice nor foul to taste. But the moment was fouler than anything ever could be. Everything was tainted.

I kept my eyes sealed closed as Robbie pulled out, leaving me, but leaving his mark forever. I heard him zip up his trousers, put on his T-shirt and leave the room. He didn't utter a word. I lay there, my heart ripping through my chest with every manic breath, his come on me, in me, my blood and his semen flowing out of me.

I couldn't open my eyes. I couldn't bear to look reality in the face, and for it to judge me, confirming what I suspected had just happened. I knew the moon would be staring in through the window, having witnessed all that had taken place; how my soul had been taken, and in its place, nothing. No, instead I kept my eyes shut. And eventually, the tears stopped. Everything stopped. But time kept moving, offering no respite.

I didn't know what hour it was or how long it had been since he left. But eventually, being the hideous person I was, I fell asleep. I actually somehow fell asleep. And somehow, that was the most disgusting thing of all.

8

I opened my Facebook profile and chuckled at my status: Paddy is Jagered beyond belief. I set it the other morning after a heavy night on the town with my college boys. What a session that had been, although far too many Jager bombs! I had come online to see if Benjy had put up the photos yet, as I was very excited to see the shot of me with some random girl on my shoulders outside the club on Harcourt Street. But before I did that, I spotted the following notice on my profile: Alice Chesterton has been tagged in three new photos. I wondered whether to investigate – was she smiling? Had she had a haircut? Were there boys in the photos with her? Did she look like a girl who only recently had split up with her boyfriend? Or did she look as if she never cast as much as a thought to that shadow of her past – that fool on the scaffolding, that toast to forever – those echoes of nothing?

I sighed. It had only been a month. I was starting to get over Alice. I sighed again, this time with a wry smile – how could I say I was over her when some stupid Facebook notice sent my heart racing? Maybe I should text her – see how she is. The lads had made me delete her number from my phone, knowing that if I still had it I would use and abuse it more than my pride would care to admit. But I was sure I could get my hands on it. Or I could send her a Facebook message . . . But sending her a message just felt wrong – to use something so ephemeral to get in touch with someone who meant so very much – my Alice.

I stared out the window. Dublin in February looked as gloomy as I felt, pathetic fallacy and all that. I was King Lear in the storm, I was . . . oh, I was feeling sorry for myself and I had to stop. I was getting stronger, remember? But maybe I would get in touch with her just to see how she was getting on. Not that I doubted she was having anything but the time of her life. I knew Cambridge was intense, but I also knew that Alice could cope. And not just cope, but conquer it all with flying colours and high spirits and love it all and grow and flourish and wow everyone with her strength and her beauty and everything that was so amazing about her.

My throat tightened. I was still weak. I was still hurting. And what was worst of all, I was still in love. I wouldn't message her today; it was too soon to get in touch. I would wait. Until then, I just prayed that, whatever she was doing, she was happy. That was all that mattered. As for me, the storm would soon pass. I had to believe that. Otherwise, I had nothing.

*

I awoke with a start, as if from a hideous nightmare. Then I remembered that it had been no nightmare, it really had happened. My eyes stung, my head pounded and I dared not move – dared not admit that I was really awake. For if I was awake, then it was tomorrow, and I would have to think about last night. And I didn't want to think.

The pale sunlight gushed in, engulfing my aching body. I glanced at my watch – nine o'clock. In the distance, bells were ringing. It was Sunday. I should go to mass. I had kept meaning to find a Catholic church since I came to Cambridge, but hadn't got around to it. Maybe today was the day. I would find it today because then today would be the day I found the Catholic church, and not the day after . . .

I realised I was going to be sick. I jumped out of bed, but knew I couldn't make it out to the toilet in time, so instead bee-lined for my sink, reaching it just in time as the tidal wave of nausea left my body. It tasted of tequila, and worse. I tried unsuccessfully to wash it down the plughole, and my stomach lurched again. I'd clear it up later. My eyes caught myself in the mirror, but instantly I turned away. I wasn't ready to look. Not now. Not for a long time.

So there I stood, in the middle of my room, in the soft light of a February morning, every inch of me throbbing, smelling, reeking of filth. I needed a shower; I needed to be clean. I gathered my things and went down the corridor to our communal bathroom, relieved that it was vacant, and relieved that no one seemed to be up yet; everyone would be nursing their heads from the night before.

My bladder about to burst, I headed straight for the loo. My pee lasted so long, all the water before bed eager to escape. As I went to wipe, I looked down, and there it was – his come was dripping out of me. My eyes welled up and I snapped them shut. I would not cry. I took a deep breath, holding it in, scrunching my eyelids together tightly: I would not fucking cry.

It was a minute before I opened my eyes again, but thankfully I had managed to convince my tears not to fall; I had won. This time. I went to wipe again, ridding myself of every last trace of him. He had to go. He had to leave and go away and never come back, never fucking come back. I flushed. Then I flushed again, sending every last drop as far away as possible. If only I could do the same to him. But that was up to me; it was up to me to cast him out. I could do that. I was Alice; I was strong; that was my thing. I blew out and shook my head and flapped my hands, banishing him from me.

And now I had to burn him away. I jumped in the shower and made the water as hot as I could bear, welcoming the scalding of my naked skin, the steam hiding me from the world. I shampooed, and then conditioned, scrubbing my scalp viciously. Next I rubbed my body with exfoliator, scratching my pores, every inch of me. Every bit that he'd touched, every broken bit— oh, shut up, Alice, just wash; just scrub it away, just get clean. My aching head was furious that I hadn't drank some water yet, so I set the tap to cold, tilted my head back and opened my mouth, drinking in the icy reward. Then I shampooed again, conditioned and exfoliated again, all under the icy cascade, which made my brain start to numb. Maybe it would freeze; maybe it would stop functioning altogether. If it didn't, I would have to make it; I couldn't let myself think.

I began to shiver – it was time to get out, time to step out of this bathroom. I will go and get dressed, change my bed linen, clean the sick out of my sink and tidy my room, I told myself, and then I will find a Catholic church and go to mass and pray and it will be fine. Really it will. It has to be.

It fucking has to be.

An hour later and my room was spotless. My bed was changed, the old linen down in the wash room, though I doubted I would ever collect it. Wait; why wouldn't I? They were only sheets. They meant nothing. I was fine. I had put on my clothes and done my make-up, and I was looking nice. There were bags under my eyes, but of course there were – I was hungover – nothing more than that – just the usual baggage, just another Sunday. I was just . . . the alarm went off on my watch. It was half ten. A wave of nausea came over me again; it was time to take my Pill. I went to the cabinet above my sink and took it out, staring at the tiny white capsule above the word 'Sun'. Yes, I was right on track – never missed a Pill – far too reliable for that. But today was different. It made me sick that this tiny dot that I had started to take so that I could make love to my boyfriend, to the love of my life so far, was now going to prevent me from getting pregnant by the guy who . . .

I took the Pill, swallowing fast, refusing to let my thoughts complete themselves. I looked at the packet in my hand. I didn't deserve this – I didn't deserve this get out of jail card – I deserved to suffer everything that came with what I'd let happen, everything that . . . oh, Alice, shut up. Shut up shut up shut up. You're fine. It's all fine. Nothing happened. Just shut the fuck up. I winced; those words, those very words had been uttered not so long ago. Oh, so you're going to flinch at every phrase that vaguely echoes what he said? Well, that's really logical of you; talk about being a drama queen. Fucking hell.

I wanted to scream. My mind was warring with itself and I couldn't take it. I grabbed my coat and my woolly hat and slammed the door behind me, leaving both my Irish and English mobiles in the room; I couldn't bear to hear from anyone. I didn't want to hear about who Millie had pulled last night and how bad Joey's hangover was, or to get a text from Róisín asking me was a free for a 'bitch + gossip', as she so eloquently put it. Because I wasn't free, quite the opposite.

I had to get out. But he could be anywhere. I could step out of my staircase, into the courtyard, and he could be standing right there. Then you just walk by, my sensible side commanded. Yes; I would just walk on by. No big deal. None of it was a big deal. None of what – nothing had happened, remember? Taking a deep breath, I blinked into the daylight, fresh air drowning my lungs as I walked as quickly as I could through court after court, head down as low as physically possible, until finally I was out of my college, on to Trinity Street, and heading towards anything, anything but here, anything but him.

The tourists were already out, ooh-ing and ah-ing at every inch of my wonderland, cameras clicking and smiles beaming. I kept my head down, not wanting to see them – not wanting them to see me. Would they take a photo and go home and look at their pic of this tower and this college and this cathedral, and this girl who the night before was . . . *shut up*! I couldn't take it. Why did my mind keep saying these fucking things? *I was fine*. I needed to calm down. Maybe I needed a drink. Ha! No, I didn't need anything. I was fine. Perfectly fine. Not perfect; nobody is. But fine.

I was in too much of a rush to look for a Catholic church – I would have to ask someone, and I didn't want to speak. The noise in my head was enough to deal with without actual words as well. So instead I walked, past King's College, and then St Catherine's, and then Peterhouse, eyes downcast. After the Fitzwilliam Museum's overpowering whiteness, I turned right towards the river, crossing the bridge and marching ever onwards as the minutes boomed by.

Eventually tourists were replaced by locals, walking their dogs through the rough grass that felt so alien compared to the manicured lawns that usually surrounded me. This wasn't the Cambridge of postcards, this was somewhere else entirely. One figure in a pale green fleece crouched to the ground, wrapping a plastic bag around his pooch's business. His fingers shook, though I couldn't tell if it was from the biting air or his age. The dog's tongue lolled nonchalantly, wondering what was the hold-up. Neither noticed me pass. My footsteps flattened the blades with menacing satisfaction, leaving a trail through the unchartered territory. I was practically running, I was walking so fast, the crisp air clawing my cheeks. Nature could claw all she liked; I didn't mind. It would do my mind good. Clear me out. Scratch me clean.

Soon I began to run out of breath, the dampness in the air translating into my sweat, pulsing beneath my many layers. I walked underneath some trees, black and naked, the other side of which was an old wooden bench, sitting there as if it had been waiting for me all this time. I plonked myself down, removing my hat and undoing my coat, shaking my hair loose to the stinging air. I heaved up my chest and let it drop once more, steadying my pulse, calming myself down. I felt better already. I felt somewhere else. No one was around; I was alone.

Except for me.

*

An hour later, I still sat. I sat still. Thinking of nothing, nothing at all.

*

Another hour. I had work to do. But maybe I would sit just a little longer. Just a little longer.

*

One more hour of nothing, just staring at the world around, no thinking allowed. Just the quiet of nothingness. A while ago a couple strolled past with their black Labrador, sweet little thing, full of energy. My energy had left me, but I didn't care – I had an essay due in on Tuesday and I wanted to make a start on it. It would keep my mind busy. Not that it was occupied. No thinking allowed, remember? And certainly no thinking aloud – just the quiet of nothingness.

*

Half an hour later and somehow I was still there. This was stupid. I had to go. I stood up to leave, but just then a figure emerged from amidst the black, naked trees. I stopped to watch her, to see where she was going. But she was coming here, to my bench, sitting down next to where I stood, her black hair tied up into a neat bun, her white raincoat glowing in the afternoon's weak attempt at shine. I put on my hat and buttoned up my coat, slowly and precisely. But suddenly I didn't want to go. Something was keeping me here.

Neither of us spoke. I had to make a decision – either say something or leave, because standing here, hovering, prob-ably made me look like a complete weirdo. But what could I say? I hadn't uttered a single word all day, not out loud, and anyway, how could I just start chatting to someone I didn't even . . .

'I'm Flo.' The girl spoke, turning to face me so that for the first time I could inspect her pale, narrow face. Her green eyes were friendlier than they should have been for a stranger, yet the tiny hand she held out to greet me looked like that of an old woman for all the lines that etched across its slender frame.

My mind moved once more back to Paddy and that last day of school when, amidst the water bombs and photo-graphs and signing one another's shirts, he and I had decided to sign something else. We went round to the side of the building, the new part, beside which picnic benches stood in ranks, all in a row like the pretty maids they weren't. This was where the scaffolding had been. This was where he had asked me out. This was where we had fallen. He took out his locker key and began to scratch a 'P' first and then an 'A', and then a line resembling a heart surrounding the two. It wasn't perfect, but nothing was, and yet back then I had brimmed with joy to know that in years to come, fresh faces would sit on that bench and look down at the faded scrawl and wonder who we were. But the scrawl wasn't the only thing to have faded, and less than a year later the wood told only a memory, not a truth.

'Oh, erm . . . I'm Alice,' I garbled, snapping back to my stranger.

'Oh, Alice,' she repeated, knowingly.

This was very strange.

'Miserable day, isn't it?' I pointed out.

What a banal thing to say. I was even boring myself.

'Hmm,' Flo agreed.

Silence once more. I really had to go. This was just awkward.

'So what brings you here today then, Alice?' she asked suddenly, eyes fixed on me once more, keeping me in place.

I considered her words. What a strange question to ask – surely loads of people came and sat on this bench of a Sunday; there didn't need to be a reason. How did she know I had a reason?

'Rough night last night,' I paraphrased, making sure I gave nothing away. But her gaze saw right through me, making me feel uncomfortable, like she could see everything, see the truth.

'I understand,' she said finally, her words floating through the moist afternoon air as she turned away from me, staring straight ahead at nothing in particular.

'So, are you a student here then?' I enquired, sitting down beside her, unnerved but intrigued by the air between us.

Flo laughed gently. 'Yeah, I suppose you could say I'm a student all right.'

'Oh, right. What college?' I continued.

'Homerton.'

'Oh. I don't know anyone at Homerton,' I admitted, its location far outside the centre of town.

'You do now,' Flo affirmed. 'You know me.'

Still she focused on something in the distance.

'Yeah, I suppose.'

The strangeness of the situation baffled me, but not to the point that I wanted to leave. In fact, the strangeness made me want to stay all the more. Because although this was confusing, the confusion that I knew would envelop me as soon as I went back to my room was not a desirable alternative. No, this was just fine.

My tummy rumbled. I hadn't eaten yet. I told it to be quiet; wretched body.

'So what do you study?' I asked her brightly, determined to keep the conversation going now that I'd decided to linger.

'Medicine.'

'Oh, cool. I used to think I wanted to do Medicine. My dad's a doctor, you see. But my real passion is History. But you know how people are about arts degrees – don't really think they're proper degrees or—'

'Well, that's bullshit,' Flo interrupted with surprising vigour. 'Especially an arts degree at Cambridge – that's as proper as you can get.'

I was glad she agreed with me.

'So are you doing History then?' she continued.

'Yeah,' I replied, telling her the name of my college.

'First year?'

'Yeah. You?'

'Yep. Scary, isn't it?' she asked.

Her empathy panicked me – what did she know?

'I love it too much to be scared,' I replied assuredely. But I was just being silly – , she wasn't trying to catch me out – she didn't even know me.

'And what do you want to do after Cambridge then?' she quizzed. 'Become a historian?'

Her words made her appear interested in me, though her eyes were still more interested in the trees and hedges which greened ahead of her.

'Well, I think my dad would still like me to go on and do Medicine. But I think my mum would love me to become a charity worker like her. So . . .'

'But what do *you* want to do?

'I . . . I don't know,' I answered honestly.

It didn't matter for now. For now I had to concentrate on getting through my degree. Nothing could get in the way of that, not even . . . the lump in my throat grew again, having only just about disappeared since this morning. I swallowed to flush it away, just like I had . . .

'Are you OK?' Flo suddenly asked, facing me again with those emerald eyes.

'Yeah.' The word broke as I uttered it. I stopped and coughed. 'Yeah, I'm fine,' I repeated, my voice composed once more.

'You just seem a bit . . . shaky.'

I frowned. How did she know this wasn't what I was like all the time? How could she know that I was acting any differently to how I normally did? I couldn't answer these questions, and part of me felt angry at her, angry that some stranger could just arrive here and tell me I was being 'shaky'.

I shook my head, not answering her question, my lips pursed and my eyes firmly fixed on a distant spot. But confusion distracted me – Flo wasn't my friend, she wasn't my mother, she was a stranger, a total stranger. I'd never encountered this breed of concern before, this unprecedented, undeserving concern. Suddenly, through the confusion, some sense began to form, for if she was such a stranger, such an unknown, if I showed weakness to her, well so what? She would never tell; we had no shared friends, no relationship.

'Last night . . .' I began, but stopped myself.

What? So I was just going to tell her? It was one thing to be a bit shaky, but it was another to actually utter the words. What was I thinking? The fact was, I needed to stop thinking at all – I needed to just push what had happened last night to the deepest reaches of my mind, not share it with some stranger. There was nothing to share. I was fine.

'Like I said, last night was just a rough night,' I said.

Flo gazed searchingly at me.

'You know you can tell me?' she promised. 'I swear I won't tell anyone,' she paused. 'Not even you.'

Somehow I knew exactly what she meant. But then again, maybe I was just being completely over the top about the whole thing – people had sex all the time, we were both drunk, no one knew – I'd probably forget about it in a week or so. Oh, why was I thinking so much? This poor girl was trying to have a conversation with me and I just kept zoning out into this other, over-analytical, self-pitying world. Come on, Alice, this isn't like you.

'No, I'm fine,' I assured Flo once more, feeling brighter already.

'Well, as long as you're sure . . .'

'No, honestly. I'm grand. However, I do have an essay to do, so I'm going to head back home, if that's all right?'

The question felt oddest of all; I didn't need her permission.

'As long as *you're* all right?' she responded, her words laced with genuine worry.

'Honestly, Flo. I really appreciate it, but I'll be hunky dory.'

My cheesy phrasing made me cringe. Thankfully, she didn't seem to care.

'Well, I come here most Sundays, so if you need to chat you'll know where to find me,' she said.

I assured her I would, said goodbye and headed back towards town, walking briskly away from that rickety little bench which had held us both in that momentary bubble, those brief minutes of inexplicable matter. My mind still tried to figure out what had just happened; that figure and that place, so random, so odd. I couldn't tell any longer what I was actually feeling. But something inside me had changed since this morning, which could only be a good thing.

As I walked, people appeared again – the dog walkers,

and then the tourists, just as I knew they would. A group of Asian tourists congregated outside Senate house, grinning so hard it must have hurt, then booing when I strolled through their picture. I didn't care; I was stopping for no one.

In no time, I was back in college, making it all the way to my room without so much as a 'Hey, Alice' or an 'All right, Irish' from anywhere. However, relief was cancelled by dread as I put my key in my lock. I wasn't sure if I was ready to be back here. But why shouldn't I be? It was my room, after all – it wasn't his. But surely he would lurk in the air?

I wouldn't let him lurk. He had done enough already without that too.

I turned the handle and let myself in, holding my breath as I did so. The room was brighter than I expected and the light welcomed me in. There was my desk and my closet, the Irish flag, and my framed photo of Róisín and me. There was my bed. I paused, expecting a shudder to come, but nothing. I sighed, relief pouring over me once again. This was all going to be grand – no one would notice a thing. There would be nothing to notice; there *was* nothing to notice. However, what I did notice was the flickering lights of my telephones, which sat beside my bed, humming with messages and missed calls. It was nearly three o'clock. I supposed they'd be worried. Sitting down on my bed, I flipped open my English mobile.

Morning sunshine. Hows the head? Im in a world of pain. Brunch? J xx

Jus tried calln u bt ur not pickn up. OMG I cant remember anything frm las nyt. CALL ME BIATCH, xx M xx

Mills+I jus poppd round bt no answer. Wher r u gay face? J x

Babe, we'r getting a tiny bit worried. Call us wen u get this xx M xx

I smiled, appreciative of their concern, but angry with myself for letting them get into this state – it was so selfish. I was off on my thoughtless ramble while they were searching high and low for me and now they'd ask questions. I didn't want to draw any attention to myself – not now – not ever. I had to call them. I would just say I went looking for a church and lost track of time. Which wasn't a complete lie.

I dialled Millie's number, but before I clicked 'CALL' my phone signalled another text. It was an unknown number. My heart beat just a little faster, wary of what was to come. I opened the text. The beating was replaced by a roar in my ears.

Thanks 4 last nite Irish. Our little secret, yeah? Robbie

I couldn't move. How dare he. How fucking dare he. Who the fuck did he think he was? My hands started to shake and I dropped my phone on my bed. What did that text even mean? The first half was like some sick way of affirming that we had had sex, to massage his disgusting ego. And yet the last bit seemed to say something different entirely – that he wanted to hide it? Surely that meant that he knew he'd done something wrong – that he didn't want to boast publicly about our night together because he knew he'd fucked up. So what, instead he thought he'd boast to me? He'd boast to me because I was the only person who knew? But I was the only person who knew what he'd *really* done. So what the hell? What the fucking . . . Alice, calm down, he didn't do anything: it was a drunken one-night stand, that's all – it's fine – nothing bad happened – not really. My eyes stung. Just breathe, I told myself, just breathe. I was not going to fucking cry. I'd spent all morning trying to bury this and I was damned if some sick little text message was going to mess things up. I was stronger than that. I picked up the phone and clicked delete, erasing his dirty words. There – it was deleted – he was deleted.

I steadied myself, furious, but more than anything, furious with myself that I could let something so pathetic as a text throw me. I caught my breath, promising I wouldn't overreact so much again. Last night was last night, and today and tomorrow and the next day, they were the future – every day was another day away from it all, and I had to move on and let it go and just get on with my life. End of.

'Darling, where the hell have you been?' Millie's voice broke through my trance as she marched into the room.

'Millie,' I gasped, startled by her presence.

'Where have you been?' she repeated, the impatient tap of her hand on her hip ringing in my ears.

'Sorry . . . I've been a bit all over the place – I thought I'd . . . I thought I'd go and find a church, and I left my phone . . .'

'We've been worried sick,' she said, clearly unimpressed. Her eyes were heavy with last night's bags.

'I really am sorry, Mills. I just lost track of time.'

'Well, don't do it again, OK? I've spent all bloody day trying to find you.'

'Millie, it's only three.'

'Alice, I don't care what hour of the day it is,' she snapped, 'it's you. You never just suddenly disappear – you always text us and tell us where you'll be if we need you. You—'

'Millie, I'm not your fecking babysitter.'

The words were out of my mouth before I could stop myself. Millie looked as if she was about to burst into tears.

'Mills, I'm sorry.'

'No, Alice, it's fine. You've made your point,' she spat, turning on her heels.

'Millie, please,' I begged, feeling my eyes well up. I couldn't bear this right now, not on top of everything else. 'Please.'

She spun around once more to face me, her face clenched in anger. But as she stared at me in fury, something made her soften. It must have been something in my eyes, because suddenly she was full of concern.

'Alice, what's wrong?' she asked gently.

'Nothing,' I lied.

Part of me was so tempted to give in and just tell her, to cry and have her hold me and tell me it was going to be OK. But what if letting go also meant letting go of who I was? I wasn't perfect, but I was OK, and I was doing an OK job of holding myself together. So why take the risk? I couldn't give in. Strength had to prevail.

'Babe, I'm fine. I just got some bad news from home, that's all.' I hated lying, especially to my best friend.

'Oh, darling, I'm so sorry. Do you want to talk about it?'

'No . . . not for now. Thanks though.'

'OK, well, if you ever do, I'm always always here for you, you know that?' she said kindly.

'I will.'

But we both knew deep down that I wouldn't.

'Are you going to come to Hall tonight?' she asked gently.

'No, probably not, babe. Just going to get an early night, I think.'

'OK, well, call me if you need me, OK? And make sure you eat something.'

I smiled. Taking meal advice from the fussiest eater I knew seemed too ironic to ignore. But I knew she meant well, and that was enough. Almost enough.

Millie left, and the room felt quieter and emptier than ever before. I worked on my essay for a couple of hours, had some dinner and then watched an episode of *Desperate Housewives* online, but soon exhaustion came over me and I willingly obeyed. I went to bed and shut my eyes. Bubbles of thought danced to the top of my consciousness, but exhaustion made them pop. My mind could manage nothing but the bittersweet promise that in the morning, it would all be OK; I would be OK. Because I had to be. There was no other way.

9

No sooner had I handed in my essay than week three was upon us and I had another essay to research, another set of books from the library to fight over, another clever argument to think up, another 3000 words to write. But I wasn't complaining: I thrived on deadlines, I loved word counts. They set limits and that made me feel safe.

'So how's it all going?' my mother asked breezily over the phone one evening. My stomach lurched ever so slightly, but I made it stop. It was only a few days since that night, but I was learning to get my body under control.

'Yeah, it's going so so well, Mum. Work's a bitch, but I do find it unbelievably interesting, so it's cool.'

'And are you eating properly?'

'The menu for Hall has been pretty shit the past few days so I've just been buying stuff from Sainsbury's and eating dinner in my room.'

'And what about RAG? Have you looked into getting involved with that yet? Alice, you know, it's such a shame not to,' Mum said.

RAG was the society in charge of organising fundraising activities for charity, so it was no wonder my mother was probably more concerned with me taking part in that than any other aspect of my Cambridge career.

'I know, I know. There's just not enough time to do everything. This place is mental,' I admitted.

'If there's time to be in the library till all hours and still go to the bar with your friends, there's definitely time to do something worthwhile, dear.'

I could feel myself getting irritated – wasn't my degree worthwhile? Wasn't chilling out and having peace of mind worthwhile? But I hated myself for getting angry with her; she meant well. In fact, I hadn't been to the bar since the bop either. No – it had been a work-fuelled week, after all, that was why I came to Cambridge – no matter how many social or sporting activities there were, the degree came first; that was what really mattered. I had the feeling that she believed all this was just a phase, a brief sojourn into an arts degree and I'd swiftly come back to my senses. Our beliefs were diverging now more than ever, mine leading me through these old streets and old books towards a new direction, a new idea of what my future would hold.

'So, how are the boys?' I asked, changing the subject.

'All great. Well, except that we were supposed to go down to Avoca for lunch on Sunday, but I ended up having to bring one of our clients to hospital after a pretty nasty fight in the shelter . . .'

I smiled to myself as we finished the conversation and I hung up my phone. Nothing had changed.

I remembered when we were younger and Mum had taken a particular interest in Jacko, a heroin addict, who was living on the streets and causing my poor mother a lot of heartache. Every dinner conversation we had, it was Jacko this and Jacko that, until eventually, one night as I tucked him into bed, my youngest brother, Nick, only aged five at the time, asked, 'Alice, who's Jacko? Do we have another brother?'

At the time I had laughed, and explained that no, we had no hidden siblings, but that night as I had lain in bed, I began to feel sad; sad that my five-year-old brother didn't feel that our mother's love was split three ways, but rather shared amongst countless individuals whom we would never know. But surely it was selfish to complain?

The fact was, these questions didn't need answers – my family was in Ireland and I was here – I couldn't distract myself thinking about things that I couldn't change. I *did* need to focus on work and I *did* need to go the library instead of the bar in the evenings, and the menu *did* look rubbish this week, so *of course* it made sense to just prepare something healthy myself. Once the menu picked up and worked eased up a bit, I'd be hitting Hall and the bar every night, just like before. Just like before I . . . my mind shut down again.

But I didn't want my lack of appearance around the college communal areas to mean that I wasn't seeing my friends; no one could notice anything. So, having had numerous tea breaks with them over the course of the week, on Friday night I decided I would organise a trip to The Cow for a big group of us.

We strolled through February's shiver, through the eerie stalls of the empty market, where bruised apples scattered the ground, and the kebab vans set up for the night ahead.

Soon we reached the restaurant, all talking and laughing, just as normal. The place was heaving, its cheap and tasty pizzas always drawing a good crowd. We were seated pretty swiftly, me opposite a very excited Millie, who was 'literally dying' to tell us some 'simply wonderful' gossip she had stored up for the evening's entertainment.

'OK, so you know that girl in our year, Olivia Fielding?' she began, like a giddy schoolgirl telling tales. 'Well, apparently she got with this guy from Christ's College the other night, and took him back to hers and . . . well, you know . . . did the deed.'

I sipped my water.

'Anyway, the next morning, there was a knock on the door – obviously the cleaner – and Olivia, rather than just saying "no, go away" like a bloody normal person would, totally panicked and told the guy to hide under the bed.'

Everyone's smiles began to grow. I ordered mine to follow suit.

'So the cleaner comes in, Olivia's trying to play it totally cool. But then the cleaner bends down to empty the bin, catches a glance of Mr Casanova – starkers – under the bed, and screams!'

The girls cringed with embarrassment. The lads found it brilliant.

'And she starts running out of the room, and Olivia jumps out of bed to go after her and apologise, but then she's naked too, and the cleaner just leaves, about to have an actual bloody heart attack, and yeah, Olivia's bin hasn't been emptied once since!'

The group exploded into laughter, relishing Olivia's pain.

'That's bloody hilarious,' one of the girls remarked.

'How had I not heard about it?' another said.

'The poor guy!' Henry giggled.

I frowned. 'The poor guy? What about poor Olivia? She must be fecking mortified!' I pointed out.

'Whatever, serves her right!' Joey joked.

'What?' I asked, shocked.

'Yeah, that's what she gets for being a slut,' Henry added.

'Look, some of us do stupid things when we're drunk. Or more precisely, do stupid people,' Millie teased, half-serious, half-joking, as the rest of the group booed and hissed, encouraging the tension that still simmered between the pair.

Henry looked as if he was about to make some witty comeback, but the arrival of his garlic bread gave him the perfect alibi for his lack of repartee, though the smile suggested he quite liked the reference to his and Millie's most recent night together. My grin was starting to stick. This mindless banter hinted to things I didn't want to think about, but I made myself stop. It felt better to just be happy.

Stabbing my knife and fork into my pizza, I snapped right into happiness; whether it was genuine or a mask, I couldn't quite tell. But, right now, it was enough.

★

I watched her from across the table. Beside me, Millie was blushing as a result of her and Henry's latest bout of flirtation, but I wasn't interested in them; I was interested in Alice.

'Joey, did you order the pepperoni?' someone screeched.

I shook my head, but kept watching Alice. But I had to stop, because if someone saw me staring, there would just be yet another gag about how I fancied her and how we were clearly meant to be together and blah blah blah. Because that wasn't it. I wasn't looking at her because I fancied her, I was looking at her because there was a tiny part of me that could have sworn that something had changed. I couldn't put my finger on it, but no matter how much I tried to suppress the idea that something about her was different, it just wouldn't go away, and that for me was proof enough.

Just now, as we'd laughed about Olivia whatever-her-face's one-night stand drama, for a fraction of a second I could have sworn I saw something in Alice's eyes that I'd never seen before: pure terror. But surely not? I mean, Alice wasn't exactly as promiscuous as a lot of girls with whom she hung out, so maybe she just wasn't as comfortable discussing stuff like that with the group. But it seemed like more than that, and it worried me. I hadn't seen much of her this week. She kept missing dinner, but that wasn't surprising, given the poxy food on offer. And sometimes people just wanted a quick bite rather than the grace and the gowns and the gigantic fuss that was piled on evening after evening.

So why did her absence strike a strange note with me? I tried to imagine why she could be down or sad or stressed – the pressure of just being in Cambridge was enough of an excuse in itself. But perhaps, in true cliché fashion, it wasn't her, it was me. Maybe the reason I cared so much, the reason I longed to stare at her and puzzle her out, was because the slagging was true – maybe I really was falling for her. Half of me flinched at the thought. That could mess everything up, it could ruin the group dynamic. But the other half of me gave in momentarily to the possibility that maybe she liked me back, and the reason she was being a bit off was because she was starting to feel something too, and it scared her just as much as it scared me.

Surely this was all in my head. I mean, was Alice really off form? Or was she just working really hard, as everyone in Cambridge simply had to? I knew her well enough by now to know that she was not the type to give her degree anything less than one hundred per cent; it was how she was built, programmed for success. But it was those rare moments, that millisecond flash in the eye like just now, that warned me not to rule out the possibility that maybe, after all, she was human too, fallen like the rest of us. I wondered if I'd ever know the truth.

*

Suddenly the weekend was upon us and my next essay was nearly finished and I was proud of what I'd written. My spirits were strangely high, so when Sunday came around, I decided to take the afternoon off and just do whatever I wanted with the luxury of spare time – such a rare concept in this hectic place.

'Irish, we're going to the pub to watch the Six Nations if you want?' Joey suggested.

'Oh my God, amazing – I'd love to. Where are you going? The May Pole?'

'Yeah, think so. You should join us, it's going to be a wicked day's rugby.'

I smiled; this was just what I needed. I had managed to completely forget that the Six Nations had started this weekend and the realisation cheered me up immensely. Not that I had been down, just dazed by the concept of an empty afternoon. But what better way to fill it!

'I'll meet you downstairs,' Joey said. 'It's just you, me, Henners, and I think a couple of the third-year lads might be coming along too.'

My heart screeched to a halt. I could feel the colour drain from my face as I turned around, away from Joey.

'OK . . . OK, well, actually, I'll . . . I'll follow you on. I said I'd . . . I'd call my parents, so I'll be there in . . . in about fifteen, if that's OK.'

I could feel Joey standing there as my body froze, though my left leg longed to twitch, to thump away the fear. I placed my weight upon it, wishing he would go. Thankfully he agreed to see me at the pub and left me rooted to the spot in my room. I closed my eyes so that it was me and me only, breathing, being OK, being just fine. It was grand – I would go to the match; I would sit there and chat with the lads and if Rob . . . if he was there, then so be it. It was bound to happen sooner or later, wasn't it? This only needed to be as big a deal as I made it. Nothing more than that; no big deal at all.

But as I slumped down on my bed, I realised that suddenly the excitement of seeing the rugby, of chilling out with Joey on my few hours off, was gone. It wasn't fair – how could *he* just do that? I just wanted to hang out with my friend and do nothing and think about nothing and nothing more. But then I remembered something – suddenly I remembered that today there *was* somewhere I could go, someone I could talk with and not have to look at him and think about him and remember . . . I knew what I had to do. And now that the idea rippled through my stiffened bones, I felt better already.

Hey m8. Change of plan – goin 2 go 2 mass instead. Enjoy d game – cheer on d boys in green 4 me. xx

I clicked send and placed my phone on my bedside table. I was not going to mass, but somewhere that would offer similar hope. I hoped.

*

I strolled through the afternoon nip and sure enough she was there, on the bench, just as I had known she would be.

'Ah, Alice.' At the sound of my footsteps, Flo turned towards me. 'Nice to see you.'

I sat down beside her and returned the compliment, genuinely meaning it.

'Good week?' she asked.

'Yeah . . . yeah it was, actually,' I replied.

And it had been, all things consid— no. It had been a good week, full stop. Next question.

'Did you sort out whatever was bothering you last weekend?' she continued, coming straight to the point. But I didn't mind.

'Yeah, I feel OK, thanks. I mean, I think I feel OK.'

I winced slightly, checking to see whether the hesitation had registered with her. But she looked serene as ever, head titled with a half-smile on her lips.

'So what exactly happened that had you so shaky?' she finally said. 'I mean, if you don't mind talking about it?'

For the second time with this perfect stranger, I felt inclined to tell her everything, despite my natural reluctance to protect myself.

'I just had . . . look, Flo, don't repeat this, but . . .' I trailed off, searching for the right words.

'Who am I going to tell?' she laughed, the half-smile becoming a full porcelain grin. 'It's not like we have any mutual friends or anything,' she pointed out.

'You never know, we might!' I laughed in return. 'Cambridge is a very small place!'

'Perhaps!'

'I'll check on Facebook when I get home,' I suggested.

'Sorry, I'm not on Facebook,' Flo informed me evenly.

'What? What are you like? Why not?'

'Just not my thing, really,' she replied.

I was genuinely shocked: every single person I had met in Cambridge was at least mildly obsessed with Facebook, and though at first I had resisted joining up, now I couldn't envisage my university life without it. A wry smile crept in – how sad did that sound? Flo must think I'm such a loser. However, she continued swiftly onwards.

'Anyway, what were you saying?'

My smile vanished. The weight which had been momentarily lifted from my heart pushed down on it once more.

'Oh, nothing, I just— Flo, this is really weird because I don't know you at all. And yet, that makes it kind of easier in a way. But it's hard because you don't know me, and you don't know how I operate, and—'

'So why don't you tell me?' she cut in, her voice now more serious.

My left leg did its twitching thing. Half of me was itching to tell her. The other half was me.

'No, it's not really very interesting,' I admitted, feeling suddenly shy.

'Alice, I want to know.'

Those green eyes were on me again, seeking me out, beseeching me to tell her everything. The moment lasted forever.

'Flo, look, there's something about you that makes me want to tell you things, and I don't understand why, but there you go. But you see, I'm not the type to tell people stuff – I barely even admit things to myself, you know?'

She didn't speak. Her green eyes waited for me to go on.

'So all I'm going to say is that something . . . something happened to me last weekend. Something . . . something bad. I mean, it's not like . . . oh, I don't know. I just . . . I'm in a bit of a weird place because of it and I don't want to be and I'm trying really hard not to be, but I'm finding that hard too. So yeah – I'm just a bit all over the place. And I'm never all over the place. So it's just scary. Really bloody scary.'

By the time I finished, I was out of breath. I hadn't told her anything, really, yet I had said more than I meant to. The breeze swirled around us, tasting of rain. The bench felt cold beneath my bum. I waited and waited for Flo to speak, though I didn't know what I expected her to say – whether she'd console me, or ask more questions, or tell me to pull myself together. But she didn't utter a sound, she just sat beside me as the sky turned darker.

'I'm glad you told me,' Flo finally said.

I waited for her to continue, but she never did. And once we said our goodbyes, her words tumbled over and over in my ears – I hadn't told her anything; that was the whole point. So why had she thanked me? Why should she? She really was an odd one. And yet I was the one who had made all these elusive confessions about 'bad happenings' and gone all pensive and weird. So who was odd? And ultimately, did it really matter?

*

The air changed. Within minutes, the heavens opened, though no angels flew out, just sheets and sheets of heavy rain, soaking me instantly. I cursed out loud. People shrieked as umbrellas blew whichever way they pleased. Cyclists stopped cycling, barely able to see through the wall-to-wall droplets which splashed recklessly on every inch of Cambridge. The rain was heavy on my body, sticking my clothes to me, my hair; everything was pushed hard against me, pushing like the weight on my heart, which had only just started to relax.

I found my way to college, already deciding that I was going to have a bath the minute I got in, dreaming of the cocoon of warmth that was only minutes away. But then my vision evaporated as a voice cut through the torrent.

'Irish! You missed a cracker of a match!' Joey announced, barely audible over the sound of the rain.

I smiled at him and he gave me a rain-soaked hug before we hurried into the first courtyard of college. But before I even saw him, before I even made out his face through the rain, I knew Robbie was there. It was as if something had smacked me right in the chest. The downpour seemed to freeze. I was aware of every droplet and its exact position between the sky and the ground, every layer of heavy wet. Yet through the blur his face was so clear it made me choke. He was chatting to Danny, unashamedly drenched, unashamedly there before me, behind me, all around me, in me . . . *agh*, I had to stop. I had to be OK. I just had to make it back to my room and lock my door and it would all be OK. Would it be? *I would fucking make it OK.* Stop it, Alice. There's no need for that. No need at all. I took a deep breath, inhaling the rain's scent. Time splashed back to life.

His eyes turned to face mine. I could have sworn he was startled by my presence, but he quickly erased all emotion from his face. I knew I could cry if I wanted to; no one would know, the rain would hide my tears. I could actually break down and be weak, and no one would have a clue, no one except for me. But if I was to cry, it would prove just how much that night had ruined me. And I couldn't do that, I just couldn't.

So instead I turned away – this time I had the strength to turn away from him – and I told Joey I was going inside and I ran. I just ran away from the rain, through the door, all the way up my staircase, into my room, ripping the sopping clothes from my skin, leaving a coat of cool droplets shivering on the surface. I drew a hot bath and immersed myself.

Here I could be strong. I knew I could.

*

One evening, when I was only six, I announced to my parents that I was going to have a bath by myself. I usually had a bath with my little brother, but this time, I was going to be a big girl and do it all myself: draw it myself, wash my hair myself, the lot. Mum and Dad didn't know what to make of this new maturity, but they didn't object.

Slowly I turned the key in the door, making sure it didn't make a sound. I knew Mum and Dad wouldn't like me locking myself in, but as I did so I didn't feel trapped, but rather strangely liberated. Turning the taps on, I watched the tub fill steadily upwards. It took me a while to get the temperature right – at one point my hand told me it was OK, but when I put my foot in it scalded badly. But eventually I got it right and climbed in.

I lolled about the tub, passing the bubbles' foam from hand to hand and blowing it into the air like swirling clouds. I had raided my mother's toiletries box, and now toyed with various lotions and potions, my skin feeling softer by the minute, and me feeling more grown up with every scrub. But I wasn't old enough yet not to want games. In the absence of a rubber ducky, I decided that I would duck my head under the water for a whole minute. I hadn't done it before, but I was sure I could. Of course I could. So here it went! I leaned back and sank under . . . one, two, three

... this was fine, very cosy, a cocoon of warmth – like a caterpillar in a cocoon but soon I would become a butterfly, spread my wings, just like I read in that book ... fourteen, fifteen, sixteen ... now I wanted to breathe, but I obviously wasn't going to – I only had to get to sixty ... twenty-seven, twenty-eight, twenty-nine ... only halfway? I was starting to struggle. Maybe I'd start counting a little faster ... thirty-four, thirty-five ... I really did need to breathe now. *No*, Alice, you're not allowed – you told yourself you'd do this so you have to do it now ... forty-two, forty-three ... my head's getting really light, my hands are grabbing the sides of the bath, but I'm keeping my head down ... fifty, fifty-one ... eyes closing, come on, you're almost there. Oh my God, I'm going to die, I have to ... no, you don't, come on, you can ... eyes closed ... fifty-nine ...

I zoomed upwards, gulping in oxygen so quickly it hurt, my whole body throbbing with panic. I started to cry – I wanted Mum – my head was spinning so fast it hurt. But you did it – you knew you could. But it hurt. But only you hurt you, no one else, so why go crying to Mummy? There's no need. You've done it – just push the pain away. Stop being scared.

Soon I was OK again. My head was still spinning and my eyes still wanted to cry, but I told them no. So I got out, got dressed and went straight to bed, heedless of my soaking hair that sogged against my pillow as I lay there bursting with pride for what I'd achieved. But I wasn't going to tell anyone. This was my victory and I was going to enjoy it all on my own because I was strong. I promised myself I would always be strong.

*

Thirteen years on, in a different bathtub, I made that very same promise all over again.

10

Hey, wana go drop our cheques in for d May Ball? Deadlines 2day!
J xx

'Feck,' I cursed, having completely forgotten about the deadline.

The May Balls were the highlights of the Cambridge calendar and all took place over the course of one week, at the end of the summer term, once everyone's exams were well and truly finished. May Week (named because it used to be held in May, though now fell in June – typical Cambridge clinging on to tradition) was the talk of the town, as tickets were going on sale. The ultimate reward for our months of hard work seemed just about in sight. Some colleges had a ball every year, some every two years, some not at all. But luckily, my college's ball was an annual event, and famed for being one of the best. Registration for tickets had been going on for the past few weeks and now the money was due and the anticipation was palpable. I knew my parents, my mother especially, would flip if they knew how much it cost, but all the older years assured me it was worth it.

I took their word for it, and scrawling my cheque for one hundred and twenty pounds, headed down to Joey's room, and then on to the pigeon hole of the Treasurer of the Ball Committee.

'I cannot wait,' Joey grinned as we deposited our cheques. 'I wonder what bands we're going to get.'

'Well, apparently Supergrass and Amy Winehouse and Dizzee Rascal have played here,' I informed him, having heard countless tales from my seniors, 'so I reckon we should have pretty high expectations.'

'Wow. This is well cool.' His eyes glazed over with delight. 'Anyway, what are you up to for the rest of the day?' he asked as we made our way back through the courtyards, the rain having finally stopped after its three-day marathon. Cambridge was thoroughly saturated, coughing up its lungs in a husky wind, having come so close to drowning away.

'I kind of agreed to go to a RAG meeting, even though I have so much work to do. I can't believe it's Wednesday already,' I said.

That was true; the days were flying by. And I couldn't quite believe I'd agreed to this RAG thing either. I already had enough on my plate between my work and seeing my friends enough so that they wouldn't suspect anything and trying to maintain contact with everyone back in Dublin . . . it was draining. So why had I agreed to go off and give up what little time I had left? I supposed the obvious answer was because then I could think about others' problems, and not mine. But with children starving in Africa or AIDS orphans or the myriad of other issues that clamoured for attention, my problems paled in comparison. Maybe my mother's approach all these years had prepared me for this, offering yet another way to stop myself thinking about what had happened. But nothing had happened, I was fine. The orphans in Africa, not so fine.

'We need to get Mills a present,' Joey said, interrupting my thoughts.

'Sorry, I was a million miles away. What did you say?'

'Present – Millie – it's her birthday on Saturday, remember?' he explained in a slightly irritated tone.

'Oh, of course. What was it we said we were going to get her? A voucher for that massage place?'

'Yeah, you said she'd like that.'

'No, trust me – she'll love it. She's been going on and on about how badly she wants one,' I said, smiling at the thought of Millie's not-so-subtle hints.

'Wicked. Well, would you mind picking it up then?' Joey asked.

'Yes of course, my dear, no worries at all. I'll go today after this bloody meeting.'

'Awesome. See you at Hall tonight?'

'Hopefully, yeah.'

And with that we parted company, and I went back to my computer to finish the RAG research I'd been doing. Suddenly it was three o'clock and it was time for me to go and save the world, to forget about my irrelevant problems and look at the bigger picture. I smiled. My mother would be so proud.

★

The meeting went on for hours. They were planning a fashion show in a couple of weeks' time to raise money for a building project in Africa and needed all the help they could get. By half twelve that night, I was exhausted, yet had still agreed to meet up with some of the committee the following day for more organising. My eyes were closed before I even fell into bed, and I was up before they properly opened again. Thursday was the same. And Friday. And then it was Saturday, and I knew I had to make a start on the reading for my essay, but it was Millie's birthday that night and I needed to get these last-minute sponsors on board, and I had to make these new posters, and frankly, everything else could wait.

When I called Mum, I could have sworn I detected a note of joy in her voice when I told her I was a bit behind on work because of RAG.

'Alice, it's just one weekly essay, but this one fashion show is going to make so much difference – it's all relative, you know?'

Part of me felt like such an attitude didn't quite apply when in such an academically driven establishment. But I promised myself that next week I would read every single book from cover to dusty cover and pen some really well-thought-out argument, something better than anything else I'd written so far. Because I was getting better already.

★

'Shit!'

I looked at my watch. It was twenty-five past seven. Millie's dinner started at half, yet here I was fiddling around on the computer, trying to word the programmes for the fashion show. It would have to wait. Quickly, I tied up my blonde mane and whacked on a bit of lipgloss. I was looking forward to an evening with my friends where I would no longer have to persuade myself I was OK, but actually, just be OK. It felt too good to be true.

'You're late,' Millie pointed out as I strolled into the restaurant fifteen minutes later.

'Sorry, babe – the walk always takes longer than you think. Happy birthday!'

I threw my arms around her and gave her a massive squeeze, my head buzzing with newfound positivity. I could feel whatever trace of anger that was in her melt away beneath my embrace, and when she pulled back and smiled, I saw nothing in those sparkly eyes but pure, untouched delight. 'Look what Henry got me!' she squealed, holding out her left wrist, where a diamond bangle glittered up at me, its wearer beaming with pride.

But shit – shit shit shit – suddenly I remembered: I'd forgotten to get the bloody present. I was such an idiot. It was just with all the RAG stuff these past few days and everything . . . oh, she probably wouldn't even notice – a couple of glasses of wine, together with all the attention she'd be getting tonight – sure, the girl would be in her element. She'd barely notice me, not to mention my empty hands.

'It's stunning,' I said, sitting into the empty seat beside the head of the table, glad she'd kept it for me, and even gladder to see Joey, Henry and all the gang.

We ordered our meals and our wine. Everyone was in great form. The gang had scrubbed up well; all the boys in shirts, and all the girls impeccably groomed. My hair felt greasier on my head than it had earlier. Surely they wouldn't notice?

Millie's glass was constantly being topped up and emptied just as quickly, so that by the time the main courses arrived, she was absolutely on her ear. But then something else hit our ears – a loud ringing that drilled through us like a thousand hangovers, so loud we could barely even think or figure out what was going on. But it didn't take long to decipher the din; it was the bloody fire alarm.

'Don't they know it's my birthday?' Millie screeched, managing somehow to sound louder than the intolerable, incessant note.

'Maybe there really is a fire,' Henry shouted, his face earnest, but a faint glimmer in his eye showing that he was only trying to wind up the birthday girl.

'Oh my God, we should get out of here,' Millie slurred, standing up from her chair so that the legs screeched against the tiled floor.

'Ma'am, if you just sit down, there's no fire – we're just having a bit . . . a bit of a problem,' our waiter said soothingly, sitting a very displeased-looking Millie back down.

'It's my birthday,' she spat, her lips pouted like an angry child.

'Well, maybe some champagne on the house would convey our sincerest apologies?' he offered.

Millie nodded her head sulkily, still not cheering up despite the waiter's generosity.

At this point, Millie spotted something over my shoulder coming in the entrance of the restaurant that made her excitement bubble more than any champagne she'd taken all night.

'Oh my God! You got me strippers!' she squawked with delight, making me spin around to see just what she was talking about.

Two firemen had just arrived and were talking to the very frazzled manager of the restaurant. I smirked, looked at Joey and then at Henry: Millie's drunken confusion was priceless. The three of us laughed harder than I could remember us ever laughing before. We tossed back our heads and shook with pleasure. I laughed, big heavy laughs that came from the bottom of my stomach, each one more cathartic than the last. But Millie's furrowed brow told us she was not impressed.

'Pet, I think they might just be *actual* firemen here to sort out the alarm, not strippers,' I suggested gently.

'Are you laughing at me?' she demanded, crossing her arms and scrunching up her cute little face even more.

Our giggles began again.

'Well that's not very nice. It's my birthday you know,' she sulked. 'Or maybe you'd forgotten – it's not like you texted me to say happy birthday. Or got me a present. Great friend you are.'

The shaking stopped. My eyes darted to see if the lads had heard, but luckily they were both cracking up too much to notice.

'Millie, I'm really sorry. I was just doing all this RAG stuff, and I completely—'

'Whatever,' she retorted, flicking her head around so that now she faced her giggling Henry.

Even though the alarm finally ceased and calm was restored in the restaurant, my calm was replaced by a feeling of panic.

But I would not let it take hold. Not after everything. No – she was being childish and silly because she was drunk. It was true – I had been really busy, really busy with really important stuff. So what if I didn't send her a bloody text? I was here now, wasn't I? That was what really mattered, wasn't it?

I tried to enjoy the rest of the meal – I was sure Millie wouldn't even remember this in the morning. Everything was fine. She was just being ridiculous. But it was her birthday and she could be ridiculous if she wanted to. For the rest of the meal, and all the way home, she didn't say a word to me.

I tried not to mind. For tomorrow, I would put my mind at ease; I would go and see Flo.

*

'I mean, don't you just think that's so unfair? Like, she probably got a million texts, all saying exactly the same thing – one more from me wouldn't have made any difference,' I ranted, pacing up and down beside the bench while Flo watched calmly on, serene as ever.

'Because, like I said, this RAG stuff has just been taking up all my time this week – I mean, I haven't even finished the reading for my essay, let alone knowing what I'm going to write about. I think if I had some free time on my hands I'd be doing that, don't you? Not sending stupid text messages or booking fecking massage vouchers. I mean, it's not like she was going to use it straight away. I'll get it for her tomorrow and it will all be grand. Why is she being such a brat?'

I stopped pacing. I was breathing heavily and a headache was starting to thud. I unclenched my brow to try to alleviate the tension.

'Oh God, why am I being such a bitch?' I sighed, slumping onto the bench beside my confidante, basking in the calm she radiated.

'You're not a bitch, you're just . . . stressed,' Flo suggested.

'But the thing is, I'm not really. I've really enjoyed the RAG stuff, and the fashion show's this week and it's just so nice to be working towards something specific. With the weekly essays, the minute you finish one, you're set the next – it's bloody never-ending. But with this, there's an end in sight. Oh Flo, it's going to be amazing. You should come. Oh my God, please do!'

My suggestion hung in the air. I always felt so at ease with Flo – almost too at ease – so why had this strange discomfort fallen between us? Maybe the thought of taking this friendship into the public – taking it anywhere but the secluded nook of our faithful bench – unnerved us both. I guess we just liked to keep our lives, except on Sundays, completely separate. I had my friends in my college, she had hers in Homerton – although she never spoke about them. I sighed. I had never asked about her friends. I just came here and blabbed on about all my problems, never once asking her a thing about her life, not one single thing. I shook my head – that was so unlike me – it was usually completely the other way round. So why now? Why was this different?

'Look, Alice,' Flo said tentatively, 'the RAG stuff all sounds great, and I'm sure you won't let it upset your work – it's just giving you something to think about other than . . . well, other than whatever it is that happened.'

But this did not sit well with me either.

'No, hold on a minute. If I wasn't doing the RAG stuff, I wouldn't be moping about and feeling sorry for myself – I've told you, I'm over that. I mean, there was nothing *to* get over – it was just a potential blip that I avoided. Nothing more than that,' I said desperately.

Flo didn't reply. Whether it was because she finally understood and saw things my way, or because she thought it better to just keep her opinions to herself, I wasn't sure. But I appreciated her silence nonetheless. We'd done enough talking for the day. I had work to do, so much work. So now it was time to go, time to go away.

★

Week four became week five, the fashion show was on Tuesday and I worked as hard as I physically could. I loved it. And as the models wowed the crowd, I felt such an immense surge of pride that a tear pricked my eye. And once it pricked, it fell, because I just wanted to cry and cry, for joy and pride and a sense of utter relief. Was it relief that the fashion show had gone off without so much as a whisper of a hitch? Or was it a different kind of relief to do with something else entirely – that specific something else? I didn't know, and frankly I didn't care. I just cried. And it felt amazing.

What felt slightly less amazing was that in the midst of it all I had to tell a white lie. I had emailed my supervisor to tell him that as I had been sick this week I had not managed to write my essay, but that I would be better soon and that my next essay would be my best so far. And sure, I felt a little guilty; I wasn't sick, I was healthier than ever – in mind and body and spirit and soul. I had just needed this distraction – this little project – to get me back on track. And it had worked. Because now I was powering onwards – everything seemed to be better than before. My mum was delighted with me, I had made a whole new bunch of friends through RAG, the fashion show was awesome and things even seemed to be back to normal with Millie. Not that they'd ever been abnormal, but I had just feared that after her birthday she would hold some sort of grudge. But I bought her the massage voucher and a ticket to the fashion show, and sure enough she was instantly pacified. It also felt good to be able to show her why I'd been so busy. And as she bombarded me with compliments after the show, I grinned from ear to contented ear. Everything was slotting into place.

★

So despite my exhaustion and my vows to knuckle down to work now that the fashion show was over, the Red Breasts had invited Millie and me on another swap with them on Thursday night, and I reasoned that a night out with my favourite girlie was just what I needed. I was on a high and I didn't want to come down. We were swapping with the Jaguars, and as I tottered along the cobbled Cambridge alleys in my highest heels, clutching Millie's hand, I knew that it was going to be a savage night.

March was looming and I could have sworn just a kiss of warmth lurked in the shadows. We reached the Jaguars' college, where most of the other Red Breasts were waiting, and once the stragglers arrived, we headed in, met the boys, sat down in their glorious dining hall and let the fun commence.

'Hi, I'm Chaz,' my next-door neighbour told me.

'Alice. Nice to meet you,' I replied, shaking his hand.

We ran through the boring questions – year, subject, home-town. Chaz was a second-year economist from Manchester, and his every word was accompanied by a lavish hand gesture, convincing me that by the end of the meal at least one glass would be sent flying by his flippant wrists. Within minutes my wine glass was refilled and a penny thrown in. Ah feck. I downed the lot. I wasn't intending to get drunk tonight – I really needed to work my bum off tomorrow. Plus I was already wired as it was. But before I knew it my glass had been filled up again, and the clink of a copper coin could be heard amidst the joking and laughing which surrounded me. Down the hatch. I thanked my lucky stars I had brought a half decent bottle of wine, but was still wishing I could just drink it at my own leisurely pace. Though I supposed, when on a swap . . .

'So, what do you want to do after dinner then?' Chaz enquired.

My stomach tightened just for a second.

'Oh no no no – I'm not suggesting . . . no, that wasn't, like, a proposition!' He threw his arms in the air, professing his innocence to the skies, my misinterpretation obviously registering on my face. 'No, God, I didn't mean . . . I mean . . . I was at least going to wait until dessert to ask you that!'

He winked. I giggled. This was fun.

'No, I just meant, some people are going on about a Drum 'n' Bass night in Fuzz tonight, but I heard one of the colleges is having a silent disco, so I'd be quite keen to try that.'

'What's a silent disco?' I asked, pouring myself another glass of wine, startled to find that my bottle was already half empty.

Chaz looked at me with a pitying grin. 'Aw, do they not have them back in leprechaun land?' he teased.

I shook my head with a smirk.

'Oh, you're so cute.' I felt warm inside; warm and winy. 'Well, basically it's a big room with no music, but everyone's wearing headphones. And the headphones have loads of different channels with different types of music, and you just set it to whatever you want, and everyone just boogies away to their own thing.'

'That must be so weird!'

'Ah yeah, but it's great when you're faced,' Chaz promised.

And I didn't need to take his word for it. Because three courses of food and one bottle of wine and a whole lot of pennies later and I was, as Chaz so eloquently put it, 'faced'. I'm not sure when exactly my memory cut out because when I think back on the rest of the evening, the details just begin to blur. There was dessert . . . and then the bar – yes, I remember their college bar . . . sambucca . . . more sambucca . . . and then we were outside, and it was cold, very cold, and I couldn't find Millie . . . .and then a big, quiet room . . . strangely quiet . . . and headphones . . . big yellow headphones . . . and my eyes were closed and I was spinning around . . . and then Millie was there . . . then in the toilet, and Millie telling me I was too drunk . . . feck off . . . then more spinning . . . these headphones are so heavy on my head . . . and then Chaz . . . and then Chaz trying to kiss me . . . and then . . . did I . . . where is . . . how did I get . . .

★

I opened my left eye. It stung. I closed it again. My tongue was stuck to the roof of my mouth with a foul paste – the tacky remnant of several sambuccas. Eventually I opened my right eye; less sore than the other, but still not ideal. But I forced it to stay open so I could survey the damage. It was morning; the blinding light told me that. My eye watered. Still wearing my skirt. No top, just bra. Just . . . my eye needed to shut. No more opening. No more.

★

Ten minutes later, I tried again. Right eye, followed by left eye; Houston, we have vision. Well, minus the clouds that seemed to be in the way. Ugh, this is awful. I don't even remember getting home . . . I don't even remember . . . anything. I groaned, but that triggered my head, which then triggered my stomach, as my body slowly began to come back to life, the most vicious of chain reactions. Pain. Absolute fecking agony. Not now.

★

One hour, one shower, seven glasses of water and two Panadol later and I was less pained, but only slightly. I looked at my watch – half eleven? I frowned; I could not afford to feel like this right now – I had so much to do. I needed to move. I needed to go see Millie. I needed answers.

Every step vibrated up through me, resonating in the cave of my skull so that it shook my brain just the right amount not to kill me, but enough to make me hurt an awful lot. This was awful. But it was fine – I'd go see Millie, hear all about last night, hear about who she'd taken home, blah blah blah – no more thinking. I reached her door, but I paused when I heard Millie's voice.

'Oh, Joey, you should have seen her – she was a total mess. I've never seen her like that before.'

'That is really weird all right,' Joey replied. 'I mean, she's always been pretty sensible when it comes to drinking and stuff.'

'I guess that's what drinking societies do to you,' it was Henry's turn now.

I cursed inwardly. I didn't like that he was there – the other two were my best friends, but why was Henry commenting too? Why were there comments at all?

'The thing is,' Millie began, and I wished I could see her face to check if her eyes were as sad as her tone, 'I just . . . I'm starting to get a bit . . . I don't know . . . a bit worried about her.'

My body froze.

'Yeah, I know what you mean,' Joey agreed. 'These past couple of weeks she's been acting awfully strange.'

There was a pause. I wondered if I should just burst in

and tell them I was fine, and not to talk about me ever again because I was always fine and that was that. But my feet were stuck to the ground.

'Guys, are you sure you're not just overreacting?' Henry suggested. 'I mean, what's a couple of weeks? It's hardly something to get worked up about.'

'Yeah, but everything's so concentrated during term time that a fortnight of weirdness is definitely something to get worked up about,' Millie retorted.

'Especially when it's Alice,' Joey added.

Silence hung once more, and I was sure they'd hear my heavy heart thumping only inches from where they stood.

'You know, she pretended she was sick last week and didn't do her essay,' Millie informed the boys.

Bloody gossip.

'And she hasn't been to Hall in weeks,' Joey added.

Oh, so they were keeping tabs on me now?

'And she practically forgot my birthday,' Millie whined.

Right, I'd had enough of this. I wasn't going to just stand there and listen while the three of them ganged up on me for no good reason; I was fine! So I wasn't even allowed to get drunk now without everyone worrying about me? They could have their little bitching session, but I had an essay to write and a hangover to combat without their speculations getting in the way as well. I would talk to them later; maybe I'd send Millie a text to say thanks for minding me last night. After all, we all knew how much she cherished text messages.

Fuming, I returned to my room. I felt sick. How could they say those things? How dare they? I needed to get out – I wanted to just go for a walk and forget it all. Oh, why wasn't it a Sunday? All I wanted was to see Flo – she'd know what to say to calm me down. I couldn't believe I hadn't asked her for her number – how stupid of me. But this weekend I would tell her all about my friends' little chat. Until then, I had an essay to write, the best I'd written so far, remember? I had to forget about my thumping head and my 'concerned' friends. No, it was just me, and me only. Just how I liked it. I put on my imaginary headphones and listened to my own thing – moved in time to *my* rhythm, not theirs. This time it didn't feel strange, it felt right.

II

'I don't know, Flo, maybe I'm just realising that the friends I made last term aren't really the people I want to be friends with, you know? Like, Millie told me a story her mum told her: apparently you spend your first couple of terms in college grabbing on to anyone – making friends with everyone you can, because you're so petrified of being alone. And then you spend the rest of your three years trying to lose most of them, because you suddenly realised you only bonded with them in mutual panic, not because you were actually suited.'

My theory was a bit grim, but it matched how I was feeling. And I resented my 'friends' most of all for that.

'I was in such a good mood this week, Flo – seriously, you should've seen me. After the success of the fashion show and raising *way* more money than we'd anticipated, I was reeling. And then at that swap on Thursday night I was having such a laugh. But then apparently I have to feel bad about that. I mean, it's so fecking hypocritical, you know? Millie gets drunk all the time – really drunk – the girl doesn't eat, for God's sake, so of course she does. So why, when it's me just this once, am I being made to feel like it's suddenly the worst thing in the world?'

I sighed. Flo looked somewhere over my shoulder, contemplating all I'd just said, concocting some wise response no doubt. My eyes traced the outline of her face, her pale white face, wondering when was the last time she'd been on holiday, the last time she'd really seen the sun. No freckle or blemish tarnished her porcelain skin. For the first time I noticed that she was actually very pretty. I wondered why I hadn't noticed that before – it wasn't like it wasn't plain to see. But I supposed it was hard to focus on Flo as a whole, when you were just constantly being lured in by those eyes, those piercing emeralds.

'Alice,' she finally spoke, the emeralds upon me now, 'I think . . . I think you have to appreciate their concern to some degree, you know? I mean, you have been having a tough time recently, and it's nice to know that at least they've noticed. It shows that these aren't just "panic" friends – they get you.'

'But Flo, I don't think that's true. I'm over what happened – I'm fine now. better than fine. Sure, I was a little weird for a couple of days, but they didn't notice anything then. And it's only now, now that I'm feeling better, better than better, that they've decided to talk about me behind my back. In all honesty, I think that just proves how they really don't get me one bit.'

I lost the emeralds to the trees now. I felt bad – poor Flo was just trying to give these people the benefit of the doubt. And I liked that about her – I liked how she tried to make me see the positive side of things. But maybe I was more of a realist. Maybe I wasn't afraid to call a spade a spade or see some bad friends for what they were. No, that wasn't fair – they weren't bad friends. I guess they just weren't as mature as me. Which was a pity. To think – everyone thought me and Joey should be together! Now more than ever I realised how ridiculous that would have been. But for some reason, I wasn't sad about any of this because amidst it all, I had come across someone who *did* get me, who understood me more than anyone else in my entire life.

'Flo, thank you so much . . .' I began.

'Don't be silly,' she replied warmly.

'Seriously,' I continued, 'I don't know what I'd do without you,' I admitted. 'In fact, the other day, I really wanted to speak to you, but I realised for some reason I don't have your number – how silly is that?' I laughed.

But Flo didn't laugh. 'I'm afraid my phone's broken at the moment,' she explained flatly.

I shuffled where I sat, discomfort now pushing in. It unnerved me to know that the person who was fast becoming my best friend – my rock in a strange time – couldn't be contacted whenever I needed her. It disconcerted me more than I cared to admit. But I supposed it did help me to stay strong, because the knowledge that I could only see Flo on Sundays gave me a deadline – a point up until which I had to stay strong. I did like deadlines, after all. Flo made me feel safe. And even when I left the safety of our wooden haven and returned to the 'real' world, that was enough. I closed my eyes. Almost.

★

I decided to go round and see Alice. I needed to talk to her – to see if she was OK. The whole thing was starting to worry me a bit. Well, quite a lot more than a bit, to be honest. In fact, obviously I would never tell anyone this but like, last night when me and Henry were having sex, for a split second, my mind flashed to Ally – I actually found myself thinking, 'I hope this all sorts itself out.' I mean, obviously I made myself stop straight away – that was just weird. Then again, it was probably the closest Henry was ever going to get to a threesome with my best friend and me!

But as I walked to her room, I wondered, was I still able to call her my best friend? Were we still on those terms? I knew Henry thought I was overreacting and that these issues had only been going on for a couple of weeks, but I kept telling him that Cambridge time was different. It moved so quickly, and yet stretched forever because you fit so much more into a day than back in the real world. Plus, Henry was such a little hypocrite – the other morning he persuaded me it was OK for us to have sex again, even though we already had half an hour ago, because in Cambridge time that had been a whole two days, and he was feeling deprived. Cheeky monkey! Things were going really well with him. I couldn't believe how much . . . but that wasn't the point. Right now I had to focus on Alice and sort things out between us once and for all. It was week six of uni now, and in only a fortnight, term would be over and she'd disappear back to Ireland, and what then?

I knocked on her door, my eyes tracing the scratches which surrounded her keyhole. How had I not noticed them before? They were deep.

'Oh, hi,' Alice said as she opened the door, clearly surprised to see me. But her voice was flat, and standing there in her hoodie and jeans, she seemed rather disconnected.

'Can I come in?' I asked.

'Actually, Mills, I'm kind of in the middle of my essay and I'm on a bit of a roll,' she explained.

I wanted to slap her. I wanted to grab her and shake her and tell her to stop being crap and to bring Alice back.

'Ally, I just need to talk to you,' I said.

'About what?' she asked, face totally deadpan.

Suddenly I realised – maybe she really didn't have a clue what we were all so concerned about – maybe she didn't even know we were concerned at all. Perhaps to her, there was no problem – everything was how she wanted it to be and nothing had changed and that was that. But surely not – Alice was the most perceptive person I knew. Surely she must have been aware, or at least have an inclination, as to what we were feeling. I decided to lay all my cards on the table.

'Ally, I'm worried about you,' I finally declared, hoping to snap her out of her emotionless state.

Her paleness infuriated me, she looked so lifeless.

'I'm fine,' she assured me in a monotone.

Now I really was getting frustrated. 'Well, can we at least talk?'

'Millie, I've told you – I really do need to crack on with this essay. I've done enough talking for today – can we just leave it?'

'Oh, did Joey catch you then?' I asked.

We had agreed I would talk to her first, but maybe he had bumped into her or something and told her how we were feeling. But that still didn't explain why her expression was so blank.

'No, no, I had a big chat with my friend Flo, and—'

'Who?'

'My friend Flo. But listen, Mills—'

'Who the hell is Flo?' I pursued, my blood starting to simmer.

'She's this girl from Homerton I've been hanging out with . . .'

'Why haven't you mentioned her before?'

I knew I was starting to get angry with her, but I didn't care. Who the hell did she think she was, going off and getting new friends and not telling me about it? Finding some new buddies while I was sick to death worrying about her? Maybe it was one of her cool RAG friends – some freaking hippy no doubt. But why on earth would she rather chat to some 'save the planet' stoner than to me?

'Look, Millie, can we do this another time? Please?'

Her voice was weary. But it wasn't the right kind of weariness – not like she was weary with the world or weary from having had a big heart-to-heart with her gypsy mate, or weary because she had to go back to a mountain of work. No, this was a very distinct kind of weariness, and it cut me to the core: she was weary of me.

'Fine, well, good luck with your essay, I suppose. I was going to say we're all going to Hall later for Sunday roast, but you'll probably be off drinking green tea and singing kumbaya with what's-her-face, so . . .'

'What?'

'Oh never mind, Alice. Goodbye,' I spat, spinning around and strutting away with such vigour that I barely drew breath before I was back in my room, lying face down on my bed, willing the burning tears that singed my lids to go away. I wasn't going to cry – I wasn't going to cry because I knew that she was just sitting upstairs, at her desk, not giving a shit, and then I'd just be even more of a fool for caring. Alice didn't cry or show her emotions, and I wondered if maybe she just didn't feel emotion anymore at all – maybe that side of her had just died away.

My tears burst through and I convinced myself that I wasn't sad about the fight, but rather I was in mourning – mourning the Alice I knew, the absence of whom broke my heart.

*

I tried to focus on the darkness, but it spiralled around me. Then the images came circling back, closing in on me. Just now, he had been on me again, on me and in me, exactly as it had been. I was panting and pushing and trying to call out. But I made no sound. I willed myself to wake up, to open my eyes, to pretend that all it had ever been was a bad dream. But it didn't stop. It went on and on, reminding me of every awful moment, every filthy touch. And then he came, and I bit my lip, and hot blood oozed down the pale, blinkless face of me. I awoke.

The room was silent, but I could scarcely catch my breath – it was running from me and I was chasing it, but it was minutes before I actually grabbed it and pinned it down. I got out of bed, as if to distance myself from all I'd just seen. As if it was that simple. I stared out the window. The Cambridge skyline scraped the inky black with threatening talons – nails on a blackboard, but worse.

'Fuck,' I cursed, the word reverberating off the shadows of my four walls, my little cell. How the hell had this happened? I was fine – I was totally fine. Only a few days ago I'd had a good chat with Flo and I'd written an awesome essay and my head was completely sorted. So why now were my dreams – the one thing that I couldn't control – turning on me? There had been nothing to trigger it – I hadn't seen him. In fact, since I hadn't been to Hall or the bar for weeks now, I hadn't clapped eyes on him in almost a month. Which was a miracle really, given the close confines of college life. But miracle or not, I was fine – I had laid all this to rest. So why the bloody nightmare? Why remind me of my bloody lip and the pain and the hurt and the thrusting deeper and deeper into my soul . . .

'Fuck!' I repeated, flinging out the venom which burned in my system. I was fuming. Why was my body playing tricks on me? Millie was worried about me, Joey was worried about me, and now my stupid subconscious had decided to infiltrate my peaceful sleep. Was this some big conspiracy theory to try and break me down? First Rob . . . first he does . . . whatever it is he did . . . and then the rest just jump on the bandwagon. But what am I supposed to learn? That I'm weak? That I'm weak and that Rob . . . that he managed to break me? But that's just ridiculous – all it was was a stupid one-night stand. Granted, they're not exactly my thing, but I can't just turn around and say it was something else just because I can't admit to myself I got drunk and acted the slut. Because I did act. I let him kiss me and then I let him finger me and then I touched his cock – *I touched his fucking dick, for God's sake*. He didn't force me to – not really – no,

I willingly got him really hard, and then when he turned around and said 'I want to have sex with you now' suddenly I was the shrinking violet. Suddenly I felt like a victim and I started saying 'no'. Did I actually say 'no'? I mean, did I actually say it, or did I just think it? Maybe my body was playing tricks on me then too, and in my head I said 'no', but my dirty, slutty body was actually loving it – loving being dominated by this hot third year – loving the adrenalin of it all. Maybe I'm one of those sick people that gets a kick out of knowing something's wrong – maybe I did say 'no', but I didn't really mean it – maybe I just had to say that to stay true to my old, prudish self, but actually, since coming to England, since breaking up with Paddy, all I'd been gagging for was a good vicious fuck. And Robbie knew that – yeah, that's right – Robbie. I can say it. And he knew that I was just saying it, just saying 'no', but not meaning it. So he thought he'd give me what I actually wanted instead – he could see right through my innocent little act – it was like some sort of sick role play. But he knew I wanted it. He knew it. And I did want it. I did, I swear. I did I did I did . . .

My breathing started to get hard, wheezing in my tightening chest as if someone was strangling me, squeezing shut my throat. I tried to inhale but my lungs were closing. I fell to my knees, gagging. My head grew dizzy and the shadows began to dance, leering over me, ready to suck my soul. I was going to be sick – a strange, airless sick. I ran to the sink, but nothing came. Still I couldn't draw breath. The fist that had clenched within me for weeks was now twisting my insides tighter and tighter till I thought I would snap. A glass sat beside my toothbrush, half empty. Maybe drinking would help. But I already felt like I was drowning. My chest tightened even more and I looked up at the girl who watched on, the girl I'd become. She was ugly. Maybe she deserved to suffocate. Why should she breathe? She looks foul. I grabbed the glass of water and hurled it against the hideous image. Shards flew everywhere, a firework of jagged edges. My face fell apart, into the sink, and then there was blood spilling freely over the shards of mirror, the shattered smithereens of me. So much blood for one small scratch.

I snapped back out, coughing viciously with agonising whoops. Air flooded through my lungs. My head still spun and I remembered the time, age six, when I'd held my breath under the bath water for those sixty seconds. Now, like then, I relished every breath. But that time, I had made myself stay under – me and no one else. As I sat down on the ground of my collapsing world, I knew that this time was different. Very different. And it made me more terrified than I had ever been. I was alone.

It was only five o'clock. Carefully, I picked the pieces of mirror into my bin, ensuring I didn't cut myself again. Tidying up the glass was better than sleep. The thought of closing my eyes and falling asleep and losing control and for that awful nightmare to take over again . . . no, I would stay awake. I would just clear up this mess, bit by broken bit, and time would pass and soon it would be morning. Things were always less scary in the morning. When I was younger, when we went on holiday, I would go on the airplane, and I'd be petrified if we were flying by night, but if it was by day, I'd be OK. It wouldn't be too bad crashing in daylight – they'd find us straight away. But the dark was scary.

The birds began to sing their morning hymns. I checked my watch – almost six. This was ridiculous. I needed to get away, but where to go? There was only one place I could think of, but there was no point – it wasn't Sunday, she wouldn't be there. Disappointment seeped into my every pore. Could I go anyway? I dressed quickly and silently, tiptoeing down the stairs and into the crisp morning air. March had finally arrived and the nip was beginning to fade from the wind's salute. I set off on my route, relishing the emptiness of the streets. In only a couple of hours, crazed cyclists would be racing to lectures. But for now, the cobbles were void of traffic, save for the Sainsbury's trucks which were unloading a new day's supplies. Men in navy uniforms lugged boxes of goods in and out of the store like zombies, just like they had done yesterday, just as they would do tomorrow. I walked as if in a dream, feeling as if I, or everything, could fade away at any moment. Just like that. I knew my route so well by now, feeling the road become grass, and then longer grass, until at last, the bench, my bench, came into sight.

*

'This will always be our bench,' Paddy insisted, wiping away the remaining splinters which poked from his handiwork.

He put his arm around me and wiped his brow with the other, beads of wet brewing on his hairline, weary from effort. And love did take effort. But as I stared down at the carving, I knew it was worth it. He had done a good job. I traced the outline of the heart with my eyes, running it against the grain. But in the top right curve, his hand must have slipped, for a jagged mistake etched downwards, pointing to the centre where our initials hung close. My own heart lurched. Was that a crack? A sign? I sighed, laughing at my superstition, squeezing Paddy just a little tighter.

But I wondered if I went back there now, back to that bench, if the crack would have grown; whether it would be the then or the now which was reflected. What would the looking glass show? Or was it broken? Broken like us?

★

As my new bench came into sight, my heart stopped. Shit. There was someone there. Oh no, not now – not now that I needed it more than ever. I could feel rage brewing, but there was no point. Oh, maybe I should just head back. Because now there was a real, other person sitting there, with a bun in their hair and a bright white raincoat . . . but then again, could it be?

'Flo,' I called out.

The person turned around to face me, and even from where I stood, I could see those emerald eyes smiling.

'Oh my God, I can't believe you're here,' I exclaimed, practically running to join her.

'What brings you here so early in the morning?' she quizzed.

But I didn't answer. I just couldn't believe it. I wanted to grab her and hug her and thank her for being here – for knowing. But I realised that I had never hugged her before. How strange. Maybe we just weren't close enough for that

yet. But I already felt closer to her than I did to anyone –
like I had known her my whole life. And seeing her here
dispelled the knot of tension which had been twisting up my
insides.

It took me a few minutes to settle my breathing and focus
my mind. I wanted to pinch myself to make sure it was real.
But we didn't touch, so I just had to feel her with my eyes,
work them over every inch of her to make sure it wasn't all
in my head.

'Why are you so edgy?' Flo finally asked, noting my
excitable disposition, my left leg twitching like a dog in heat.

I made it stop. That's when reality arrived once more. I'd
been momentarily so distracted by the joy and sheer luck of
finding Flo here that I'd almost forgotten about why I had
come in the first place. The cut on my finger screeched as
a reminder. I pulled my sleeve down over it. But what was
the point in hiding? Her question still hung in the air. The
cut still screeched. There was only one way to silence it. I
took a deep breath. This time, I would answer.

'Flo, I had the most horrible nightmare last night,' I began.
Her flawless skin glowed in the morning light.

'But the thing is, it wasn't a nightmare . . . not really. I
mean, it was more . . . it was more of a . . . of a . . . a flash-
back,' I eventually managed.

A gust blew between us, clearing the space.

'OK. Why don't you tell me what happened?' Flo suggested
tentatively, smooth syllables pouring out. 'In the nightmare,
I mean.'

I paused on the threshold of truth, inches from revealing
everything. But shouldn't I just shut up? Then again, surely

talking about it would make it real and it would just be better . . . Alice, you can't do that anymore; you can't pretend. Because your dreams know the truth. And even if you keep denying it, they won't – they'll keep showing you, reminding you what a filthy liar you are.

'Well, in the nightmare,' I began, 'I'm in my room, after a bop. And this guy called . . . Rob . . . Robbie, he's in third year in my college . . . well, he's there too.'

I looked to Flo for reassurance. The emeralds offered it in abundance. I just had to keep going. Don't stop, Alice. Don't think.

'And we're in my bed, and we're kissing, and then . . . and then he wants to . . . he wants . . . but I don't . . . I mean, I don't want to . . .' I shut my eyes. 'But I do . . . I mean, I say no, but . . . but he still . . . and my lip bleeds . . . and he . . . oh God . . .'

Tears began to form behind my clenched eyelids, and in the darkness, the image started to form again – that same image – the nightmare all over.

'No,' I screamed at it.

'It's OK,' Flo soothed, still not touching me, letting her words feel their way. It felt good.

I steadied my breathing and wiped away pre-tears that had managed to escape. But no more. No more crying. But more importantly, no more pretending – if I wanted to get over this, to get on with my life and just forget that this ever happened, first I would have to remember. I would have to accept the truth and then walk away from it. Run away and never come back. Just say the words, Alice – just say the words and you'll be cured – you'll have accepted what happened to you and then you can let it go and move on.

I turned to Flo and then turned away again, looking straight ahead at where a blossom tree began to open its petticoats to the world.

'Flo . . . Flo, I think . . . no, I don't think – I know . . . I know I was . . .'

One last deep breath. Just one. Come on.

'Flo, I was raped.'

Just as I uttered the final word, the wind howled, muffling the sound. But I wasn't going to let the breeze take that away.

'One month ago, almost to the day, I was raped. I don't really want to talk about it, because there's nothing to say, except that I was raped, and now I'm accepting it, and then I'm going to move on. And I'd like you to be a part of that.'

I couldn't believe I'd uttered the 'r' word. Up until now, 'Robbie' was the thing beginning with that letter which had troubled me most of all, but then, as if out of nowhere, I'd gone and said it: 'rape'. I hadn't even let myself think the word, never mind saying it; saying the single syllable that was foul on my lips. But now I knew that it was me saying it – that at last, I was in control of it. I knew, from now on, I was going to be fine. I shut my eyes. Almost.

12

I met with Flo again on the Sunday. I used the 'r' word a few more times and each time I could feel myself healing. But for some reason, Flo wasn't letting me get away with it that easily.

'You know, you should really talk to someone. There's plenty of counselling services in Cambridge – maybe you should give one of them a call.'

I closed my eyes, suppressing my frustration. 'Flo, I *am* talking to someone – I'm talking to you.' How many people did I have to bloody well talk to? I was over it, so why couldn't Flo be over it too?

'Ally, come on. You're doing so well, and it's so good that you've finally told me about it all, but if we're being honest, I don't really have a clue about any of it; not really. You need to talk to a professional – see what they have to say.'

The logic of Flo's words frustrated me further. I knew she was right. But it was still irritating to know my plan had backfired – I had thought that once I used the 'r' word – once I finally gave a name to what had happened – that was it. Acceptance was the first step to recovery, right? I had secretly hoped it would be the only step, that I could accept and move on. But I know saw that using the 'r' word had

141

implications; apparently now I should talk to a bloody counsellor, a therapist. There was an awful joke the boys in school
used to tell: 'Why do shrinks make you lie on couches?'
'Because they're really the rapists.'

The relevance made me shudder. But this was ridiculous.
I was fine.

'Alice, if you want, you don't even have to meet someone
face to face – you could just call someone up. There's loads
of phone lines and stuff for this sort of thing. Just see what
they have to say and then at least you can know you made
a conscious effort to sort it out, to sort yourself—'

'I don't need sorting!'

I didn't mean to snap. I just felt like I was going backwards, not forwards, and it was driving me crazy. This bench
was supposed to be my place of solace, not somewhere to
frazzle my brain.

'Alice, please. For me?' Flo coaxed, the emeralds softening so much I could have sworn she was going to cry.

And I couldn't let her cry. She had been so amazing all
along, and always right; scarily right. So maybe I just had
to take this last piece of advice and all would be OK. I had
to trust her. After all, that's what best friends do, right?

*

As I walked home, I decided that maybe one phone call
wasn't so bad. If seeking professional advice was the way to
prove that I had let it go, then so be it.

Entering my college, the stillness echoed the calm which
had descended on my mind. Presumably people were either

watching the Six Nations, or in the library, or actually embracing Sunday as their day of rest. A familiar face emerged from the Senior Tutor's door, that of a very sheepish-looking Joey.

'Senior Tutor's office, on a Sunday? Wow, you must really be in trouble,' I teased. I was happy to see him. It had been a while.

'You have no idea,' he replied, rolling his eyes.

'Go on, confess your sins then.'

He launched into his tale of woe, where too little dinner and too much lager had led to just the right amount of vomit to earn him a stern talking-to.

'Anyway, how are you?' he asked, his eyes making sure I was aware just how loaded a question this was.

But by now we had almost reached my door. Half of me wanted to invite him in for a cup of tea – to have a chat and a catch-up and while away the hours. Because I really had missed him, more than I realised. But the rest of me was so focused on making this bloody phone call – to get it over and done with so that I could then have all the time in the world for tea and chats with Joey or anyone else.

'Joey, I'm really sorry, but there's a couple of bits and pieces I need to do. But how about I call you tomorrow and we'll go for lunch or something – spend some quality time, yeah?'

I could see doubt flicker in his eyes. 'OK, well, do give me a call,' he said, though his voice sounded unconvinced.

'I will,' I said, and meant it, looking forward to proving him wrong just as soon as I'd put everything right.

*

I logged online to get a phone number. I googled 'Cambridge' + 'counselling' + 'phoneline' and a list of options instantly appeared. I clicked the first one. I wasn't going to be fussy. 'Welcome to the Cambridge Crisisline', the page greeted. But I didn't feel welcome – I felt awkward and weird and I just wanted to get this over and done with. I clicked on Contact Us, looking over my shoulder, as if someone was suddenly going to burst through the door and catch me.

'Shit,' I growled under my breath.

Due to lack of resources, their phone line was only open on Wednesday evenings, from eight to ten. That was it. One night a week, for a couple of hours. No more. Jesus, it wouldn't want to be a crisis after all, would it? I had built myself up, psyched myself up to this being it, the real it, over and out. But now I had to sit it out for three more days. The whole point of calling this bloody 'crisis line' was to make things better, to seal the deal. But I couldn't let this get me; it was just a test. Deep down I knew I could probably have found another number, another phone line. But I told myself no – I just had to wait. The time would toughen me up; I would be ready for anything.

*

Eventually, Wednesday came. I hadn't spoken to anyone since Flo on Sunday – I was too focused on making the call, to talk to that stranger, to be told I was cured. I went to

144

lectures alone and studied alone. And that was fine. Except when I realised that that meant no lunch with Joey. He had known I would bottle, and it turned out that he was right. My failure had become predictable – it was the worst thing of all.

But Wednesday evening soon arrived, and it was time for change, to break the gloomy trend which had consumed me for so long – time to escape. I held my mobile in my hand, the number dialled and ready to go, telling myself that I was in control. My left leg jolted and I slammed it still. The cheesy photo of me and Róisín grinned on; I slammed it down too. No one could watch, no one could hear. I clicked call. This was it. Every ring made my heart shudder, my butterflied stomach about to burst. The ringing stopped. A tiny click clicked. There was a voice. This was my stranger.

'Hi, you've reached the Cambridge Crisisline, thank you for calling. My name's Adele and I'm here to listen.'

My voice was completely gone; I mean, what do you say? Where on earth do you begin? From the beginning, I supposed.

'Eh . . . hi. I'm . . . I'm Alice,' I said.

I knew I could stay anonymous, but whatever – my first name wasn't going to make much difference.

'By the way, did I see on your website that I can only talk to you for twenty minutes?' I asked.

'Well yes, I'm afraid that's the case – because of our limited resources, we have to make sure we can take as many calls as possible in the couple of hours we have,' Adele replied.

'And like, can people come and meet you face to face?' I continued.

'No, again, our limited resources . . .'

'Wow, that's mad, isn't it? So are you guys all volunteers?'

'Yeah, pretty much,' she answered, disheartened further.

I tried to picture what she looked like. She sounded weedy and pale. I imagined her stooping bony-shouldered over a phone.

'And like, where do you get your funding from and stuff?'

'To be honest, most of it comes from the Cambridge RAG committee. But Alice, is this really why you called?'

They were funded by RAG? I smiled; how ironic. RAG had been my way of thinking about other people's problems instead of my own. Yet now it had come full circle. Turns out I didn't need to be a starving AIDS orphan in Africa – I was still a charity case.

'Look, I just want to keep this as brief as possible,' I stated, keeping my tone very matter-of-fact.

'OK, take your time,' Adele said soothingly.

I assumed by taking my time what she really meant was to 'take my twenty minutes'. Oh, I was being cynical.

'OK,' I affirmed, more to myself than to her. 'OK, well, basically, the thing is, about a month ago, five weeks now really, but anyway . . . I was . . . I was . . . I was raped.'

The 'r' word didn't feel as weird this time – see, I *was* better.

'Well done for coming out and saying it, Alice. I know a lot of survivors really struggle—'

'Survivors?' I repeated with an almost-laugh, the word shocking my ears.

'Yes, survivors. That's what we call women who have been

raped or sexually abused, because "survive" means to keep on living.'

'Well, it's not like he tried to kill me,' I guffawed. Clearly Adele was overestimating just what had gone on. 'Look, it was a guy in my college, a couple of years ahead. And we were both drunk. And yeah, he raped me. Look, I don't really want to talk about it – I've come to terms with it and everything, so I just kind of want some advice as to where to go from here, you know?'

I was probably one of the more frustrating 'survivors' Adele had dealt with in a while – I wasn't exactly the vulnerable little victim she could just assure everything was going to be OK. No – I wanted answers; quick, fast answers, and that was all.

'Well, it's good that you can be so strong about it. As long as you're sure . . .'

'Oh, I'm sure,' I cut in, my voice loud.

'Well, OK. That's good. So I suppose the next things to think about are things like STDs – I mean, did he use a condom?'

I almost laughed again – how much of an idiot was I not to have thought about that? How had I not thought about STDs? What a twat! Alice, that's so unlike you. Right, need to get an STD check. Grand. Next?

'OK, cool, and what else?' I continued, forming my mental checklist.

'What about pregnancy? I mean . . .'

'No, I'm on the Pill. Ironic, really, isn't it?' I snorted, a single bitter laugh coughing out. It wasn't funny. We both knew that.

'Right, well . . . I mean, have you thought about seeing a counsellor? Face to face?' Adele suggested, her tone still most gentle. Was that to reassure me? Or because she was afraid I would bite her head off? Oh, I knew I was being a bit of a wench, but frankly, I didn't care.

'I kind of have been seeing one,' I lied.

But was it a lie? Because Flo was as good as any counsellor, she made so much sense. And she made me feel so at ease. No, I could probably say that that box was ticked. Next.

'So anything else?' I commanded.

'Some survivors consider going to self-defence classes.'

Poor Adele's voice was starting to shake. Of course I assumed she usually dealt with specifics and the specific needs of individuals and individual cases. But I was keeping this as general as possible; just needed some general advice.

'No, I don't need self-defence classes, thank you.'

'Right . . . well, have you considered, you know . . . .pressing charges?'

I froze. Press charges? Go to the police? That was a bit much, wasn't it? Suddenly I could feel her sitting up, trying to instil me with confidence.

'Rape organisations are trying to get more women to report their experiences because although it is a very serious crime, the rate of convictions is so low, and it's such a shame more women aren't given the justice they deserve.'

Justice? Crime? Serious crime? These terms had never entered my head before now.

'How . . . how . . . I mean, it's not like . . . I wasn't like, walking home at night and some madman jumped out of the bushes or something. It was only . . . like I said, we were both . . . it was just drunken . . . he's in my college, for God's sake . . .'

'Alice, only eight per cent of rapists are complete strangers to the survivor. And around seventy-four per cent of rapes are carried out in the survivor's home. That jumping out of the bushes malarkey is just a very tiny portion of all cases. Yours is just as entitled to go to court.'

I had to sit down on my bed, my legs weaker than they should have been. But everything suddenly felt different. I thought it was just me trying to keep things general, but now I wondered, in reality, just how general I was – was I just another statistic?

'So if . . . if I was to . . . you know . . . follow this through. Like, how would I . . . how would I go about it?'

I didn't know if I would. But it was worth asking. I mean, I'd never even considered . . . My mind was misty, and no lighthouse guided me through. I needed Flo. She was my lamp.

'Well, you'd need to go to a police station as soon as possible and make a statement. If the case is reported soon enough after it occurs, they would do a forensic examination, but as it's been over a month . . .'

'What kind of stuff would they do?'

Even if it was too late, I was still curious to know.

'Well, if you were still wearing the clothes you wore when it happened, they would check them for hairs and fibres, and the police would keep them . . .'

I thought of my pale pink knickers dotted with roses – the ones I'd worn that night. But I'd washed them since.

Like my bed linen, I'd left them down in the laundry room, where I knew they would stay, hidden far away.

'. . . comb your hair and pubic hair, and take samples from under your nails, your vagina, anus, throat and mouth . . .'

I couldn't believe my ears – this sounded vile. It was violating in itself. Strangers touching you in all the places you've just been . . .

'Alice, are you still there?' Adele's voice cut through my sordid thought train.

'Yeah,' my voice cracked. I coughed. 'Yes, I'm here.'

'If you want me to stop at any point . . .'

'No, no, keep going. Please.'

I needed to hear this – I needed to hear because if I didn't, then I couldn't say I was better. I could bear all this, no problem.

'OK, well, like I said, since it's been a few weeks since your case took place, then it's probably too late for a forensic. So instead, you'll just give a statement and then if there's enough evidence against the attacker, he will be charged.'

'And then what?'

'Well, then you may have to formally identify the perpetrator, and then the next day at the local Magistrate's Court it will be decided whether he gets bail or not.'

'And then when's the actual court case?'

I knew it was rude to keep interrupting, but I just needed the facts.

'It's usually between six and twelve months before a case goes to the Crown Court.'

Six to twelve months. Up to a year. Another year. In one year I'd be halfway through my time in Cambridge.

'Do you think there's actually a chance he could be convicted?' I asked Adele.

'Well, Alice, I'm not an expert so I don't know. If you feel up to it, you should go to the police station and give your statement, and see what they have to say,' she advised cautiously.

I knew she couldn't give me a black and white answer. But right now, my brain couldn't deal with colour. Facts and information and statistics created a cacophony of confusion that made me want to scream. I needed to get off the phone.

'Listen, Adele, thank you very much for your help,' I said.

'You know where to find me – if you call back at the same time next week, you can ask for me.'

'Thanks.'

I had no intention of calling back, for even as I hung up the phone, regret pumped through my veins. What a stupid bloody idea it was to call. Now I felt wretched. My brain hurt and I was weary and there was so much to consider. I was spiralling downwards. I felt angry at Adele for telling me all those things, angry at Flo for making me call, but most of all, angry with myself – why had I listened to Flo's advice? Why didn't I just go with my instinct? And why was I so flustered by what Adele had said? After all, I had asked. And just because I *could* go to the police and apparently I *should* see a professional counsellor didn't mean I had to. No, it was time to rely on my instincts again. But as I searched within myself for guidance, I couldn't see. It was dark and murky and diverging paths led in different directions, none of which felt right. It took every last inch of my strength not to just admit defeat there and then. But Alice, what the hell are you talking about? You're fine; you're Alice Chesterton. You never give up. Pull yourself together, for God's sake.

So I did. Because I didn't know what else to do. I didn't even really know how to give up; lack of experience made it a foreign concept. So instead I went to bed and told myself to sleep, praying that he wouldn't be there, waiting for me, on the other side.

Thankfully, he wasn't. Maybe I was OK after all.

13

That Sunday I didn't go see Flo. I was still in shock from Wednesday's phone call. But why had I freaked out so badly? It didn't make sense. I had been doing so well. But then I decided that maybe since Adele was being so nice and offering me all these ways to 'get over' what had happened that I had started to let myself believe that I even needed to 'get over' it at all. When someone is being nice to you and piling on the compassion and advice, it automatically weakens you, because you feel like you can let your guard down because this person will look after you. And that was what happened with Flo too — she was so generous and kind and amazing at listening that I had told her things and opened up and bathed in her concern. But the bathing had made me soft, had eroded my tough skin to the point that I suddenly realised that I didn't just enjoy our Sunday chats, but I relied on them, I needed them. But I was Alice Chesterton and I didn't *need* anything. It was time to take a step back and not step off the path into that long grass towards our secret garden.

So I wrote my final essay, and suddenly it was the last week of term and I was struggling to work out where the last two months of my life had gone. But someone else was keeping tabs on my academic life for me, and I before I knew it I was off to my end-of-term meeting with my Director of Studies to discuss my progress.

'Come in,' he called as I knocked on the big oak door.

I entered with a smile, gazing at the portraits that hung on the beautiful wood-panelled walls, which made the room dark but reassuring all at the same time. I had only been in this room three times before since coming to Cambridge – at the start of both my terms, and then at the end of last term to hear a glowing report of my progress in my opening eight weeks in the university. But this was also the room in which I'd had one of my entrance interviews – that terrifying day all the way back in December over one year ago. This same tutor with his half-moon spectacles and his gentle lisp had greeted me kindly, but I had been wary of him nonetheless – I'd heard all kinds of stories about Oxford and Cambridge interviews, and I knew there was nothing kind about them whatsoever. Luckily, my interview had been very straightforward, consisting mainly of a rant about Irish history in which my tutor was very interested – lucky me! And now that he had chosen me to get in, and had been suitably impressed with my first term's work, I was eager to hear what he had to say about this term.

I sat in one of the two leather armchairs which stood either side of a magnificent marble fireplace in which a low glow flickered softly. The room was heavy with history, apt for his profession.

'Well, Alice, it hasn't exactly been a great eight weeks for you, now has it?' he began.

My heart sank. I gazed at the coals, their glow the only thing that made sense.

'Oh?' was all I could manage, my left leg beginning to shake.

'Yes – it seems you started out well, but then I believe you were sick?'

'Oh . . . yes,' I agreed, casting my mind back to the lie that had seemed so insignificant at the time. Who knew it would be kept on record? Guilt flooded through me, my left leg gaining pace as I willed it to stop.

'And are you better now?' my tutor asked, looking over his spectacles with what I assumed was concern.

But I didn't know what to say. It was a very good question: was I better? I knew we were both talking about different things, but I wished he had asked me this question ten days ago, before the phone call, before the strange and confusing thoughts which plagued my every waking minute. At least the nightmare hadn't come back. But it seemed instead it had filtered into my conscious hours, lurking in my every shadow. I *wanted* to be better; did that count for something? But things were crumbling – I was crumbling – and it infuriated me beyond belief.

'I'm getting there,' I finally replied. And it was the truth, however sorry.

'Hmm, well, I'm afraid it rather shows in your progress this term. All your supervisors' comments are much the same – that you started well, but then got steadily worse, and that your work often gave the impression of being very distracted, or preoccupied with something else.'

I couldn't bear this. I had worked my ass off, particularly

in the last few weeks – I had barely done anything else. I hadn't gone to Hall, I hadn't gone to the bar, so how could he say that I was preoccupied? I mean, I knew that there *was* something else going on, going on in my head. But I didn't realise it had affected my work. My stomach sank lower than I knew it could go. This was awful.

'Well, let's just hope your illness was to blame and that a good deal of reading over the Easter Vacation will set you up for a better term's work, yes?'

'Yes . . . yes . . . I mean, of course,' I stammered, muddling everything. 'I'm really sorry,' I added, feeling I at least owed it to him to say that – he had chosen me, for God's sake – he was the reason I'd got in. And now I'd let him down.

'Alice, don't apologise. Just pull yourself together! And have a nice break,' he concluded, standing up, indicating that that was all.

I did as I was told, getting up from the armchair and gliding out of the room in a sort of trance. 'Just pull yourself together!' His words echoed through me. I had been telling myself that all term. I just didn't know if I had the energy to pull together anymore. And that angered me the most – I'd let myself down and I was fast becoming unmotivated to do anything about it. I felt fury rise up – this was Cambridge, one of the best universities in the world. I knew how lucky I was to have got in. I'd kicked ass, for a while, and then what? Then I'd ruined everything. But no – that wasn't fair – it wasn't my fault. It was Rob. It was him – he ruined everything. Oh so what, you're just going to blame it on him? Play the victim all over again? *Well, why not? Why can't I?*

My head was screaming, my body longed to lash out, to

hit something, anything. But most of all him; to hurt him just like he had hurt me. My world was swiftly falling to pieces, and it was time for him to pay. It was the first time I had wanted revenge. I couldn't pretend anymore. It had happened, and he did it and it's time that I got my revenge. Why should he be out there having a great old time while I spent the whole term practically in hiding, focusing on my work? Well a fat lot of good that did, didn't it?

My feet started to lead me out of college and down the street. My body – the body which had been violated and hurt and controlled – was controlling my mind, taking me to the place where I, and it, could get even, get justice.

Cambridge Police Station was beside the fire station, the far side of Parker's Piece, the bustling stretch of grass where footballers, dog-walkers and unseasonal sunbathers alike congregated, while the stench from the fan at the back of Pizza Hut wafted through the breeze. A couple lay on the grass, arms intertwined as they melted into one another, kissing and giggling. But I didn't have time to be jealous, only time to put one foot in front of the other and cut through the grassy plot until finally I reached the wooden door.

The station itself was unlike any building I'd ever been in in this town – so unstylish, so bleak, so unimpressive. The sunlight didn't quite make it all the way down the length of the foyer, leaving the last metre in semi-darkness, dusky grey. There was no one else there; no civilians, that is, for which I was thankful, and I tried to remember if I'd ever been in a police station before. I was in one once in Dublin to get a form for my driver's license, but that was about it. Yet now I was here for a proper reason, to report a real crime. It was a scary thought, yet strangely exciting too. I walked to the counter at the end of the foyer, beyond which I could see desks and chairs and folders and two police officers chatting over a cup of coffee. They didn't notice me immediately, for I had tried to make as little noise as possible when moving over the tiled floor, nervous to disturb the silence, my silent film. But one of them, the fatter of the two, with short red hair, spotted me.

'What can we do for you, miss?' he asked in a Yorkshire accent.

'Eh, I'd like . . . I've come . . . I mean, I need to make a statement,' I garbled in a whisper. Why was I so afraid to speak normally? It wasn't a bloody library.

'Oh right, miss, and what exactly would this, erm, statement be about then?'

Even though I knew this was going to be one of the first and most obvious questions I was asked, it still caught me off guard. How to put it? Oh, just tell like it is, Alice. Stay strong, OK?

'Well you see, I've been . . . I was . . . I mean, about six weeks ago now . . . I was, you know . . . I was raped.'

There – I'd said it. Now it was time to compose myself again – I wasn't here as a victim, remember? I was here for revenge.

'Oh right, well, eh . . . if you'd like to come through to the interviewing room just on your right there, I'll go get the Dictaphone and we can, er, we can have a little chat,' the policeman advised.

I wondered how many nineteen-year-old girls just showed up unannounced of a Friday afternoon and declared that they'd been raped.

I entered the door to the right of the counter and was instantly disappointed with what I saw. It was just a small, grey room with a table and chairs not unlike those we had in school. My police officer bumbled in, clutching some forms and pens and a Dictaphone, a single bead of sweat trickling down his bulging forehead.

'Right, right,' he muttered as he set himself up. 'My name's Officer Marty Jones, but just call me Marty, all right?'

I assured him I would, and introduced myself in return.

'Oh, an Irish lass? I didn't notice before. Whereabouts are you from then?' Marty quizzed, his Yorkshire eyes brightening up.

'Dublin,' I answered. I wasn't here for small talk. I was here to talk about something big, really big.

'Ah, Dublin – lovely place – been there a couple of times with the wife. Now, you know you're entitled to request that a female officer be present in the room if you so wish. Trouble is, we've got none on duty at the moment, but if you'd like to come back . . .'

'No, no, that's fine. I'd just like to get on with it really,' I said. Frankly, I preferred there to be as few people in the room as possible. Minimal fuss.

'Right, well, I'll just click record and then you can start to tell me what happened – if you could give us dates and times and that sort of thing, and if you know the perpetrator, and if there was alcohol involved . . .'

Marty rambled on, until finally he stopped, and it was

my turn. I was more nervous than I expected – even though I'd told Flo about it, I had never given her the details. But now I was being asked for a blow-by-blow account, and I knew that, if I let it, this could be like the nightmare all over again. But I just had to think of them as facts – facts and figures that were all pieces of evidence. So I began at the beginning, and I didn't stop until the very end – until he had come and my lip was bleeding and I somehow fell asleep and the next morning and then his horrible text message . . .

'Do you still have it?' Marty interrupted for the first time. I had paused very little during my account. To pause was to think, and there was nothing to think about; these were just facts.

'No. I deleted it,' I admitted sheepishly.

How bloody stupid of me was that? That was proof if ever I had any, a single shred of concrete evidence. But back then I had just wanted to erase it all and pretend that it just hadn't happened – to fool myself into denial. Oh, how naïve I had been. How naïve and bloody stupid.

Marty wiped his brow with the back of his hand, yet I felt so cold I was almost shivering.

'Now, Alice, I'm going to need to ask you a few questions about your own sexual history. You don't have to answer anything you're not comfortable with, OK? So just take it handy,' Marty advised, though not making eye contact with me. The poor guy – he probably had kids my age, maybe a daughter.

'So, before the . . . the rape, were you . . . were you sexually active?'

'Yes, I'd had sex with my ex-boyfriend.'

'Right. And anyone else?'

'No.'

'No other sexual partners?'

'No.'

'And when was the last time, before the rape, that you'd had sex?'

It had been the day Paddy and I broke up. I could remember it so vividly in my mind. And yet the detail which stuck out most of all was those awful words, that awful question he'd asked about it as we were ending things: 'What was that, my goodbye fuck?' The 'fuck' tainted our last time together, and I resented Paddy for it; why had he done that? But I supposed in his eyes, I had tainted everything; I was telling him that I had fallen out of love with him, and I couldn't help but admit that his anger was probably far stronger than mine.

'It was about three weeks.'

'Right, OK . . . well listen, Alice, if you want to go outside and take a seat in the foyer, and I'll just write this up and then I'll call you back in to read it and sign it and we can talk about what happens next.'

Marty was very good at making it all sound just like a procedure – just another case. And I liked that; that was how I wanted it.

I stepped back into the foyer, the dim light still momentarily blinding compared to the interview room. I sat down on one of the steel benches beside a pathetic-looking potted plant, wilting in the gloom. It felt strange to have been asked about Paddy, to think about our last time together, the last time we made love. Maybe I should give Paddy a call? I'd be home in just over a week – maybe we'd meet up? Part of me wanted to see him and see how he was and just to look at him again. But the other part wondered how I could be around him. How could I just chat and laugh and tell him I'd had an amazing term, when so much had changed, when I had changed. Because what scared me the most was that Paddy knew me so well, better than anyone. So what if he could tell? What if he just looked at me and said, 'Alice, something's up', and then worked it out? A bit of me wanted him to hold me, and to bury my head in his shoulder, and hide in his arms. But what then? Would he want me back, want us to get back together? I couldn't even begin to think about something like that. I was struggling to even think at all.

I waited in the foyer, with all this going through my mind, for what seemed like an age.

'Right, Alice, if you'd like to come back in,' Marty finally said cheerily. I entered the grey room once more. 'Now, either you can read this to yourself, or I can read it out to you.'

'You read it,' I interjected without really thinking.

I listened to Marty read the statement. It was strangely odd to hear him read it, as if I was listening to a story about someone else entirely.

'Right, well, if you think that sounds OK, I'll just get you to sign at the bottom now, and then we'll be in touch about what happens next – whether we feel it's still worthwhile doing a forensic examination, though I think it's unlikely, whether we're going to press charges – all that sort of thing. I mean, I don't want to get your hopes up too much because these are always very tricky cases, you know? And you'd only be a witness in the case.'

'What?'

'It's the state that makes the case – you're just a witness.'

I couldn't believe my ears.

'So it's not actually me who brings him to court?'

'No. You barely appear in the court at all – only when it's your turn to be in the witness stand.'

'And what about the rest of the time?' I asked, my heart beginning to thump violently.

'Well, you'd be in the waiting room really. But some girls find that very difficult too, because often the lad's family is in there with them.'

My left leg was off again, quicker than ever. How could this be true? This was *my* case, *my* payback.

'But listen, we'd still encourage you to give in your state-ment and we can decide where to go from there. So if you just sign here . . .'

My mind was numb, feeling everything and nothing all at once.

'Just here, yeah – just your initial and surname on this one . . .'

I took the pen Marty handed me and stared down at his scrawl – the messy words that told my messy story. *My* story. How dare they try and take that from me, just call me a witness, an onlooker to the whole thing. Because I had done so much more than watch. And now I had to watch it over and over again every day, in my dreams and in my mind's eye. And not just watch it, feel it, to feel him on me and in me . . .

'Alice? Are you all right?'

I nodded my head and began to sign, just like he said; initial and surname. My hand shook . . . A . . . I could feel him even now . . . C . . . would he ever go away . . . H . . . come on, Alice, pull yourself together . . . E . . .

I stopped and stared down at what I'd written: ACHE. And that's when it hit me – I *did* ache. I ached in every way imaginable. I was bruised within and without, and I couldn't face feeling like this and going over and over it all for another whole year. Soon I would be twenty, and would I really want to leave my teens behind and yet be forced to cling onto the thing I wanted to lose most of all? By the sounds of things, I had so little evidence that the chances of him being convicted were slim to none anyway. So he would just win all over again? I'd have to drag the whole thing out, to ache more and more, and for what? So that he could just beat me down, humiliate me once more?

I let the pen fall from my fingers as I stood up in a daze. I could hear Marty saying my name, asking me what was wrong, but I needed to get out. Those four grey walls were closing in, pushing me to do something I just couldn't face. Even if he *was* convicted, where would that leave me then? Did I really believe that it would just erase all the pain that throbbed through me? The thought of sitting in a waiting room with his family, the thought of their eyes burning on me, probably believing that I was some lying little bitch, some stupid Irish girl that was trying to humiliate their poor innocent son. And meanwhile, their son would be in the court, with his lawyers, covering all the angles, covering his back. And who had my back? That wasn't for me to know;

it wasn't my case. I wasn't the defendant because I hadn't been able to defend myself then, so why should I get the chance now?

The foyer was brighter than before, startling my eyes again as they winced to cope. Marty was calling me back, but I needed to get out. I felt bad – he'd spent all day tiptoeing around me, being the perfect gentleman, and now I was leaving without so much as an explanation, a reason. But reason had left me, and emotion; that thing I so rarely let take control now led me out of the station, away from it all, away from the ache. Only I was the ache. And it shadowed my every step.

*

I don't think I spoke until Sunday; thirty-six hours of silence, aching silence.

I spent Saturday on the internet, looking up facts and statistics about rape, storing them up in my already overloaded head, so that by the time I met Flo on Sunday, they were bursting to pour out.

'And did you know, if he's found guilty, the sentence can be appealed, but if he's found innocent, it can't,' I recounted, my voice hurried and desperate as I listed off yet another bleak truth. 'And apparently there's evidence to indicate around one in six women have experienced some form of sexual victimisation since the age of sixteen. One in six! Can you believe it?' I shrieked, sending a blue tit which had been hopping nearby fluttering away in terror.

'No, no I can't,' Flo replied calmly, her gaze upon me as

I tried to catch my breath. 'But Alice, what do all these statistics mean? What are you trying to achieve?'

'I just don't know,' I admitted. 'I guess I just thought it would be another way of coming to terms with it all, you know? Flo . . .' I sighed, staring down at my lap, ashamed of it all. 'Flo, I've tried everything – I've tried pretending it didn't happen, I've tried talking to you, I've trying calling the fecking Crisisline, I've tried going to the police – I've literally tried everything. Why am I not better?' I begged, praying she knew the answer, praying she knew why every day was warmer, brighter, and yet I was sinking into a swallowing darkness.

'Ally, you need to give it time. It's only been six weeks; six weeks – that's it. You can't just expect to get over it in—'

'But why not?' I shouted, the tears breaking free now. 'Why can't I? I'm going home in a couple of days and if they see me like this – if they notice that something's up . . .'

'So what?' Flo questioned, her voice more powerful than I think I'd ever heard it. 'So what if they do notice? You're perfectly entitled to be stressed after an entire term at Cambridge, rape or not. So even if you don't want to tell them exactly why, would it really be so bad to just admit that you're down? That you're a bit weak?'

'*Yes!*' I screeched, my frustration overflowing, 'Flo, you don't understand. You have to stop telling me it's OK for me to be weak, because that's *making* me weak.' My voice broke beneath the weight of my tears.

'Is that why you didn't come and see me last week?' she asked.

A horrible tension loomed over us both; the eye of the storm.

'I'm sorry,' I finally muttered.

'Don't apologise,' Flo replied, though not in an 'it's OK' kind of way, but rather in a way that implied that such an apology was pathetic, pathetic and unappreciated.

'But Flo, you have to see; this isn't me. I don't get upset and I don't cry.'

'Alice, you were raped!' she interjected with frightening strength. 'You're allowed to be upset, for God's sake.'

'I know I'm *allowed* to be,' I retorted just as powerfully, 'if I was the kind of person who tended to get upset. But I'm not. So do you not see? This is changing me – I'm starting to lose who I am, and it petrifies me.' My voice trailed off into a whimper.

'So let people see that, Alice. You don't have to be perfect. Just because you've spent your life looking after your brothers and your friends and everyone else doesn't mean you have to be perfect. Nobody is.'

I frowned, resenting the implication that I thought I was.

'Flo,' I continued, desperate to make her see, 'it's not about being perfect – God knows I'm not. But you have to understand – this was my big adventure. I've told you how my friends felt about me leaving Dublin; they were scared and sad and I think deep down they resented me a bit for abandoning them. So what, now I'm supposed to come back and say, actually, no – I've failed; I've failed my big adventure.'

'But you haven't *failed*,' she jumped in. 'Something just happened to you, something terrible.'

'And do you not think that would just scare them even more?' I snapped. 'Do you really think my parents would ever let me come back here next term if they knew? If they knew that I wasn't able to look after myself?' I questioned, my heart sinking with every angry word.

'But Alice, you *are* able to look after yourself. This was just—'

'No, Flo – apparently I'm not. I mean, look at me.' I indicated towards my face, red and blotchy from the furious tears.

'You just need time,' Flo tried.

'Fine. Fine. I need time. But until the time comes that I can actually know that I'm better, I have to pretend; I have to get off that plane in Dublin Airport on Thursday afternoon and I have to be OK. For their sake as much as mine, Flo.'

My voice had taken on a new air of conviction, that Flo must have known there was no point continuing this conversation. There was another silence, the most awkward of them all.

'So you're leaving on Thursday then?' she asked, barely audible.

'Yeah.'

'How come so late? Term finished on Friday.'

'Want to make a start on my reading. Got a shit term review from my Director of Studies.'

'Really? You never said . . .'

'Just another sign of me failing.'

I sighed. Maybe I was feeling sorry for myself. Maybe I was depressed. Or maybe my world just was that gloomy. On top of everything, things now felt weird with Flo, and that was the bitter icing on top of the mouldy, crumbling cake.

'So, will I see you before you go?' she continued, looking into the distance as if she didn't care.

'Probably not, to be honest. I'm just going to be in the library and packing up my stuff. My flight's pretty early on Thursday. But if you want to call around for tea or . . .'

'No, I'm pretty busy myself,' Flo said.

I hated myself for assuming she was lying.

'Right, well . . . is your phone fixed yet? It's going to be really weird not talking over the holidays,' I admitted, trying to salvage something.

'No, still broken, I'm afraid.'

'OK, well, what about email – if it's the best we can do?' I laughed gently, trying to lighten things up – trying to undo the indignant attitude I'd adopted before.

'Don't have internet back home. But listen, you need to focus on stuff at *your* home this holiday. Just think about what I said, OK?'

'OK,' I agreed, hoping she knew that I really would. 'But I'm coming back a week early before next term, so will you be around? I mean, will I see you here?'

'I'll be here,' Flo affirmed, her voice softening enough to let me know that I hadn't ruined things completely.

I wanted to hug her, to apologise and to tell her I'd miss her and that in all honesty, I didn't know how I was going to face three weeks at home without her. But something held me back. And suddenly we were saying our goodbyes and I was heading back into town, the tears welling up once more. But I knew it would be OK with her; I had to know that, otherwise why would I come back next term? I hadn't spoken to Millie or Joey or anyone else in so long now that

Flo was pretty much all I had; she was all that was keeping me from being totally and utterly alone. So I couldn't push her away, I just couldn't. And I just prayed to God that I hadn't.

14

I stepped through the automatic doors into Arrivals, vaguely scanning the faces in the crowd as if by some miracle any of the Chesterton clan had bothered to make the trek out to the airport to collect me. A blur of signs and smiles fused together for others, but not for me. But suddenly I spotted a familiar face.

'Róisín!' I chirped, slightly startled by her presence.

'Hey, biatch, how's it going?' she said, throwing her arms around me and squeezing tightly.

I realised it was the first time in ages that I'd been hugged. It felt good; better than good. It felt like home.

'Come on, I'm parked on a double yellow and if I get clamped you are so getting your ass kicked.'

We bundled into the car and made a speedy getaway, just as a very aggravated taxi man beeped his horn with unnecessary ferocity.

'So, to what do I owe the honour of such a lovely chauffeuse?' I asked brightly. It was so nice to see someone new, someone who didn't know about all the mess, or who didn't know I'd been acting weird this term.

'Well, I rang your gaff yesterday and asked if anyone was going out for you, and your mum said your dad would be working and that she had some client to visit . . .'

'Ha, what's new!'

'Well, anyway – I just felt bad about you coming back to the motherland without a friendly face there to greet you. I was going to make you a sign and all, but I couldn't find my sister's fecking glitter glues. Maybe she's been sniffing them, the dark horse – get high and look pretty – now there's a concept . . .'

'Oh, Róisín, you're such a sweetie – I really appreciate it.'

And I did. More than she could know.

'Hmm,' she grumbled, suddenly less enthused.

'What?'

'No, nothing,' she covered, focusing all too intently on the road ahead.

'Go on,' I coaxed.

'No, it's just . . . well . . . oh, it's nothing really. I just met Paddy in town on Saturday.'

My stomach lurched.

'Ha ha, don't look so petrified,' Róisín teased. 'No, don't worry, he didn't say anything weird. We got talking about you and, well, it just made me think . . . oh I don't know, I don't want to go into it now, you've only just arrived.'

'Ah, Róisín, come on – tell me what it is.'

It took her a moment to finally get the words out.

'Look, Alice, I'm not having a go at you because you're only just home, but I just . . . you were just . . . you were really shit this term.'

I felt myself tense up. I couldn't take another friend having another go at me for being distant. What did they want from me? Why couldn't they all just leave me alone? I wished we weren't in a car – I wanted to just walk away from her, to tell her I couldn't do this, not now.

'Look, you don't have to say anything, because I know what you're going to say – that work was mental and like, you had so much stuff on your plate, and blah blah blah. I just want you to know how I feel, OK?'

I nodded slowly. I didn't want to fight with her.

'Anyway, that's all I wanted to say. Let's just forget about it, yeah?' she paused, letting the dust settle before stirring it all up again. 'So did you hear about PJ's party last week? There was this absolute hottie there – kind of a cross between Antonio Banderas and Heath Ledger, but a bit less Spanish and a bit less dead . . .'

And off she went into a torrent of mindless gossip, my body filling with relief as she filled me in on how everyone back in Dublin was, who was kissing whom, who was pissing off whom – all the usual. It felt so good to hear about other people again, their lives and worries and various goings-on. It was only then that I realised how wrapped up in myself I'd become, how self-involved. Without any friends in Cambridge besides Flo, to whom I only ever really spoke about myself, it felt like an age since I'd thought about anyone else. It was as if I'd done a complete personality transplant this term, from selfless to self-obsessed, and only now that I had taken a step back across the Irish Sea had it become clear to me. How hideous. No wonder Róisín was annoyed. But I knew how to put things right.

'And what about you,' I asked Róisín, brimming with interest. 'Any men on your scene?'

Róisín giggled more than ever. See – I could do this – I

was born to do this, and as we zoomed down the M50, I felt I'd found my cure at last.

★

By the time we reached my house in Ranelagh, I was so relaxed I could barely recognise myself. Róisín pulled over the car and said goodbye with a hug. Another embrace. It felt just as good as the last one.

'So look, I'll let you go spend the evening with your 'rents and bros and whatever homeless chap your mum is courting at the moment, and then tomorrow we can hang out, yeah?' Róisín suggested with a grin.

'Yeah, sounds good,' I agreed.

But then I remembered – no, there was something I wanted to do tomorrow. Just one last thing. I needed to see if I was completely clean; I needed to get an STD check.

'Oh shit, Ró, I'm really sorry – I can't do tomorrow.'

'Why not?'

'I just . . . I just can't,' I fumbled, my mind too light to think of an excuse. Why did it matter? I had three whole weeks at home. It was going to be great.

But Róisín didn't see it this way. 'So what, you're only back a few hours, and already you don't have time to hang out with me?' she complained.

'Oh come on . . .'

'What?' she spat. 'You can't even come up with a decent excuse.'

'Ah, Róisín, it's not like that – there's just something I have to do,' I said, still smiling; this didn't need to be a big deal.

'Oh, whatever, Alice. Now I really am glad I collected you from the airport – probably the only time I'm going to see you this holiday.'

'Ah, Ró, don't be like that,' I begged, worry beginning to seep in. 'Saturday I'm all yours, OK?'

'OK,' she conceded reluctantly. 'Just don't screw me over or you're dead, OK?'

'Wouldn't dream of it.'

'Right, well I might go get a bikini wax tomorrow instead then – I've got so many ingrown hairs down there I swear my minge is about to turn itself inside out!'

And with that, off she drove, leaving me mildly disgusted, but happy – or almost happy. Why did I feel like I had to sign a contract with my friends the minute I was home as to where and when I would see them? Why couldn't I just do my own thing? But I reminded myself that my own thing didn't matter anymore, that after tomorrow, there was going to be no more thinking about me or what I needed, because, after all, I didn't need anything. My old philosophy back intact, I strolled up my driveway.

*

The next morning, once my parents had gone to work and my brothers to school, I made an appointment at my GP's clinic because it was familiar and it felt safe.

The bus to Monkstown bumbled along, the windows staring out to the sea, and beyond, Howth Head, which curved round in the foggy distance. Cambridge felt a million miles away, and with it, everything else. The rape felt like a lifetime ago, and even though I was still doing something related to it, it was a mere procedure, a means by which to check out and clear up any physical traces of that awful night. Simple as that. And emotional traces? Had they been checked out and cleared up? For now, it certainly seemed so, and though they say you can't run away from your problems, it certainly felt like you could hop on a Ryanair flight across the Irish Sea and feel a hell of a lot better. Because maybe this had been my wonderland after all.

*

'Well, Alice, what can I do for you?' the small, grey-haired doctor asked me, lipstick smudging the left incisor of her otherwise very friendly smile. 'You usually go to Dr Banks, don't you?'

'Yes, yes I do. Well, basically I wanted . . . I need . . . basically I've had unprotected sex and I want to have an STD check,' I blurted out.

'Right . . . right . . . well, usually we'd send you down the corridor to the nurse for this sort of thing, but I suppose it's good for me to keep my hand in, isn't it?'

I didn't know whether the joke was intentional or not, but I couldn't help but smile as she donned her rubber gloves and told me to hop up on the bed and take off my knickers. Rolling up my skirt, she told me to spread my legs, knees up.

'If you just spread as wide as you can, love, and when I count to three, you take a deep breath in, OK?'

'Ooh,' I squealed.

'Sorry, I forgot to count out loud. Just breathe in now, love,' the doctor instructed.

I did as I was told, though doubting how much it would help now. But despite the whole thing being a less than pleasant experience, at least it was brief; I'd give her that.

'Now, if you'd just take this and . . .'

'No worries,' I interjected, taking the plastic pee-sample jar and leaving the room, down the corridor on the left and into the loo to give the lady what she wanted. Soon I was back in the doctor's room as she sealed up and signed off various plastic bags filled with, well, filled with me.

'Now, it will take about two weeks for these to come back, OK? But we'll give you a call when they do. Would you prefer if Dr Banks . . .'

'No, no, that's fine, thanks   I'd rather you called,' I insisted.

I thanked lipstick-teeth profusely and left her room, paying at reception, and then jumped on the bus for home, all the while marvelling at how quick and easy and remarkably stress free that had been. I really was better. I really was fine.

*

The days blurred into one another as I flitted from friend to friend, catching up and chilling out and basically refamiliarising myself with my Dublin and my old self. Brown Thomas's waft of pricey perfumes was stronger, O'Connell Street's spike caught the sunlight brighter and every busker sang sweeter than I had remembered. Dublin was setting me right, training me back to my roots in no time. And then just as no time was becoming no time left, a big part of the old me, my old Paddy, got in touch.

Hey Ally, how u doin? Heard u got bak a while ago. Was jus wonderin if u wantd 2 catch up dis wkend – maybe dinner on Sunda? My treat. Wud b gd 2 c u, bt I totaly understand if ur busy. Hope all is wel, P xx

I smiled. It was nice to hear from him. Before I'd come home I'd been worried if I met him that he'd be able to see the truth. But no one had so much as blinked an eye at my demeanour since I'd returned. In fact, they'd all commented on what great form I was in. How I wished I could see the looks on Millie's or Joey's faces if they heard that. I guess after all it did just prove that the problem was them and not me. After my first term in Cambridge I'd secretly suspected that my new friends would be the ones I took with me into the future, but what the past two weeks had proven was that no, the opposite was true; the Irish crew were the ones who made me feel happy, relaxed, back to the old Alice who hadn't been raped and who looked after everyone and who never showed any signs of being weak. That girl was back, and I knew that it was my friends, my real friends, that I had to thank.

That said, I did miss Flo; or at least, I did think about her. But having suspected before I left Cambridge that her sympathy and generosity had indulged my neediness, my time at home proved that to be the case. My friends here didn't have a clue about what had happened, which made me start to forget about having it too. So how could Paddy? No, I would see him – I would let him buy me dinner on

Sunday – and I would prove to him, but most of all to me, that I was better, better than ever.

★

The Newcastle sky couldn't make up its mind. One minute it was bright, the next, dark, and the next, nothing at all. Just a void of white that left me feeling unenergised and uninspired.

'But Joey, surely you could just chase your tail for hours on end and have an awesome time,' Alice had once teased when I expressed a similar lack of motivation one Cambridge afternoon.

I smiled at the memory. I missed Alice and I had missed her all term. All term, as Henry and Millie's romance had bloomed and Alice had faded further and further out of my life. I still had lots of friends – the football team were all legends, and provided me with a great sporting alternative to tail-chasing. But it wasn't the same; it wasn't the same as knowing I could just wake up in the morning, pop down to Alice's room and chat the hours away. And why couldn't I? That was what troubled me. Because she had never explicitly said: 'Hey, Joey, feck off out of my life, would you?' Not once. That said, I knew Millie would argue that it was in fact Alice who had 'fecked off' out of ours. But had I given up too soon?

Everyone in Cambridge knew about Week Five Blues – the depression and exhaustion that seeps in just after halfway through term, when it's all getting too much, but the end still seems so far out of sight. What if that was what had happened to Alice? What if her Week Five Blues had just hit her harder and longer than anyone else's? And where had we been while she was struggling? We'd been down in our rooms, complaining about what a rubbish friend she was being, comparing notes as to when she'd let each of us down on various occasions.

Millie had surmised that the Ally we'd met in first term wasn't the real her, and now we were only finally realising what she was actually like. But I wasn't convinced. I wasn't convinced that my instinct – that connection I'd made with such an amazing girl from day one – was wrong. No, the more I thought about it, the more it seemed like something was up.

Now she was back in Ireland and no one had spoken to her in ages and I couldn't deny the guilt which tiptoed through me. Should I call her? Send her an email? Or was it too late? And if it wasn't too late – if there was still a sliver of hope that all could be restored – would some petty, impersonal email really be the way to make it better? No, frustrating as it was, I just had to wait until next week – until we were all back in Cambridge and things could finally be put right. Till then, I just prayed that Alice was all right. Because something deep down within me wasn't so sure.

*

'So what have you got planned for your last few days then?' Mum asked as I helped her fold the laundry while Dad and the boys were out at mass.

I knew I should have gone with them, but a big night out with the gang last night had made me sleep in until almost midday. I hoped God would understand. Then again, Róisín had always assured me that a hangover was a very viable excuse for not going to mass: 'Sure after all that water to wine malarkey, Jesus must have had a few seedy mornings himself, let me tell you.'

'Well, I'm going for dinner with Paddy tonight, and then Róisín's throwing some farewell thing for me on Tuesday evening with all the girls. And then my flight's on Wednesday afternoon,' I said, amazed at just how little time I had left.

'And when does term start then?'

'The following Tuesday. I just want to get back early to get some reading done, you know?'

I hadn't told Mum and Dad about my end-of-term report from my tutor. There was no need. It was a mere blip. And I was going to do everything in my power to get things back on track next term.

'So, dinner with Paddy, then – how do you feel about that?' Mum teased, elbowing me as I searched for order amongst a pile of odd socks.

'Mum!'

'What? I mean, you left so soon after you broke up, I never got a sense of how you felt about the whole thing.'

'Oh, so you did actually notice we broke up then?' I joked. Mum and I had never had one of these 'sisterly' relationships that many girls boasted they had with their mothers. So I didn't quite know why she now appeared to be showing some kind of interest in my private life.

'Ah, Alice. That's not fair,' she replied, her voice low.

We carried on folding, but her motions grew more agitated as she wrestled with the clothes, turning out an inside-out sock with increasing vigour until finally she flung it away.

'Look, Alice,' she began, suddenly locking my gaze. Her eyes were the very same blue as mine. And yet we were so different. Or were we? Maybe we were actually quite alike. I put up my front and she put up hers.

'Look, Alice, I know I spend a lot of time at the shelters and whatever, but—'

'Mum. Don't.'

I held her stare for a moment and then looked away – turned away from those eyes that mirrored mine.

And there we sat, amongst a heap of crinkled clothes. My head ached. It was fine. I was fine. I was finally OK again, despite everything. Flo had been right; I had needed time. Time and a change of scenery. But soon it would be time to change back again, and I only prayed that I could take back across the water whatever newfound contentment I'd discovered, or more precisely, uncovered. I didn't need to find out what Mum seemed so desperate to spill. It was too late for that. But it was time for me to finally find myself. Again. To be found.

*

'I hope you found your way OK?'

'Paddy, I've been here a million times. I was hardly going to get lost, now was I?'

A waitress showed us to our table, the warm buzz of the restaurant as alive as I'd remembered it as we trotted up to the mezzanine to our table beside the glass balcony which looked down on the humming below. I loved this place, and I knew that Paddy knew that, so was glad he'd chosen it. Very glad.

'You look great,' he said as we sat down.

'Thanks!' I tried to ignore the butterflies which suddenly awoke from their long, unhappy hibernation.

With every second I was trying to gauge how I felt about being there. Was I nervous? Of course. Excited? Well, why not? I hadn't seen him in so long. Hopeful? A bit. But hopeful for what?

'Will we get wine?' he suggested, scanning the menu.

'Yeah, sure, why not?' Some alcohol was just what was needed to put those butterflies back to sleep. 'The rosé is gorgeous here.'

'I remember,' Paddy said, catching my eye with a smile.

As he sat there in his pale pink shirt, the one I'd bought him for some anniversary or another, I wondered if perhaps I did want something to happen. Surely not? But nothing seemed sure anymore. Only time, and the rosé, would tell.

'So, how are you?' Paddy asked, his tone indicating that this was not just an off-the-cuff question.

I paused, gathering up all the newfound positivity I could find.

'I'm brilliant.' My own conviction almost startled me, though I didn't know why – it was the truth.

'Well that's good. Cambridge still as amazing as ever?'

'It really is.'

And that was the truth too – no matter what, Cambridge really was incredible.

'And work going good?'

'Ah, it's still tough. But I got another really great end-of-term review from my tutor, which was so nice after slogging my guts out, you know?' Wait, that wasn't quite the truth.

'And all your friends?'

'Sure, they're amazing. Millie and Joey are well. And I've made this new best friend called Flo.'

'Is she in your college as well?'

'Yes, she's in my college,' I fibbed, not knowing quite how to explain how we'd really met.

'And does she get on with the rest of your crew then? Or is Millie starting to get a bit jealous if she's a new best mate?' Paddy laughed.

'Oh no, they're great friends too. No fights over me as yet!' I laughed back.

What the hell was I doing? Why was I saying these things? They weren't true; none of it was true. I grabbed my glass and took a long, relieving gulp of rosé, praying it would sort me out.

'God, you really do like it, eh?' Paddy teased.

I smiled and engrossed myself in the menu, giving myself a few seconds to pull myself together.

After we ordered our meals, Paddy remarked, 'I knew you'd pick that. I don't know why you were reading the menu so intently. I've never known you to order anything else!'

'Oh, I just wanted to see if they'd added anything new since I'd left,' I covered. But shit, shit shit shit, already he was noticing; he noticed everything. I took another glug of my wine, hoping, commanding my nerves to settle.

'So how about you then? How's college treating you?' I inquired, turning the focus on him.

'Oh yeah, really well thanks. We've got a really good mixture of people on the course, you know? Some who are experienced, like me, and then some who are coming to it completely new. But it's really interesting because you can tell that the tutors must have been able to spot their potential at the auditions because they've already come on in leaps and bounds,' he explained. As always, his eyes burned with intensity when he spoke about drama.

I wondered what was going through his head right now, whether he still had feelings for me, or whether he was completely over the whole thing. Who knew – maybe he had a new girlfriend. My shoulders tensed. I hadn't thought of that. Could he have a new girlfriend already? Why shouldn't he? He was a good-looking, funny, warm, generous guy. Plus, hanging out with drama freaks all the time in college now, he'd probably found some beautiful budding movie star with whom he could chat Shakespeare and Synge till the cows came home. My heart sank, but I forced it to rise back up again. Why should I care? That wasn't why I was here. No, not at all.

★

'Look, Henry, it's no big deal,' I said, having pulled away from him just as things were starting to get hot and steamy, 'but I just wanted to say: I missed a Pill yesterday.'

It really wasn't a big deal, but I felt I ought to be honest, or more precisely, I was physically unable to keep a secret – 'Millie the Mouth' – that's what they called me at school! But this had to be brief – my parents were out for the evening, so Henry and I had the house to ourselves and the privacy was sheer bliss.

'Shit! OK, well, what does that mean?' he asked, pulling away from me even further, his face turning all tense and serious. He looked so handsome like that.

'Baby, it doesn't mean anything – I just wanted to tell you,' I replied with a giggle, delighted I had told him if only to see him get all cute and concerned.

'No, Millie, seriously. Should we use a condom or something?' he fussed.

'Oh, you're such a prude,' I teased. 'You sound just like Alice!'

The words were out of my mouth before I could stop them. I stopped giggling. The room was very silent. I hadn't spoken that name all holiday.

'Have you been thinking about—' Henry began.

'Don't,' I interjected. We weren't having this conversation. My parents were only gone for a couple of hours and . . .

'Come on, Millie. We knew this was going to come up sooner or later. Have you heard from her?' he asked, ever the optimist.

My heart sank. I hated where this was going.

'Unsurprisingly, no,' I replied, folding my arms.

'And have you tried contacting her?'

'No.'

'Well, maybe . . .'

'Henry, why are we having this conversation? I mean, why are you even thinking about her – we're about to have sex, for God's sake.'

I knew I was being a hypocrite. I'd thought about Alice at times like this before. And I'd thought about her yesterday, and the day before, and the day before that . . . but that didn't mean I had to call her. Because why should I be the one to break the silence? She was the one who had the apologising to do – there was no way I was giving her an easy way out by just phoning her up and pretending everything was OK. Right now, she was back in Dublin, and I didn't want to think about it. I just wanted to be happy – happy and horny with Henry. Nothing more.

But the moment had passed.

'I need a glass of water,' I grumbled, rolling off the bed and stomping out of the room in a huff, every frustrated step leading me further away from him. It looked like we wouldn't need a condom after all.

*

'Can I have a glass of water, please?' I asked the passing waitress, my head spinning ever so slightly as I made my way through the last of my main course.

'And then,' I returned to my story as Paddy shook with laughter, 'we had a History meeting with this tutor in Jesus College—'

'There's a college called Jesus?' he interrupted.

'Yes, yes, now shut up. So we had this meeting in Jesus college, but Joey got lost, and apparently he tried calling me but my phone was off, so he rang a few other people, but the only person he could get through to was our friend Rachel, who was fast asleep. But the phone woke her up, and she answered it, and Joey, who by this stage was in such a panic, just goes, "Where's Jesus?" And obviously Rachel doesn't have a fecking clue what he's talking about – she doesn't even do History so she didn't know about the meeting or anything. So she's like, "What the hell are you talking about?" and he just keeps saying, "Rachel, where's Jesus – I need to find Jesus." I mean, can you imagine how bloody confused she was?' I spluttered, my laughter becoming too much.

'Did she honestly think he was asking some profound question?' Paddy asked, eyes streaming now.

'Yes! And the best bit is – she's Jewish!'

That was the final straw – the two of us were off and there was no stopping us. My sides ached from shaking so hard and I knew my mascara was probably all over the place, but I just couldn't stop laughing. It felt fantastic. I watched Paddy as he laughed too, his eyes screwed up and his mouth wide open. He had the best smile. So infectious, too. I remembered when we used to fight, and he'd think I was getting too worked up about something, and he'd start smiling, and then I couldn't help but smile. And it was so frustrating – because I really was angry. But there was something about it that I just couldn't resist, and I'd realise how much nicer it was to smile than to fight, so I just would. Conflict over.

The waitress came over to take away our plates, while I excused myself to go to the bathroom to try and sort out my make-up, my laughter starting all over again as I saw my blotchy reflection. I fixed myself up as best I could and gave myself a few minutes to catch my breath. My head was still light, but I knew that, rosé or not, I was happy. I stared into the mirror, at the girl I used to know. Where did you go? Why did you leave me? It doesn't matter – I'm back now. I smirked – Alice, if anyone saw you talking to yourself in the mirror they would think you were gone in the head. But my head was more right now than it had been in months. There was nothing left but to enjoy it.

'I didn't know whether you wanted more wine or if you want to go get a drink somewhere else?' Paddy asked as I returned to the table.

'What? Have we finished the bottle?'

'Don't look so innocent, missie, you drank most of it,' he teased.

'Did not!'

'Anyway, do you want dessert?'

'I physically couldn't,' I groaned, my stomach throbbing from too many noodles.

'So, will we get the bill or do you want more drink?'

'I think I need a walk,' I conceded, my head craving fresh air.

So we got the bill and headed out into the night air in rosé delight. It was April now, and in true Irish fashion, the weather was milder than it probably would be all summer, balmy against my naked arms. We walked and walked, the streets of Ranelagh in their Georgian beauty guiding us wherever we wanted to go. My eyes smiled the entire time, and I breathed in Paddy's scent, the one I used to adore, the one I vowed would always be sweeter than any other. It was strange how things worked out. I mean, when I came home at Christmas, there felt like there was this massive gap between us, this huge separation that had grown over the course of my first term that left us awkward and confused. That's when I knew I didn't love him anymore. And yet, now, I felt just as comfortable with him as I ever did. Just two old friends wandering through Ranelagh, and life, content with it all.

'Do you want to come in?'

Our stroll had brought us back to Paddy's house, habit I supposed – I'd hardly noticed we were heading there.

'OK,' I replied, my head spinning more than ever. Was this really a good idea? I mean, maybe I should just call it a night.

'Are your . . . are your parents here?'

'No, silly, I told you earlier they're in Bordeaux on a wine-tasting trip.'

'Oh yeah,' I lied – I couldn't remember him saying that at all. Maybe I was drunker than I thought.

It was strange being back here, to step into the vast hallway where an ornate ceiling towered above, each cornice just as I had remembered it. Strange, yet utterly familiar. I knew to leave my shoes at the door, and then moved into the kitchen, grabbing a grape from the blue china bowl which always sat on their worktop.

'Did you get the kitchen painted?' I asked

'Yeah, a couple of weeks ago,' he replied, head in the fridge.

'Hmm . . . I preferred it the way it was.'

'Me too. Just don't tell my mother that. Now, do you want another glass of wine, or something stronger?'

I considered my options. Maybe I shouldn't have anything.

'Oh my God, we should make mojitos!' he suddenly announced.

I closed my eyes and grinned. This really was a trip down memory lane. I'd lost track of the amount of times that I'd come back to Paddy's after a meal or a drunken night on the town, and we'd always convinced ourselves that a mojito would be the perfect nightcap before we went to bed. Then one would inevitably turn into two. And then another. 'Just one more – we'll put in extra mint so it's basically instead of brushing our teeth, yeah?' Then the next morning we would eventually surface, sore heads all round, and find the kitchen in a total state of disarray; sugar and mint leaves flung all over the place and the bottle of rum a lot less full than it had been when we'd got our greedy mitts on it.

'Oh, Paddy, I don't know. I'm pretty drunk as it is.'

'Oh come on! One won't hurt,' he coaxed, now armed with a bottle of Bacardi and that bloody smile that got me every time.

'We'll regret it in the morning,' I insisted, reaching to grab the bottle out of his hand.

But suddenly we were very close. Closer than we had been all evening. Neither of us spoke. The air between us felt alive. I could smell the rosé we'd drunk on his breath. And then his scent. I closed my eyes. This isn't a good idea, Alice; you know it's a bad idea. It's too complicated. But it doesn't have to be. I'm leaving on Wednesday, and we've had such a great evening together . . .

'We'll regret it in the morning,' I repeated.

'But it always seems like a good idea at the time,' Paddy whispered, still leaving a shred of possibility that he was just talking about the mojitos. Did I want that? Did I want to just pull away from this and have a drink and get a taxi home? Or did I want him to grab me and kiss me and . . .

Too late. He already had. Before I could even consider what was happening, we were kissing. His lips were on mine, those sweet lips I knew so well. And it was so gentle, so light, that we were barely kissing at all. He knew what that did to me. And as he ran his hands down my arms, his touch made my skin prick with delight. Was this really happening? Ten weeks on, having kissed no one in between . . . well except for . . . *no*. Don't you dare go there. No, Paddy is the last person you kissed, and now here you are, kissing him all over again. And it felt as if the time in between just hadn't happened. I grabbed him closer; I wanted to feel him right against me. This felt so right.

'I can't believe this is happening,' Paddy said. He pulled away and stared at me so hard I thought I might break. 'I've missed you so much.' He kissed me again, wrapping his arms around me so that I was completely shielded from the world in our cocoon. I was safe.

He lifted my top up over my head, and I did the same to him. It felt strange to be standing there, in my bra, in his kitchen. Strange because it wasn't strange. We'd had sex in his kitchen before, for God's sake – I think his mother would be much more disturbed by that than by me telling her I didn't really like the new shade of blue. But now we were moving out of the kitchen and up the stairs. He led me by the hand, and I followed, squeezing my eyes shut just for a moment, wondering what on earth I was doing. When I opened them, I met the gaze of his parents. My heart lurched anew. The family portraits stared right at me, those eyes which I had known for so long. And I knew them so well; I knew that Paddy's dad was strangely superstitious and wouldn't get into a car with the number 13 on the registration plate; I knew that Paddy's mum had had an accident when she was younger and lost half of her right index finger. I knew it all. Before I knew it we were in his room. I smiled. Back to square one indeed. I hadn't been here since the break-up, but it looked just the same as ever – there was his notice board, tilted slightly to the right, packed with ticket stubs from plays and concerts and exhibitions, the edges curling upwards, folding themselves away in time. And there was his bed, his double bed. And now we were on it, and we were kissing once more, and my butterflies could barely take it. He started to undo my jeans, and I could feel that I was wet with desire. No matter what my mind said, it was obvious what my body wanted. Next my bra was off, then his trousers, and then he stopped, looking down on me, keeping me safe.

'Alice, I just want to say, I didn't plan any of this. I just . . . I can't help . . . I know this makes things complicated, but I think . . . I'm still in love with you,' Paddy declared through gasping breaths, and my mind fuzzed more than ever.

He was right – it did make things complicated. And what was I supposed to say in return? Because I couldn't think except to know that right now I wanted him more than I had ever wanted him in my life. I needed him. And although that scared me a little, I knew my needs were about to be fulfilled.

I grabbed him to me, kissing him deeply as my hands moved to his boxers, pulling them down, taking them off.

'Alice, I want you so badly,' he groaned as his hands moved south too, playing with me, teasing me, driving me wild.

I couldn't bear it; I needed him now. So I took off my knickers myself, letting him know it had to be now; now or never.

'Do I need . . . you know . . .' he pulled away and asked, nodding towards his bedside table where he used to keep the condoms. I stopped; I still hadn't had the results from my test. But how could I tell him? But what if I had . . . what if Rob . . . *shut up* . . . don't you *dare* say his name. Not now. Not . . .

'No,' I replied, both answering his questions and silencing my mind.

The lust encouraged the silence. I was about to explode. I wanted him inside me. I wanted him to come inside me and to wash away . . . *stop it*. Stop thinking about . . . just want this because you want it – not because it will erase . . . *there's nothing to erase*.

Paddy entered me, sliding in as pleasure travelled through me, all over my naked, wanting body. It felt so right for us to be reunited. How had I ever wanted him to go away? How had I ever thought that we weren't meant to be together? Because we were. Everyone knew that. And now my body knew it, as he thrust deeper and deeper into me, bringing us closer and closer.

'Oh, Alice, you feel amazing,' he moaned, feathering my neck with the lightest of kisses.

My skin was hot with love. Because maybe this time we really were making love. I did love Paddy. How could I not? If he could make me feel this amazing, and this comfortable, when all along I'd secretly thought the next time I'd have sex would be weird . . . *shut up*. Why would it be? You're fine. Come on, Alice. Stop thinking. Just think about now. Think of how good this feels.

'Alice, this feels so fucking good.'

'Oh, Irish, that feels so fucking good.'

I froze, my sweat suddenly cold against my skin. Did Paddy say that? Or was it my cruel imagination?

'Are you OK?' Paddy's tones suddenly cut through my thoughts.

'Yeah, sorry, I'm fine,' I assured him, willing my body to relax, to just go with the flow. It felt good. It felt amazing. Nothing else mattered.

'I told you I'd have you, Irish.'

No, I willed. No, fuck off. Go away. Not now. Please, not now . . .

'I told you I'd have your tight little Catholic pussy.'

I slammed my eyes shut. I had to make him go away. I was fine. I had been doing so well these past weeks; being home had put everything right. Come on, Alice. Pull yourself together.

I opened my eyes and stared up at the man I loved, his head raised in ecstasy. This was good, so fucking good. But when his head lowered again, it wasn't Paddy's eyes I saw. And it wasn't Paddy's lips on mine. Robbie was on me. On me and in me, his eyes burning through the darkness, a hideous grin ripping across his face; that foul smile glowing out through the choking shadows as he fucked me harder and harder, making me ache within. Please go away, I willed, staring up at him, tears pricking my eyes. Please. I'll do anything. Just go away.

'This feels so *fucking* good.'

It was louder this time, knocking my head to oblivion. I was back in my room, back in Cambridge, but it wasn't back then, because the mirror was gone, the mirror I'd cracked. And the twinkling shards scratched my mind, and Paddy was scratching the bench, etching his words, our words. But Paddy was only in my mind, only a memory, because the now was someone else.

'I going to come. I'm going to fucking come,' he growled.

I bit my lip. This couldn't be. His breathing quickened and quickened and I bit harder and harder to stifle the wailing that wanted to escape. It wasn't real. It wasn't fucking real . . .

'*No!*' I screeched, pushing him from me with all my strength. My tears poured forth as I jumped off the bed, my face screwed up with the bitterest of rage.

'Alice, what's wrong?'

I could hear Paddy's voice somewhere in the distance, but it didn't matter. I had to get out. *Get me out of here!*

I gathered my clothes, limbs lashing as I tried to put them on, to cover up my hideous flesh.

'Alice,' Paddy tried, 'Alice, please, what's wrong?'

But I couldn't even begin to answer him. I couldn't speak and I couldn't think. I just had to get out.

'Alice, if you just calm down,' he continued, reaching out to steady my shaking frame.

'*Don't touch me!*' I screamed, his fingers burning my arm.

I had wrenched on my clothes save for my top. Where the fuck was it? Then I remembered – the kitchen. I stormed downstairs, past the seeing eyes of the portraits, needing to get out of there as soon as possible.

'Alice, please, can we just talk about this? I'm sorry things got out of hand. Maybe . . .'

But I didn't listen. What was the point? Paddy just thought I was freaking out because us having sex was a bad idea, and I wished more than anything that that could be the case, that it could all be that simple. But it wasn't him. It wasn't him at all. It was *him*; that fucking wanker that was trying to ruin my life. Trying, and succeeding.

My top was on now, and I marched to the door, wiping away the flood of tears that just wouldn't stop. I tried to put on my shoes, but I couldn't focus. I was drunk. Why had I let myself get drunk? None of this would have happened if I'd been sober – none of this and none of . . . *just leave me alone*. I couldn't do it, my body was a mess. So I just picked up the shoes and opened the big, Georgian door, the cool night air greeting my aching body.

'Alice, come back. Where are you going?' Paddy begged, following me down the steps and out onto the street.

The trees loomed upwards, just like the Cambridge towers. But so different; so much was different.

'Go back inside,' I commanded.

He was in his boxers. He needed to leave me alone. This didn't concern him; this didn't concern anyone but me and

I had been a fool to think that I could just pretend it didn't exist anymore, to pretend that being back in Dublin and talking about the same old shite with the same old people would make me better. Because the truth was I was worse than ever. I was wretched.

'Alice . . .'

'Paddy, *please*!' I shouted, stopping in my stride, every inch of me shaking.

Out of the corner of my eye I noticed someone on the other side of the street, strolling briskly but clearly listening to my every vicious word. But it was too late for shame.

'Alice, just tell me what's wrong,' Paddy pleaded, his voice quieter now, more soothing.

I could feel him right behind me. I could hear his breath, feel it just inches from me, warming the biting air that flowed between us. I knew if I just turned around, he'd be standing right there. But I couldn't. I couldn't bear to look at him.

'Paddy, just go back inside,' I whispered. 'This has nothing to do with you, I just . . . just leave me alone,' I finished, sadness pouring over me.

How could I explain? How could I make him see that this really didn't have anything to do with him? It was so unfair. And I hated myself for it. It was one thing to make me feel like shit; I'd been feeling like that for months now. But not Paddy; he didn't deserve that. How dare Rob . . . how dare *he* hurt my friends as well. Hadn't he ruined enough? He'd ruined me, that was for sure.

I heard Paddy's footsteps retreat, his bare feet sounding lightly on the gravel. I knew he'd be walking backwards, keeping his eyes on me, searching for even a flicker of something that would hint at what the hell was going on. But this *was* hell. And this time, I couldn't get out; I couldn't pretend that I could just run away and hide. Hell had found me and I knew I would never be free again.

*

The next day the doctor rang to say that my test results had come back. They were all negative. I was clean. Little did they know I was dirtier than ever.

> Hey pooface. Why u no answer ur fone? Am preparin ur gdbye feast as we speak. Mine at 7. B there loser. Or better stil – don't go Ró xx

*

My eyes unwillingly opened again. I looked at my watch. Six o'clock. I checked my phone. Four missed calls. Ugh. Go away. I rolled over against the suitcase I was supposed to be packing. My mother must have thought I was insane – I'd spent the last two days up here 'packing'. What did she think – I was putting everything in alphabetical freaking order? Not likely. Though I wished I had done at least something, because the case was still completely empty. And my room was chaos, but I just didn't have the energy to put it right. All I'd done was lie here and slept and cried and slept. But I was leaving tomorrow morning. Oh, I could just do it this evening. But what about Róisín's thing? Oh feck that, I am in no fit state to see anyone . . . But she'll be so pissed off . . . so let her –

that's the least of my worries right now . . . So what, you're just going to wallow in self-pity and not even say goodbye? . . . Yeah, that's right. Come on, how am I supposed to even make myself presentable – I feel like shit . . . Just go for a couple of hours; she's gone to so much fuss . . . But I don't want any fuss – I just want to be left alone . . . Maybe it will take your mind off . . . *no*. I've tried that. And look where it got me . . . Knowing Róisín, if you don't go, she'll probably drive round and get you herself . . . I won't answer the door . . . You'll just start another fight – can you really bear another fight? *Fine, you win.* I'll go. Bloody hell.

It took all of my strength to get up from the bed and run the shower. After I'd dried myself, I threw on a pair of sweat-pants and a hoodie – I couldn't do better than that – they could feck off if they wanted me to dress up. I dried my hair and put on some mascara – there – was that enough for them?

'Mum, I'm going over to Róisín's,' I called into the kitchen, turning to leave.

'Do you want a lift, love?' she offered, bursting into the hallway, obviously glad to see me finally out of my bedroom. I hadn't come down for dinner last night. I'd told her I'd already eaten while she was at the shelter. She had believed me. Naturally.

'No. I think I'll walk.'

'Alice, it will take you ages. Come on, I'll grab my keys.'

I didn't have the energy to object.

Neither of us spoke for most of the journey, Lyric FM filling the void between us, until finally: 'So, are you all set then?' Mum asked, full of unnecessary enthusiasm.

My head ached. 'Yeah, still a bit of packing to do.'

'Really? You've been at it long enough. But I suppose you just want to be as ready as you can be.'

'Hmm.'

But I wasn't ready, not for anything. Time was just pushing me on, whether I liked it or not.

'Still, it will be nice to see all your Cambridge friends again, won't it?' Mum continued, trying desperately to get any reaction from me.

And she was right – it would be nice – nice to see one person, that was. For the past few days I couldn't stop thinking about Flo. I wished more than anything that I had her number; I needed to speak to her so badly, to tell her all that had happened, to tell her about Sunday night. I knew she'd listen and understand and tell me what she thought, but I didn't care anymore whether she was sympathetic or generous or let me be weak. Because I *was* weak. And, more than anything, I needed someone who knew that.

'Right, well here you are. If you want me to pick you up later just let me know. I'm staying in for the evening anyway and your father—'

'Thanks,' I cut in.

I kissed her cheek, a cold, worthless kiss, and got out of the car. I paused on Róisín's doorstep, taking three deep breaths and trying to locate some sort of enthusiasm. Come on, Alice – just one last push, then you can go back to Cambridge and see Flo and do whatever you want to do. But you have to perform just one last time.

★

'About bloody time,' Róisín boomed as she opened the door to me, 'dinner's just served. Not like you to be late, gay face.'

'Sorry. I was packing and—'

'Never mind,' she interrupted, grabbing my hand and yanking me into the kitchen where everyone else squealed loudly on my arrival.

They were gathered around the table, all bright colours and bright eyes, bodies leaning across one another as arms grabbed from the overflowing serving bowls. My eyes tried to make sense of the chaos which spread out from all directions.

'We've got lasagne, salad and fuck-it-atcha bread,' Róisín informed me in true Róisín fashion.

Everyone else burst out laughing. I smiled. I was trying, but there was only so far I could stretch. I was exhausted. However, luckily for me, everyone was so wired as it was that I wondered if they would even notice if I wasn't there, the mindless banter flowing around the dinner table, wine and friendship mingling freely.

'Do you remember my driving test?' Róisín recalled, launching into one of her favourite tales. 'The guy asked me like, what you needed to check you have before going on a long journey – meaning like, petrol and oil and all that kind of shit – and of course, I was there driving along, absolutely shitting myself, and without thinking I just reply: "Er, sandwiches?"'

We'd all heard it before, but it was still funny.

'I mean, what kind of a total freaking idiot am I?'

'I still don't know how you passed,' one of the girls remarked through a mouthful of lasagne.

I was distracted by the sight – how refreshing to see a friend actually eat carbs. I thought of Millie. I unthought of her just as swiftly.

'I bet she took advantage of him.'

'Now, Martha, stop that – that's called rape!'

'Nah, it's not rape, remember – it's surprise sex!'

And off they went again, whooping and giggling at the top of their lungs. Still I smiled.

'So anyway, Ally, what time are you off tomorrow?' Róisín asked, suddenly focusing the attention onto me. I wished to God she hadn't.

'Erm, I think my flight's at about midday,' I replied, still smiling.

'And are you all packed?'

'Yeah, just about,' I informed, unable to manage anything more detailed or witty than that.

'Well, just make sure you don't make the same mistake I did coming home from Malaga.'

'What was that?' Martha inquired, eagerly taking Róisín's bait.

'Well, I packed my chicken fillet things in my hand luggage, and let's just say trying to explain to the Spanish security guard that they were cleavage enhancers and not liquids for a bomb was a rather interesting game of charades!'

The giggling erupted again.

'Sounds like . . . Frubes!' Róisín mimed, acting out a rather phallic impression of eating the tubey yoghurts, and then grabbing her breasts, much to the amusement of everyone else.

'Then again, it's not like Alice has to worry about things

like that,' Martha announced. 'Her tits are already big enough as it is.'

All eyes were on me again.

'Yeah, I bet you the lads over there would love to get their hands on them,' Róisín joshed.

'Ah yeah, and you know the Brits are into all their kinky shit,' Martha continued. 'I bet she could give them some fairly impressive tit jobs.'

'Yeah, maybe!' Róisín shrieked, grabbing my breasts and moving them in a rather vile backwards and forwards motion.

I felt sick. 'Stop,' I said.

But no one was listening to me, just watching my heaving bosom as Róisín acted the clown.

'Róisín please, stop,' I repeated, louder now.

'Oh come on, you love it,' she cackled. 'They don't call you Chesty-ton for nothing, do they?'

'Róisín, I said stop!' I yelled, close to tears, pushing her hands from me.

Her hand hit a glass and, as if in slow motion, I watched it topple and smash. The shards flicked outwards, a firework of jagged edges, landing on every plate, glinting in the now cold light. Silence fell. They all stared at me in shock. I knew that look. It was the same frightened, startled look they'd given me when I'd told them I was going to Cambridge, like they didn't even recognise me. Truth was, I didn't recognise me anymore either.

'Sorry. I'm sorry, I'm just a bit . . .' I tried, but I could feel everything slipping out of reach. I reached for a towel, but Róisín stood in my way.

'No, go on, you're what? You've sat there in silence from

the minute you got here. What the hell is wrong with you, Alice? Or are you dying to get back to your English friends – back to their civilised ways and their PC humour – because we're just a group of uneducated slobs?' Róisín spat.

'No, please, it's not like that . . .'

'So what is it then? Because there is seriously something up your ass tonight, Alice.'

Ten sets of eyes fixated upon me, urging me to answer. I couldn't take this. I knew coming had been a bad idea. I just wanted to curl up into a ball and for it all to go away. Still they stared at me. Róisín's eyes were full of anger. I recognised that jumper she was wearing, the pale blue against her pale face. It had been a birthday present from me. Back in time. But time was on me now, crawling up my skin. I had to say something. Come on, Alice, think – just think. Tell her something or she's going to go crazy and lay into you and you can't take that; you can't physically bear it.

'I just . . . I don't know how to say it, but . . . please don't tell anyone, but . . .'

And then finally I thought of something, divine intervention perhaps. Yet why was I thinking of Flo; why did it feel like she'd come up with this? For a split second, I felt safe again.

'I'm just a bit all over the place because . . . well, basically, me and Paddy had sex on Sunday night, and it was a really bad idea and I feel like such an idiot and it's really affected me more than I thought it would, so I'm sorry, but this is all really lovely, really it is.'

I sighed, hoping that would do the trick. And it hadn't really been a lie – I *had* had sex with Paddy and it *had* affected me more that I thought it would; it was only the reason why that I was leaving out.

No one spoke. The broken glass still flickered, winking at me. I prayed they'd believe me, hoped I'd done enough. Thankfully, for once, I had, as they all gushed to tell me how sorry they were. Even Róisín seemed satisfied, or at least I thought so. Her smile was there, but something else wasn't. Then again, my judgement was so all over the place at the moment that it was probably just my imagination.

'Look, men are shit,' she announced, silencing everyone else. 'But I know two men who will happily keep us company in the sitting room.'

'Please God tell me this is one of your crappy Ben and Jerry's jokes?' Martha begged.

Róisín nodded and for the squeals which ensued, we may as well have been a group of five-year-old schoolgirls. Everyone jumped up from their chairs, running to their ice cream treats as I cleaned up the mess I had caused. But Róisín ushered me after the others, saying she'd do it later. Some ice cream was thrust in my direction, but I already felt ill. I wanted to go. You can't leave now – they're looking after you – you finally have an excuse to be down – just roll with it, just for another hour; you can do it.

So I sat on the couch and counted down every minute, a clock ticking somewhere in the far distance. Soon, I could take no more. 'Listen, girls, I think I'm going to head. I've an early start,' I announced, getting up.

'Awwwwww,' they complained in unison, each begging me to stay longer and chorusing about how much they were all going to miss me.

I kissed them all and promised I'd be in touch, but eventually I escaped, reaching the door none too soon, as Róisín saw me off.

'Thanks for tonight, Ró.'

'No worries. Wanted to give you a proper send-off, you know? We really are . . . I really am going to miss you,' she admitted.

'Yeah, I know. And I'm really sorry about the glass.'

'It's fine,' she interjected, 'it was an accident.'

I nodded. But it didn't just feel like a clumsy mistake; it felt like everything I touched, everyone I touched, broke.

'I'll miss you,' I said, and meant it. I turned to go, but Róisín wasn't finished.

'Ally, are you sure you're OK?' she asked, concern in her eyes.

'Yeah, I'm grand,' I lied. *Just let me go, please – I need to go.* 'Just upset about Paddy, really.'

'Hmm. I just . . . it's so weird seeing you like this. I've never seen you like this.'

'But Róisín, I've told you why,' I interjected wearily. Why was it never enough for her?

'Yeah, I know that. But Ally, you never tell us stuff like that. You never let stuff like that get to you in the first place. It's just a bit scary, seeing you so blue,' she explained.

'Look, I'll be fine, OK?' I assured her, though my tone lacked any real conviction.

'Well, keep in touch,' she said sternly.

'I will.'

'No, *actually* keep in touch this time.'

She smiled. I tried to. But my energy had literally run out.

I could barely lift my arms as Róisín wrapped hers around me.

When I pulled away I avoided her eyes and turned on my heels. As I walked away I felt as though a massive question mark was emblazoned across my whole being. Who knew what was to come? Who could even believe that this time tomorrow I would be in Cambridge? It was all too hard to try and process, so my brain shut down as I walked the long walk home and went to bed, where sleep was the only respite from this messy, messy world.

15

Once again, I sat in a plane, somewhere between Dublin and London Stansted, on my way to start a new term at Cambridge University. I was numb. My body had shut down. On Sunday night – that night with Paddy – my body thought that it finally had a chance to wash away or undo or cover up all that had happened, so that he would be the most recent person I'd had sex with, he would be the last person who'd been inside me, not . . . But it hadn't worked. And now my body wouldn't work. A tiny part of me feared that if I did actually know the truth of how it was I was feeling, there wouldn't be a hope in hell of me going back to Cambridge. But now, I was numb, and I was on my way . . .

'Any snacks or drinks, miss?'

I shook my head. I was on automatic pilot. My surroundings made me almost smile at the joke, but smiles meant feeling. And I couldn't feel. All I could do was sit there and read my history book and get off the plane and get my bags and get on the train and get a taxi and get my key from the Porters' Lodge and go to my room and unpack. As robotically and impersonally as that. I had done this all before, I would do it again. Only this time, I didn't put up my Irish flag. What was the point? Why did I want to be reminded of home? I hadn't felt at home there. Not by the end. And my mirror wasn't there; it still hadn't been replaced. No need for reflection, really. And this time I didn't expect a knock on the door from Millie or Joey or Henry. No, this time was different. And how did I feel about that? Couldn't tell you. The only person I would be able to tell, if there was anything to tell, was Flo.

The walk to our spot seemed longer than ever. Probably because I feared that when I finally arrived, she wouldn't be there. Why should she be? It was a Wednesday. But maybe I had told her when I was coming back; maybe I had told her the specific day. Because then she might come. But I couldn't remember if I had. And yet why, with every step, did I feel more and more sure that I'd find her there? Cambridge was bathed in a glow so full of summer. The colleges were no longer grey, but a pale yellow, all dressed up for the impending season, their Gothic points softer in the light. I walked by them all. There was that one time I found Flo there by chance on a weekday. Chance? Or something else? Alice, what something else could there be? Maybe she just came there every day – I mean, I'd never asked her if she did. I'd never asked her much, except her opinion. And I needed that opinion now more than ever, because if I couldn't think or feel or know what was going on, maybe, just maybe, she could tell me. It was worth the risk, worth every step.

The ground felt so different under my feet than it had all those months ago when I'd first done this walk. I remembered that morning being cold, the grass damp beneath me.

Now the sun shone and the blades were lush and upright. Pastures fair but not pastures new. But so little had changed, really. That night had still happened and I was still broken. I wondered whether I was broken for good.

But the answer to that was sitting, as I'd hoped and prayed she would be, on our bench.

'Flo!' I called as I approached.

She turned to greet me, her emerald eyes full of life.

'I was hoping you'd show up,' she announced as I sat down beside her, smiling for the first time in what felt like a lifetime.

We talked for hours. Or, more precisely, I talked. I told her everything, from start to finish, from flight to weary flight. She said very little, allowing me to take my time, particularly when I recounted the tale of my night with Paddy. I welled up a few times, but never cried, my body still unable to engage in such a level of emotional display.

'I'm just numb,' I admitted at the end, telling her what I had been telling myself. 'I don't know whether I'm glad to be back or scared or more driven or just upset – I just don't know. I am happy to see you though,' I assured her, hoping she realised the importance of this given my otherwise barren state of feeling.

'Well, I'm happy to see you too,' she replied sincerely, 'but I'm sorry to hear that you're feeling like this.'

'But like what? That's the thing!'

She looked away, her porcelain complexion glowing in the sunlight like a brilliant lamp.

'Alice, you just need to take every day as it comes. I think we've . . . I mean, I think you've learned by now that there's no point having a game plan or building things up to be the cure or the solution or whatever. Because it doesn't work like that. This isn't like an illness where you can go on this medication and the side effects will be X and Y and the results will be Z. And I know that's how you like things; I know you like deadlines because they make you feel safe, but I'm afraid you just have to just take it as it comes. And I know that that makes you even more afraid, because there's nothing exact – nothing certain—'

'Except you,' I interjected.

Flo paused, startled. 'What?'

'I mean, *you* are certain. *This* is certain. This bench and us and Sundays and . . . at least I have that.'

Flo smiled. I knew she felt happy because she was appreciated. Of course she was. And although it was clutching at straws, it was better than nothing; she was better than nothing. Much better.

For another half an hour we talked or just sat in silence. Only when the time came to go did something occur me. 'Do you like seeing me?' I asked.

'What?' Flo said, startled once more.

'I mean, I know what I get out of our time together. But you . . . do you like it?'

'Alice, where is this coming from?'

'I just . . . I mean, do you have many friends in Homerton? Surely you must spend time with them and have fun with them and stuff, but this can't be fun for you; it can't be fun at all. So why do you come?'

We were standing now and I realised how much smaller Flo was than me. And thinner; much thinner. The figure of a child. But she was so wise, full of wisdom beyond her years that belied her slender frame.

'I come because you need me,' she replied.

And I had to admit that she was right. Me – Alice Chesterton – who needed no one, needed Flo. And though there was something strange about that, for some reason I didn't pursue it, and it was with those words that we parted.

★

I found my way back, step after step, just like Flo had said, one at a time. The early evening skyline was even more beautiful than I'd remembered, and the river line too, punts basking in the extended warmth. On they floated towards Queen's wooden bridge, and then round the corner towards King's, looking up at the chapel no doubt, its rose window the only circle in a structure of points. And then under Clare Bridge, the stone spheres lining the edge, one of which was missing a quarter; everyone had their own version of why it was missing. And then that one they all called 'Orgasm Bridge' because of it's sharp, climactic incline, and then Trinity Bridge, the college's columns vaster than they looked on land, more Roman than the others. And then under the prettiest of them all – St John's pride and joy – the Bridge of Sighs. On an evening like this, one could easily be forgiven for thinking you were passing under its counterpart in Venice. But it was unmistakably Cambridge, with its ancient splendour and grimacing gargoyles. Like me, they were stone, but they were so very alive. I prayed that somewhere, beneath the numbness, I was too.

16

People had warned me that Cambridge was different in the final term of each year, when everyone was locked away in the libraries, some armed with sleeping bags so as to keep trips home to an absolute minimum, while outside the streets were empty. But nothing had prepared me for this. It was like a ghost town, like one of those movies when there's been an earthquake or an alien invasion or a comet has struck, and everyone hides in their underground bunkers, desperate to be safe. And then finally, an individual emerges, blinking into the light and strolling through the once-chaotic streets, totally alone. I was that individual, that lone ranger. I'd spent most of the end of last term *being* quite alone, but that was by choice; that had been my decision. Yet now I really was alone; I couldn't just immerse myself in the hum of Cambridge life, because the hum was silenced: No Humming in the Library.

The atmosphere was surreal and it matched uncomfortably well with my own state of mind, my emotional flat line. The town was flat. The gatherings of pigeons twittered about restlessly, lacking the usual convoy of pedestrians which disturbed their cooing corners.

First-year English and History students were the only

ones in the university who didn't have end of year exams, and while everyone always remarked how lucky we were right now, burying my head in a stack of ancient books was just what I needed. Of course I still had my weekly essays, and I signed up for some more RAG stuff, but every time I left my room, the emptiness made me feel almost nervous, more exposed and, as a result, more lost. I was a ghost of my former self – or my former fantasy of myself – strolling over the cobbles of my ghost town. A shadow of the past.

But then, one Thursday morning, I bumped into a figure from my past, that long, slender figure I had always so admired.

'How weird is this place?' Millie began, her big eyes wide.

'Yeah, it's really surreal,' I agreed. 'I mean, people did warn us, but Jesus, this is just strange.'

I smiled at the irony. The empty streets were nowhere near as strange as the fact that we were talking for the first time in what felt like a lifetime.

'So how was your holiday, then?' she asked, her tone more hostile that she had been at first.

She looked thinner than I remembered, her fingers skeletal as they fiddled with her bracelet, flicking it tensely.

'Good. Quiet. How about you?'

'Really good, thanks. Henry came to stay for a bit, and . . .'

'Oh, so you guys are like, official?' I asked, surprised. I didn't realise it had all escalated to such a degree as holiday family-home visits.

'Yeah, we've been properly an item now for ages.'

Millie's voice trailed off, because the more she emphasised

the length of their relationship, the more she emphasised the length of our silence. She stared at the ground. I stared at some pigeons who stared back. I watched their twitchy movements, their nerves adding to my own.

'Look, Ally, I think Joey and I are going to drag Henry away from the library tonight and make him come to Wagamama. Why don't you join us?' Millie suddenly said, her tone like that of a child unable to maintain a huff any longer.

It took me a minute to register the invitation because something had pulled me up short; she had called me 'Ally'. How had I not become just Alice, or just some girl in her year with whom she'd once been friends? How was I still 'Ally'? Hearing those syllables gave me a brief glow through the numbness, like someone who's been paralysed but then suddenly figures out how to wiggle their toe. It surprised me.

'Yeah, that'd be . . . what time?' I stumbled.

Surely this was massively significant, but what did it mean? And what did I want it to mean?

'Meet outside college at seven,' she said and headed off, leaving me rooted to the spot.

That evening I showered and got dressed and went down to the front of college to meet the others. It felt strange to be meeting them here – back in the day I would have just called into one of their rooms and strolled on together from there. But, I reminded myself, it was even stranger that I was even meeting them in the first place. And strangest of all was that I felt as if I was in a dream, like someone else was meeting up with them and I was just an observer, watching but not participating.

'Hello, stranger.' Joey threw his arms around me; I was startled by the sudden contact.

He was wearing a T-shirt and jeans but he looked well – I'd forgotten how handsome he was. As always he was full of energy and while Henry and Millie both looked awkward as they strolled up behind us, I knew that Joey would be doing everything in his power to make sure that everyone was at ease, or at least as easy as we could be given the weight of all that was being left unsaid. What did they call it; the elephant in the room? Well, ours was officially thrashing around Wagamama, evidently in search of something satay-based, but we just ignored it. We ordered and chatted away, hiding beneath frivolities. That said, I contributed very little, because I had no witty anecdotes or gossipy nuggets. Just my spaced-out, empty self, my shell.

'So I've got a dinner with the Peacocks tomorrow night,' Henry informed the group as we tucked into our grub.

I couldn't remember the last time I'd even thought about drinking societies – I'd almost forgotten they existed. I'd been receiving the emails from the Red Breasts inviting me on various swaps towards the end of last term, but had just kept clicking delete; I hadn't thought I would be the best of company for a group of rowdy, randy boys.

'A dinner? In exam term? I had to drag you kicking and screaming out of the library tonight, yet suddenly the Peacocks click their fingers and you go running?' Millie complained, clearly unimpressed, her accent more cut-glass than ever.

'Baby, it's not like that . . .'

'And you're just going to spend the evening on a swap

217

with a group of girls you've never even met, and yet you hardly ever see your girlfriend.'

'It's not a swap!' Henry interjected, mildly triumphantly, obviously glad he was in some way able to prove her wrong. 'It's a lads' night out. Danny's got a friend in Jesus who has hooked us up with some dinner tickets for their Hall, so we're just going there.'

Joey started laughing.

'What?' Henry asked.

'No nothing . . . "a friend in Jesus" . . . gets me every time,' he giggled.

Henry and Millie rolled their eyes. I smiled, Joey's innocent humour unabashedly cute. Our gazes met for just a second, while the others returned to their argument. Joey's eyes narrowed as he stared at mine, obviously trying to dig out something from beneath the dust. I looked away.

'Henry. You know, if the Porters catch you riding it . . .'

'What?' Joey inquired, having returned his attention to this conversation too.

'You know the statue of the horse they have in Jesus,' Millie explained. 'Well, apparently the Peacocks want Henry to ride it tomorrow night.'

'It's the start of my initiation,' Henry defended, as if that made any difference.

'But baby, you could get into *serious* trouble.'

'When's the rest of your initiation?' Joey cut in, leaving Millie, mouth agape, furious that she was being totally ignored.

I smiled; it was like a comedy sketch. And still, I was the passive observer.

'Well, as far as I know I'm being initiated properly on Caesarean Sunday.'

'When's that?' I asked, forming words for one of the first times all night.

It took Henry a moment before he replied, clearly taken aback by the alien sound of my voice.

'It's in . . . it's a couple of weeks away.'

'And like, what's the story? Why is it called Caesarean Sunday?' I continued, having heard the name before but never known the details.

'Well, basically the Jesus drinking society and the Girton drinking society come to the park and have this massive scrap. And all the drinking societies from the whole university go along and everyone gets drunk and has picnics and loads of people are being initiated – it sounds awesome,' Henry relished, the idea of such carnage obviously appealing to him a lot more than it did me. Or Joey, apparently.

'Do you not just think it's weird that Cambridge is so traditional in terms of the fancy dinners and the gowns and the grass you can't walk on and shit,' Joey reasoned, 'but then there's like these ridiculous things – like intelligent lads beating the crap out of each other for no reason, and intelligent men and women going on along and watching and stuff and like . . . I don't know, it's just weird!'

'Wouldn't have expected such madness in exam term either,' I added.

'I think all the drinking societies treat it as their one day of freedom, you know? That's why everyone gets so fucked,' Henry replied.

'And what are they going to make you do for your initiation?' Joey pressed.

'I don't know yet. Though I did catch Danny in the computer room ordering some absinthe off the internet so . . . baby, why are you looking so grumpy?' Henry was suddenly distracted by his girlfriend's obvious huff.

'No, don't mind me,' Millie hissed, looking away with indignant fury.

'Ah, baby, come on . . . .'

Joey and I turned to face one another, leaving them to it.

'Lovebirds, eh?' he said, cocking his head with a wry grin.

'Yeah, the Peacock and the Robin Red Breast,' I replied, matching his smile.

Joey almost did a double take at my joke. I smiled, wanting to say something like 'I haven't completely lost my personality', but it sounded so contrived. Plus, I wasn't sure one vaguely witty quip could count as an actual personality defibrillation. Joey asked me about my Easter break. I knew he probably thought I was boring, or bored, not bothering to offer him any interesting answers. But what was there to give? To tell him about Paddy? To tell him that I'd spent time with my friends but then it had all gone tits up and had now rendered me like some kind of zombie? No, better just to say it was 'fine' and 'nice' and 'grand' – all those bland adjectives that thwarted his attempts at conversation. The bill arrived just in time.

We walked back through the silent streets, a homeless guy strumming his guitar with even more desperation than usual, the lack of punters leaving him with only a few measly coppers lining the bottom of his tattered case. 'Everybody huuurts,' he wailed in breathy tones, cracking with beery excess.

'Jeez, I would've thought he'd at least have a more upbeat setlist in exam term – people might bloody kill themselves.'

'Henry!' Millie shrieked.

'What?' he asked, holding up his palms with mock innocence.

'No, seriously, baby, did you not hear about that girl in Magdalene College . . .'

A story about suicide passed by my ears, but I didn't let it in. I just wanted to walk home, then go to sleep. It had been a pleasant evening – nothing memorable given the circumstances – but it certainly beat eating alone.

'Thanks for inviting me along,' I said when we finally reached the entrance to college.

Henry was going back to the library and Millie was going to walk him there, probably to shout at him some more about his dinner tomorrow night, while Joey was off to check his pigeon hole. The three of them stood in a group, and I opposite them, alone.

'Well, nice to see you, Irish,' Henry finally blurted as he stepped across the dividing line to give me a limp hug.

'Yeah. Pity we didn't get to talk more, but . . .' Millie trailed off, her hug not much more convincing than her boyfriend's.

'We'll probably be going to Hall tomorrow night if you want,' Joey offered as he grabbed me and squeezed me tight.

'Oh . . . OK, yeah. Sounds good,' I replied, knowing they all thought it was rubbish.

I mounted the steps to my room, the sound of each footfall reverberating off the cold, stone walls, my echo offering me company. It was just how I'd left it, everything perfectly in order. I washed and undressed and slid beneath my sheets, running the night over in my head but realising I remembered very little of it. Or maybe there had just been very little to remember. Sleep came and sleep went, no dreams, no nightmares. I just turned off and turned back on again like the robot I was, the tin man with no heart. And no Oz to give me one. I smiled to myself, but I had no use for jokes. No use and no time and yet all the weary time in the weary world. Another weary day. Another nothing.

*

She walked into the hallway like she was sleepwalking. I was in the queue for the dining hall with Millie and Henry, and I could see her eyes scanning the crowd for our faces. People pushed past her on both sides, eager to get a good spot in the queue so that they could eat and get back to the library as quickly as possible. I wondered when the last time she'd been here was. Definitely last term, but how far back? How far back in my memory did I have to go to find an image of us eating together, sitting in Hall by candlelight in our navy gowns, nattering away without a care in the world? She looked tired – her skin was pale and I suspected she'd lost a bit of weight. Oh, who was I kidding – I didn't just suspect it, I knew it. Because I knew everything about her. Or at least, used to know. A lump formed in my throat. Where had it all gone wrong? And why did it feel like, even though things seemed to be going right again – even though she had come out for dinner last night and had shown up tonight despite all our doubts – she was further away than ever?

'Alice,' I called, trying to snap myself back to my usual lively self. I was tired and it was draining, but I had no choice.

'Thank God! It's absolute carnage in here. I didn't think so many people would leave their beloved desks,' she remarked, her voice even, giving nothing away.

'Apparently even geeks need to eat,' Henry chirped. 'Hi, Irish, by the way.'

'Oh . . . hey. Not at your Peacocks' dinner then?' Alice noticed.

'No, he's being a good boy,' Millie replied, unable to see the gruesome face Henners was pulling behind her back.

That boy really was whipped. But they were in love, there was no denying that, and as much as I hated admitting it, I was jealous. As the queue started to move, Henry grabbed onto Millie's hand and pulled her with him, through the madness, keeping her close and keeping her safe. Cambridge felt like madness sometimes; pure, intense madness, and while the highs were so very high, the lows could sometimes be . . . well, let's just say I wished someone would grab my hand, or at least, I had someone's to grab.

'Joey!' Alice shrieked as the throngs of hungry nerds began to sweep her away.

I found her wrist through the chaos, and yanked her back up to the step on which I stood.

'Thanks,' she said as we continued up to where dinner was being served.

I looked at her, trying to see whether maybe, just maybe,

her cry had been as symbolic as I hoped. My heart soared. Maybe now we'd both realise that actually the rumours were true; maybe we were meant to be together. Maybe . . .

'Someone said it was shepherd's pie tonight. Ugh, I'm not really in the mood,' she remarked, eyes glazed over just like before.

My heart sank. Turns out I was the one who'd been carried away. Disappointment overwhelmed me, leaving me unusually quiet during the meal, as I joined Alice in just listening and observing as my three courses came and went and the candles burned slowly downwards, forming rivers of waxy melt. And that's when I realised that maybe she wasn't the only one who was lost.

*

I went to the bar with them after dinner. Rob . . . he wasn't there – obviously on that Peacock dinner. I only stayed for one drink, then returned home. And then the next night I went to Hall with them again, but not to the bar; not because I was worried he might be there, but just because there was no point; the bar was pretty much empty anyway – people literally sprinted back to the library the minute they put down their cutlery. I wondered if I'd be like that next year. Probably. But what if instead of that, I was just . . . like this? What if, even this time next year, I still just felt nothing? What if I floated through the rest of my time at Cambridge like some drugged-up freak with nothing to say and nothing to show for my entire university experience except three 'friends' who probably only still spoke to me out of pity?

Because it certainly wasn't for my riveting conversation, that was sure. Then I supposed there was Flo, but even when I went to see her on Sunday, we'd had very little to say.

'I guess it's better that you're like this than . . . you know . . . feeling upset,' she tried, the emeralds lacking more lustre than usual.

'Yeah, I guess . . .'

But that was just it – that was all I had, guessing. Because my body was still keeping secrets from me, still not talking to me after all that had happened, and in fairness, I couldn't blame it. I couldn't blame it and therefore I couldn't complain that this was what I'd become. I knew that people were commenting about how they hadn't seen me around in ages, and that now that they did, it seemed I had changed. And they weren't wrong. So I just had to endure the whispering and the nudging and the eyes across the dining hall and just get on with my life; not living, but observing – ever the witness.

★

'Irish, where have you been all my life?'

'Danny, long time no see,' I remarked as I poured the tonic waters into the gins which I was about to deliver to the booth where Millie and the boys were waiting for me.

'Seriously though, it's like you vanished from the face of the earth!' he exclaimed. 'Wait, let me guess – you've gone and found yourself a boyfriend, haven't you?' he said, eyes twinkling as he smacked his hands and rubbed them together.

I shook my head, but he was having none of it.

'So who is he? What college? He must be an animal in the sack because you've obviously been spending a *lot* of time over at his place,' he continued.

'I'm afraid you're deluding yourself, Danny – there's no—'

'Ah, Irish, you're going to break a lot of hearts. What about poor Robbie? I thought . . .'

And suddenly, my heart jolted into life, hammering against my chest. The room became a blur and it was as if Danny was speaking in slow motion.

'Hey guys,' he called to the booth where the rest of his third-year mates were sitting. Including him. There he was. 'Guys, listen to this . . .'

I picked up my drinks; I needed to go back to the booth.

'Irish has a new fella on the go,' Danny declared, loud enough for the entire bar to hear. 'Yeah, she's been shagging him for ages!'

I froze. All eyes were on me now; I could feel every single one, burning against my skin, burning through the numb. But one pair hurt most of all. Robbie looked at me, grinning like his friends at good old Danny, embarrassing the little first year. But there was something in his eyes that made his expression so very different from his comrades'. I wanted to scream – how could no one tell by the way that he looked at me what a monster he was? What a hideous, awful, disgusting . . . I looked away and I found a new pair of eyes – Joey's. He stared at me with a mixture of pity and confusion. Surely he didn't think Danny's fabrication was true, and even if it was, what was it to him? Why was he looking at me like that? Why were his eyes hurting me too, hurting me like Rob . . . like his, merging into one? My heart thumped so quickly I thought I would explode. Danny was still laughing and everyone was still staring and I wanted to be dead. Suddenly I thought of Paddy, of our night together, of how great it had been until suddenly, he'd looked down on me, and his eyes had become Rob . . . had become *his* eyes . . . those eyes that were staring at me now . . . and now Joey's eyes . . .

Everything stopped making sense, all blurring into one. *They* were all one; every way I turned, everyone's gaze was on me, on me and in me and . . .

And then through the chaos of my mind, a silence suddenly descended, a loud, aching, heavy silence. And then a smash. I'd dropped the glasses. Shit.

*

'Alice, Alice honey, now be careful there, dear – I know it's a beach, but there can be a lot of broken glass – just mind your feet, OK?' Mummy called as I skipped through the glorious sand.

She was right up against the shore's edge, teaching Nick how to skip stones. Suddenly something sharp stabbed through my big toe. I fell to the ground. I spun around, but they weren't looking anymore, too focused on Nick's latest attempt, its resounding plop making them all giggle with joy. I was in agony, but they couldn't see; I wouldn't let them. I yanked the glass out of my eight-year-old foot, breathing in sharply as it jagged through me on the way out. But then it was gone. Blood seeped out. I clamped my finger against the hole to stop it, pressing with all my might. Come on, come on, they'll be here any minute . . . I can't let them see . . .

For the next week, walking pained me a bit, but I hid my limp. I hid everything. I was an expert. I was Alice.

★

Reality smacked me right in the face.

'I'm really sorry . . . I don't know . . . I'll just . . .' I bumbled to the barman who had appeared within seconds.

'It's OK, love. I think this young gentleman should be in charge of cleaning it up as penance for causing such a racket in my bar, don't you?' his cockney lilt bellowed out.

'Yes . . . I mean, no . . . I mean . . .'

'Irish, it's grand. Relax,' Danny chuckled.

But I couldn't relax. Because the ice was starting to thaw – my toes were starting to wriggle – the paralysis was lifting. Why the hell had I wanted it to? Why, no matter how much I had told myself it was better to feel like that, better to feel nothing than to feel bad, had I secretly wanted to snap out of it? I was just greedy – I was just scared that I would spend my whole life in this state of limbo. But had I really wanted this? Had I really wanted to cause a scene in the bar and have everyone's eyes on me and for my heart to be throbbing and for him to be right there and still be able to . . .

I started to run. Out of the bar and out of the building and into the dusky courtyard. I could hear footsteps behind me, hear Joey's voice calling my name, and Millie's too, but I couldn't stop. They couldn't see me crack. I just had to hide my pain. I had to hide everything. Come on, Alice, you're an expert, remember? But I couldn't remember. I couldn't remember and I couldn't forget and as I locked my door and threw myself on my bed I had nothing left but to repeat the words I'd been saying for so long now, too long, too long for them to be true. But they had to be true. They fucking had to be.

'I'm fine, I'm fine, I'm fine, I'm fine, I'm fine, I'm fine, I'm fine, I'm fine . . .'

The words became my tick and my tock, whiling the time away until eventually, exhaustion put me out of my misery. But I knew deep down that it would all be waiting for me in the morning. Always waiting.

17

Joey and Millie came round early the next day. I couldn't pretend I wasn't in. They came into the room and asked me what had happened last night and I told them that I had just freaked out because Danny was really annoying me and that I hated that there had been a big scene because, as they knew, I hated big scenes. And they said they did. And then I told them that I'd got scared because they had been looking at me like they believed what Danny was saying and I really didn't want that, because it was bullshit, and it just panicked me to think that they would think that I had changed all because of some stupid boy. But they said of course but was I sure I was OK. And I said yes. And then they invited me to Hall that night. But I said I had a RAG meeting at seven so I probably wouldn't be able to make it. And then Millie told me to check my email because there was a thing there about the Red Breasts initiation for Caesarean Sunday this Sunday. And I said I would. And then they left. And I started my essay. And I didn't stop until it was finished, nine hours later. And when I finished I sighed. And then the numbness was back. Thank God for that.

*

My Darling Breasts,

As you all know this Sunday is Caesarean Sunday, and of course as one of the university's most popular drinking societies, we will be attending the afternoon's festivities in full force. The day will commence with a champagne breakfast in Hall, and then we shall head to the park to watch the fight, whilst also initiating four of our youngest members: Millie, Rachel, Rebecca and Alice.

So see you in Hall at 10 a.m. sharp looking foxy and fierce, and initiates: good luck.

All my breasty love,
Tina xxx

I replied, telling Tina that while I was honoured, I wasn't really up for getting initiated, but that I would come along on Sunday nonetheless. I knew he'd be there too, but that didn't matter. Nothing mattered. I felt nothing.

*

Sunday arrived, and after a pleasant breakfast, the girls, including Millie, were sent away to get changed into their initiation attire, leaving me with the girls from the older years as they discussed their evil plans. Hall looked different during the day, the colours of the stained glass more primary now, the portraits displaying their details with pride.

'Don't forget the garlic.'

'Or the dildos.'

'Did we end up getting the mouldy cheese?'

'Wait, Alice, I thought you were doing it too?' one of the second-year girls suddenly inquired, causing fifteen perfectly styled heads to pivot round and stare at me.

I didn't know what to say. Panic set it. But thankfully . . .

'Girls, three is enough. Alice will do it some other time,' Tina quickly said, loosening the knot of tension which had begun to tie itself around me.

Everyone seemed satisfied with this and returned to their discussion. I caught Tina's eye, wondering why on earth she'd saved my ass. Her eyes smiled, even if she didn't, looking at me as if she knew something. A note of panic struck again. She was friends with Rob – maybe she knew. But he had wanted to keep it a secret – why would he tell the biggest gossip of them all? No, surely she couldn't know. So why was she cutting me so much slack? Maybe I'd misjudged her. Maybe Tina was OK after all. Though as my three friends returned dressed in the ugliest jumpsuits I'd ever seen, and putrid swimming caps on their eggheads, I remembered that actually, Tina would always be a bitch. But I appreciated her saving my skin nonetheless.

The initiations began as the girls downed strange concoctions of vodka and sweet corn juice and licked cream cheese out of each others' armpits, carrying out these bizarre acts with glee. I smiled and winced as was appropriate, through glazed eyes – at least it was a novel way to spend my Sunday afternoon. Then I thought of Flo. Would she be upset if I didn't turn up today? But what was the point anymore? I had nothing to say for myself. No, far better that I now wandered with the rest of the girls towards the park, where hundreds of drunken students stumbled about, some in fancy dress, some with funnels of beer down their throats, some puking into bushes despite the fact that it was only one o'clock in the afternoon. No, this was much better than forcing myself to try and open up. That was hopeless. Far better to watch the two male drinking societies beat each other up while everyone took photos and cheered as bloody noses and vicious rugby tackles poured from all sides. A raw chicken flew through the air. Over there a group of sportsmen in their Blues jackets were being flocked to by scantily clad blondes. And over there a guy in a tutu was being made to eat dog food while a group of lads shouted angrily, 'If you want to be in, you better chop it down, you useless fresher.' I moved through them all in a daze.

'Alice, have you seen Millie? Apparently she's passed out.' Henry's anxious voice met my ears.

I shook my head. He carried on walking. So did I. I passed a group of guys setting some poor lad's boxers on fire. And then two girls wrestling in bikinis for some other boys' amusement. If only the tourists could see this – if only they could see how the most intelligent youths in the country let off steam in exam term. I would have smiled if I'd had the energy, but what was the point, who would see it? Who saw me? I was invisible. I was nothing.

I saw him twice that day. But he didn't see me. Then I saw him again on Monday in Hall. But I left straight after, so I don't know if he saw me. Then on Tuesday I thought I saw him from my window, walking along the street with Danny, but I wasn't sure. I didn't have the energy to focus. Then twice on Wednesday, not at all on Thursday or Friday, once yesterday and not at all so far today. I touched wood. But what was the point? I didn't think luck even knew I existed anymore.

*

The following Sunday we sat around the long wooden tables of Hall, eating our brunches, the conversation reverting back to this day last week and the glorious drunken antics of Millie Blenchworth, newly initiated Robin Red Breast and bookies' favourite to be president of the society in her third year.

'So let's just get this straight, you passed out at half two in the afternoon?' Joey chuckled, tucking into some very greasy-looking hash browns.

'No, come on, we've been through this – it was definitely after three,' Millie insisted.

'That's bullshit!' Henry contradicted, 'By the time I found you it was just after three and you'd definitely been out cold for a while.'

'I meant to ask you – I thought you were supposed to be initiated last Sunday too?' One of the girls asked Henry, changing the subject slightly, much to Millie's obvious disappointment.

'Nah, they've decided to wait until Suicide Sunday instead. Probably for the best – I was too busy looking after drunky over there,' he said, pointing towards Millie.

I drank some orange juice, but I wasn't hungry. I stared at my bacon and eggs – runny, just how I liked them – but I couldn't eat them. The banter raged on.

'But Henry, just to clarify, by looking after you obviously mean taking advantage of her, yeah?' Joey teased.

I looked up, the comment lilting through my daze. That wasn't usually the kind of joke he made.

'Oh yeah, took her home and had my way with her,' Henry growled. 'Who needs Rohypnol when you've got vodka?'

Everyone laughed. I looked away, discomfort crawling up my back. Why would they say something like that? It wasn't funny. My left leg betrayed my silence.

'Alice, you all right?' Joey asked through the hilarities, noting my discomfort.

'Yeah, fine,' I replied, still not looking at him.

'Alice, seriously, what's wrong?' Joey pressed.

'Nothing,' I insisted. Come on, just block it out.

But a voice so strong it couldn't be ignored suddenly cut through.

'Don't mind her, Joey. Alice just doesn't like talking about initiations,' Millie announced loudly, making me spin back around to look at her. 'She's far too mature for all that sort of thing now,' she added.

'What?' I managed.

Suddenly the group was silent. My gaze flitted from face to face. I was uncomfortable with the change of focus. 'Oh, I saw you last Sunday, watching us do all those stupid things while at the back of your mind you were just thinking "what a load of twats". I mean, I know you thought you were above being initiated yourself, but that gives you no right to look down on me just because I did it. It's just a bit of fun, for God's sake. Or wait, have you forgotten what that is?' she spat.

I was shocked. Where was this all coming from? And why

was she being so mean? Everyone was silent. I felt so exposed, the brightness of the hall illuminating my fear. But Millie wasn't finished.

'Well say something, for God's sake! I think you've said about five words all term, Alice,' she continued, laying into me harder and harder. 'And then you go and drop those glasses and cause a big scene in the bar and then everyone thinks "oh, poor Alice, is she OK?" But what about poor Millie? Or poor Joey? What about the ones who keep trying to be nice to you even though you've just turned into this boring little shit? I mean, I know they say Cambridge isn't for everyone, but seriously, Alice, I'm surprised you even came back this term. You're clearly not happy here, you've got no bloody friends – you've got bloody nothing. You've *become* nothing.'

By the time she finished her voice was almost a shout, catching the attention of neighbouring groups who stopped, mid-bite, to watch the attack. I could barely breathe. It was so unexpected that my numbness had been caught off guard. Her words cut through me.

'Excuse me,' was all I could manage, my body shaking as I got up from the bench and walked out of Hall.

I could feel them all watching me go. I knew Joey would be torn as to what to do; whether to go after me or to stay with Millie – his loyalties were divided. But according to Millie, they shouldn't be. Because he wasn't my friend. Because apparently, I *had* no friends. Apparently, I had nothing.

★

'Apparently, I *am* nothing,' I hissed, marching in circles as a startled Flo watched on, trying to learn quickly from where my uncharacteristic rage had come.

'Is that not just the harshest thing you've ever heard? What a bitch,' I continued, every bit of me seething, burning through the ice, melting it away by the furious second.

'But you know she doesn't mean it,' Flo tried.

She never wore any make-up, but today she needed some. She looked drawn.

'So why bloody well say it? In front of everyone?' I shrieked, still dumbfounded. 'And they *are* my fucking friends.' I yelled. 'Fuck her! I knew she could be a bitch, but never to me. But she's right – we're not friends anymore. And thank God!' I flung my arms upwards with relief, delighted I'd finally seen through such a hideous person.

'And I could just see that the others were so bloody uncomfortable by it all – like, who does she think she is to tell me that? *I'm* nothing? Coming from the girl whose life revolves around drinking societies and having sex with some twat? I mean, if I'm pathetic, then what the hell is she?'

My breathing sped up. My body had gone into emotional overdrive, feeling so much at once after its long hibernation that it was too weak to deal with the intensity. I leaned upon the bench, my hand feeling the grain. I looked at Flo, at those emeralds. They would make me strong. Come on, Alice; pull your fucking self together.

'Alice, it's only because she misses you. And it must be frustrating when she doesn't know why you've been . . . well . . . different,' Flo tried, my venom shrinking her smaller than ever.

I hated myself for frightening her. But I hated Millie more. But there was someone I hated most of all.

'It's all his fucking fault,' I shouted, my voice carrying up into the trees above. 'He's made her turn against me. He's made me turn against myself. I fucking hate him. I fucking hate him so much,' I screamed, straining my neck, feeling the veins bulge just beneath the surface. There was so much in me just bursting to get out. 'I just want to be free.'

I thought briefly of that girl in Magdalene . . . oh shut up, Alice, you're not going to bloody kill yourself . . . but why not? If I bloody well *am* nothing, then why not – what have I left? Stop that, you're being ridiculous. Millie's wrong – you do have stuff – you even have her; Flo's right, she's just frustrated because she loves you – she hates seeing you like this . . . so why don't I just put us all out of our misery . . .

'Alice, you need to calm down,' Flo tried to soothe.

'I can't do it anymore,' I yelled, my voice hurting now from too much shouting. 'I can't fucking do it,' I repeated, falling to my knees.

I held my head in my hands, tears streaming forth. I began to sob. I was making a scene, but I didn't care. I didn't care if Flo saw, because it was just me and her and the towering trees, architecture in themselves, all part of this wonderful town. But was it really wonderful? Millie's words echoed through the madness: 'Cambridge isn't for everyone.' What did she mean by that? Like she thought I had cracked under the pressure? How dare she. How *dare* she think I was that weak. For, broken as I was, that was because of something different; something very different . . .

But what does it matter now, Alice? He's won. Look at you, for Christ's sake. 'Ooh, I'm Alice Chesterton, I'm so strong, I never get upset' – you're a quivering wreck . . . but it's not my fault . . . it doesn't matter whose fault it is, Alice. He's won. You've got nothing. You *are* nothing.

My heart sank down deep. All my life had been leading up to this moment, or indeed, leading down. I had failed.

'I am nothing,' I whispered.

I watched as the tears fell from my face, raining onto the ground. I pitied the daisy that would grow there – it would be the saddest daisy of them all. Sad and hopeless and would never survive. But what was there to live for anyway?

'Alice, you can't say things like that. You have to have hope,' Flo affirmed with increasing desperation.

I shook my head. She was so naïve. How could I have hope anymore?

'You've got so many people who love you. Me, Paddy . . .'

I froze. I wished she hadn't said that name. Because now I thought of that night; our night, when he had become . . . *him*. My memory became so vivid I could feel Paddy all over me. But it felt nice. I felt safe, a split second of air in this drowning frenzy.

'Alice, I just want to say I didn't plan any of this. I just . . . I can't help . . . I know this makes things complicated, but I think I'm still in love with you.'

The words teased my soul, telling it that everything was OK; Paddy loved me, he would keep me safe. I rocked where I sat, my head dancing with thoughts.

'Oh, Alice, you feel amazing.'

See – we were amazing together – I wasn't nothing, I felt

amazing; Paddy told me so. I wished he was here. I longed for it.

'Alice, this feels so fucking good.'

And then everything started to change, to spin, and it was him; it was HIM.

'Oh, Irish, that feels so fucking good.'

Why was the nightmare here? I was awake. I was awake and outdoors and . . . and . . . I was with Flo – not now. But I couldn't see Flo anymore. My eyes were glazing over with images; dirty, sordid images. And suddenly I was back in my room, and it was after the bop and I was drunk and Rob . . . he was there, and . . .

'I told you I'd have your tight little Catholic pussy.'

No! Why didn't I just say no? I did say it . . . but not properly. Why hadn't I screamed? Why hadn't I screamed and screamed until someone came in? Just think, everyone would have known how evil he is, and it wouldn't have gone all the way. I wouldn't be fucking tainted. The scene burned into my eyes. I looked up at him, tears streaming down my face. But it wasn't him anymore, it wasn't him at all. It was Paddy, my Paddy. What the hell are you doing? Paddy, it's not meant to be you. Stop . . .

'I''m going to come. I'm going to fucking come.'

Paddy. Get off me. Why are you here? I slammed my eyes closed even tighter, squeezing away the terror, wringing out the pictures so that they poured away. I opened them.

'I'm going to come. I'm going to fucking come.'

Why wouldn't it end? Why wouldn't he . . . or Paddy . . . or whoever it was . . . but now it was someone else. Those eyes I knew so well and held so close. But now he was disgustingly close, touching me and fucking me and groaning like a sick dog as his stare burned through the darkness, that foul smile glowing out through the choking shadows. Not a dog but a cat, the Cheshire Cat . . .

'Joey?' I whispered, the words barely daring to cross my lips.

The large grin ripped across his face as he thrust his cock into me so hard that it stung between my legs. What was going on? How did he . . . why was he . . .

'Alice,' a voice somewhere very far away called out as Joey gained momentum, his panting breath making me want to be sick.

'Alice, Alice please – wake up,' the voice called again, louder now.

But I couldn't wake up because I wasn't asleep. This wasn't a nightmare; I was awake. This was hell. I had finally made it here.

'Alice,' the voice shrieked.

I knew that voice. It was Flo. It grabbed me and pulled, but Joey pulled me down, yanking my hand to keep me with him.

'No,' I told him, begging him to stop.

Still the voice called my name. I longed to follow it, to escape. But then I thought of the other day, and the thronging crowds of the dinner queue and how I'd nearly been lost. But then Joey's hand had pulled me back, saved me. Where was that hand now?

'Alice,' she called, he called; I don't know.

'I going to come. I'm going to fucking come,' he called, she called; I couldn't tell.

'You're clearly not happy here, you've got no bloody friends – you've got bloody nothing. You've *become* nothing.'

No; no that's not true; that's not fair.

'Alice, Alice honey, now be careful there, dear – I know it's a beach, but there can be a lot of broken glass – just mind your feet, OK?'

I could feel the ocean's breeze. Where was it coming from? But it washed over me, filling me . . . but now it was water; it was water and I was drowning, I couldn't breathe. Thirty-four, thirty-five . . . I really did need to breathe now; *no*, Alice, you're not allowed – you have to do this – you told you you'd do this so you have to do it now . . . but I didn't tell me – I'm not six anymore and I'm not in the bath and this isn't a game, this is real . . . forty-two, forty-three . . . my head's getting really light . . . fifty, fifty-one . . . eyes closing; I hope I'm not going to die. Come on – you're almost there. Oh my God I'm going to die, I have to . . . no you don't, come on, you can . . . eyes closed . . . fifty-nine . . .

A scream suddenly rang out, its high pitch piercing through the confusion. I opened my eyes, trying to comprehend. It must have been Flo. I stared at her in disbelief. The wind brushed my hair, every strand disturbed into dancing through the stillness.

'What the hell did you do that for?'

Why the hell had she screamed? Why hadn't she grabbed me or shaken me or slapped me back to life? Why wouldn't she touch me? Was I too hideous for her? Was she afraid what she might catch?

'I was trying to wake you up,' she replied, her voice calm, always calm, frustratingly calm.

'How dare you?' I snarled. 'I'm supposed to wake me up, I'm supposed to pull my head from under – that's how it's supposed to end,' I spat, my body tensed up with rage.

But I was being pathetic. She was only trying to help, only trying to do the one thing I'd ever asked her to do. Who cared how she did it? This really was pathetic. Alice Chesterton and Flo . . . and then I realised . . .

'I don't even know your surname.' My voice was a whisper again.

'What?' Flo asked, my statement too random to make sense.

'I don't know even know your full name,' I repeated, the words whirring me into the frenzy from which I'd only just escaped. But I hadn't escaped, she had saved me. So why did I still feel trapped? Because *I* hadn't saved me.

'Alice, what are you talking—'

'This is ridiculous. This is actually ridiculous,' I declared, my words getting stronger now, filled with anger. But not anger at her, anger at this, all of this, this stupid bench and these stupid trees and the stupid fluffy clouds which just lolled above. No wonder I was still a mess. No wonder, because for the past four months of my life I had been hiding away on the outskirts of Cambridge with a girl I barely even knew. A practical stranger. And yet she wasn't a stranger, she was my oldest friend . . . Alice, what are you talking about? Just because she listens to you whinging on doesn't mean she's your friend. It's pathetic.

'I mean, Millie's right . . . I have nothing,' I realised, my eyes flickering from side to side as I tried to grasp this ridiculous reality. 'All I have left in the entire world is some girl I barely even know who has nothing better to do with her life than to listen to my self-indulgent rants.' My voice rose higher and higher, squeaking with incomprehension.

'Alice, I *do* have better things to do. But I come because you need me,' she insisted.

'I don't need you,' I corrected instantly. 'I thought I did, but I don't. The woman from the Cambridge Crisisline told me I needed professional help and do you know what I said? Do you know what I thought? I thought: "Oh no, it's OK, I've got Flo." What the hell! I mean, I don't even know you. Not really. I mean, who are you? Why are you here? Why do you come here every Sunday to listen to all the terrible things that have happened to me? Do you like it, eh? Get some sort of sick kick out of it?'

'Alice, that's enough,' she said firmly.

'No, come on, Flo,' I pushed, my voice mean and sarcastic. I wanted to stop but I couldn't; an unknown source of bitterness had been unleashed and every hideous word stung my lips. 'Come on, Flo. Just answer me this: why are you here?'

'You know why I'm bloody well here.' Her voice was louder than I'd ever heard it. 'Why are you doing this? Why are you being such a bitch?' she quizzed, the emeralds now full of an alien emotion, rage pouring out, dulling the dazzle.

'I'd rather be a bitch than a weirdo,' I replied, spitting the words. 'You know everything about me – every last thing – more than anyone in the entire world. And yet you won't tell me a thing about you, not one single thing. I know nothing, nada, zilch. And do you not find that a little strange?' I quizzed, my face only inches from hers, seething against the porcelain.

'This whole fucking thing is strange,' she exclaimed. 'But

it doesn't mean it doesn't work – it doesn't mean you have to suddenly turn against it.'

But I wasn't finished. 'And every time I come here, no matter what day or what time, you're here. Do you not think that's a bit fucking odd? I mean, what are you, stalking me?'

'Alice, just listen to yourself, you're being awful. Do you want me to just leave?' She turned away from me so that now her back was the canvas for my taunts.

'See if I care,' I hissed. 'I don't need you. Or do you have nowhere to go?' I coughed out a disgusted laugh. 'I mean, it's not like you ever talk about your friends – do you even have any?'

I was hideous. I sounded like Millie. I was repeating the words I'd loathed so much.

'Well some friend you're being to me. After all I've fucking done,' Flo spat, still facing away.

Her words echoed through the stillness, the world completely motionless; no breeze, no noise, everything on the brink of the next step.

'But if this is your way of getting rid of me, then fine.' Her voice was calmer now, as if she was over our fight, as if she was over me.

'So what, you're just going to give up? Just like that?' I shrieked, trying to provoke her again, wishing she's just put up a fight – wishing she'd save me from myself.

But she didn't. She just started walking away.

'Fine!' I shouted. 'Good bloody riddance,' I bellowed after her, the sun glowing off her white coat. Wasn't she warm? It was May, for God's sake.

'That's it – just fucking walk away. Just leave me on my

own. Don't mind me – I'll be fine,' I screeched. 'Yeah, I don't need anyone. Don't mind the fact that I just let you in and now you're just fucking off – no, don't mind that at all!' The volume built and built, my rage seething over, until: 'Jesus, you're just like my fucking mother.'

Did I really just say that? Did I . . . did I really mean that? Where did that come from? No – no – I don't; I don't care about my . . . so why . . .

'Come back,' I whispered, not knowing quite to whom. To Flo? To myself? My mum?

'Come back,' I tried once more, a little louder. But the wind blew the words away, just as Flo moved ever further from where I stood shaking. So this was how it ended?

★

I stumbled back through the Cambridge streets, my face puffy and sore, and yet the sobbing wouldn't stop. I thanked God that it was exam term and there was no one around to see me like this. But even if they did see me, who would care? And why were you thanking God? Fat lot of good he's done you; fat lot of fucking use.

I felt like a mad drunk thrashing through the streets. A group of pigeons blocked my path. I sent them flying with vicious, imbalanced steps. Are you happy now? You've got what you wanted. And what had I got? Please stop this; I just want to go home. But where is home, Alice? Do you mean your room? Or Dublin? You have no home because . . . *stop it*. Please. I can't do this anymore. I can't go on . . . I won't go on . . .

I reached my college. I raced through the courtyard, yearning to be back in my room, to lock the door and pray that somehow I could lock the voices out. The gargoyles relished my pain, sticking out their tongues with taunting glee, licking my soul with their evil eyes. In the door and up the steps I ran, away from myself. It was impossible. I reached the top step. My door was ajar. Shit, I must have forgotten to lock it on my way out. No matter, I'm here now; here at last. Away. Far away. My body shook as I pushed open the door, dying to slam it shut once more, to shut it all out. But as soon as I entered, I froze. Everything froze. Everything was just as I'd left it, perfectly in its place. Except for one thing. The nightmare was here – it had caught up with me. Because there he was – the one who only half an hour before had been in my mind and inside me, breaking me down, harder and harder . . .

'Hello, Alice.'

I stood on the edge of the cliff, ready to fall. Or ready to jump?

This was it. It was time.

18

I was sitting on the couch with my mum, watching *The Simpsons* and wondering what time she was going to send me to bed. I wasn't tired. I knew it was 'bed time' – that stupid fixed o'clock – but I wasn't ready.

'Come on, Ally-poo,' she commanded, just as I'd feared.

'Mum, I'm not tired,' I informed her, coolly and calmly, like an adult, not a whinging child. Because I wasn't a whinging child; never had been, never would be.

'Ally, I'm wrecked. I had a long day in the shelter and I'd really appreciate it if you'd just do as you were told.'

Now who was the child? I didn't like her bossing me around. She was being silly; I just wasn't tired.

'Come on, honey, or I'll have to drag you by your toesies,' she joked in that stupid baby voice she always used on my brothers, grabbing my right slipper and yanking it right off.

'Mum,' I groaned, unimpressed by her immature joshing.

But the smile had gone from her face. 'Ally, what is that on your foot?'

I moved my leg, tucking it under the cushion. 'Nothing,' I replied, wishing she'd just go away.

'Ally, give me a look at that, it looks awful,' she said, grabbing my leg to her.

I wanted to wrench it away, to tell her to mind her own business. But I didn't want to be a brat. She looked tired and much older than she was. But she also looked like me. We had the same bright hair and eyes, those eyes that were made to look, to look after, to comfort.

'Alice, it's infected. When did you get this?' she quizzed, examining the yellow pus which oozed from the wound.

I hoped she wouldn't touch it; it was really sore and it had been aching all week. But I had hidden my limp well and now I was annoyed that my cover had been blown.

'Mum, it's nothing. I just stepped on some glass when we were on the beach last weekend.'

'Ally, I told you you shouldn't have been walking bare-foot – that place is full—'

'I knew you'd say that,' I cut in.

I didn't want to hear it; I didn't need to hear how I'd messed up and how she was right and I was wrong. I got it; I'd made a mistake, and now I was paying for it, pus and all.

'Ally, it's OK,' she soothed, placing her hand on my shoulder and trying to look into my eyes. I turned away; I didn't want her to see the tear which had begun to form.

'Ally, look at me – are you all right?'

'I'm fine,' I assured, still turning away, looking at the photo of my parents on their wedding day. Mum was prettier back then. Dad looked just the same then as he did now, but happier. I felt sad.

'Look, let me just go get the first aid kit and I'll try and sort you out, OK?' she said.

But I didn't want her help. My foot still hurt but it was

a lot better now compared to a couple of days ago. 'Why can't you just leave it to heal on its own?' I asked, still looking away, still waiting for that single tear to drop.

'Because, honey, not everything can heal on its own, you know? I know it might hurt, but sometimes you need someone else to help make it better, OK?'

I had decided there and then that I would spend my entire life trying to prove her wrong.

But already, that felt like a lifetime ago.

*

I stared at him, wondering how long he'd been sitting there waiting for me. The afternoon light cascaded through the window, but the shadows concealed the details of his features. Maybe I was just dreaming again, or imagining or whatever I had been doing earlier. How would I know if this was real? How would I ever know?

'Come here,' he held out his hand.

His voice made all the others stop. Surely that was a good sign, right? But how did he expect me to take his hand, to trust him, to sit beside him on that bed when not so long ago my mind had been showing us on this bed and him . . .

'Please,' he added, his eyes begging with me.

I remembered the first time I had seen them, on my very first day in Cambridge. We had been in the bar, and he was paying for a pint of a magenta concoction the likes of which I'd never seen before in my life.

'It's Snakebite,' he had informed me with a grin, noting

my disgust. 'It's really nice, I swear – do you want to try some?'

'It looks radioactive,' I had replied, mesmerised by its fluorescence.

'Yeah, it's like the Pink Panther took a piss in a glass, isn't it?' his strange accent had chuckled. 'I'm Joey, by the way,' he said, holding out his hand.

'Alice,' I took it and shook it, its firm, warm grip making me instantly comfortable.

And I had never looked back. And as I looked back at that memory and then looked back to where Joey was sitting now, still offering that same, firm grip, I knew what I had to do. Perhaps my instincts were all I had left. And this felt right. So I took his hand after all these months and, after all these years, I took my mother's advice.

*

I didn't say anything, just put my arms around her. She felt so small beneath my embrace, a fraction of who she had once been. Her hair smelled stale, but still of Alice, a musky version of that scent I knew so well. She buried her head in my chest, clutching me tightly, showing me that she still had some strength in her. And I hadn't doubted it. But I knew there was little left, and now finally, I needed to know why.

'Ally, you have to talk to me,' I whispered, rocking her gently like a tiny child. She felt even more fragile than if she had been one, like she could break at any minute. Though I feared she had already broken.

She didn't reply, but I wasn't going to push her. I gazed

around her room. It was more empty than it had been last term. Even the mirror above her sink was gone. How odd. It was as if she just hadn't unpacked, as if she needed to be ready to leave at any moment. I thought of what Danny had said about her having a new boyfriend, and what Millie had told me about some girl called Flo whom Alice had mentioned, but as far as I could tell, she had no one. Which was why I was here. When she had dropped those glasses in the bar the other night, she caught my eye and looked truly terrified, like a deer in the headlights, but with its feet stuck in the tarmac.

'I don't know where to start,' she whimpered, still holding tight. I wondered when was the last time someone had hugged her and made her feel safe.

'It's OK, just take your time,' I soothed, stroking her head now.

She let go of me and pulled away, those blue eyes so full of sadness it broke my heart. She looked so beautiful like this. But there was no point thinking thoughts like that. We needed to get to the point; she needed to take me there. Finally she spoke.

'Joey, can I trust you?'

'Of course.'

'No, I mean, *really* trust?'

Her tears were drying up, answering her question for her, but still I nodded, never breaking her gaze.

She took off her flip flops and pulled her feet up underneath her, crossing her legs. I looked at the tiny foot which sat beside me, the slender toes like those of a child. They were so white. The sole was wrinkled, but looked soft, except for a small scar at the base of her big toe. I wondered how she had got it. It was more silver than the rest of the foot, a tiny line from which two other lines diverged, like a crack on glass.

'Joey, something happened to me at the start of last term,' she began, her voice wary, as if she was still debating whether this was a good idea. I let her pause. 'Something that really hurt me . . . and I know I should have told you at the time, but I just thought if I forgot about it, then I could just . . . I suppose . . . forget about it, and then everything would be OK,' she explained slowly, as if trying to work out the logic of it all herself.

My mind raced with possibilities, as it had done for months now. Had someone died? Was she sick? Pregnant? The last was obviously a stupid suggestion, given Alice's constant cautiousness with everything.

But before I could conjure up any more ridiculous notions, she took a deep breath, about to say the words that would hopefully make everything click, that would finally explain why things had turned out the way they had. She turned around to face me straight on. My heart stopped. My ears opened.

'Joey, I was raped.'

The room began to spin. My mouth fell open, but not to speak. For what could I say? What could I actually say? I looked at her, wondering had she really just said that, but the blue eyes told me the truth. A million questions rushed by, but I couldn't grab them. I couldn't move. I could only hear the words over and over in my mind. She had been raped. I wanted to be sick. Who the fuck did this? Who the fuck had dared to touch her? I knew it didn't matter; I didn't need to know the details, this should be enough. But I had to know. I had to know what sick freak . . .

'It was Robbie. Robbie in third year.'

The words hit me like a punch in the gut, quickly giving way to blinding rage.

'I'll fucking kill him,' I snarled, my veins pumping with pure hatred.

I wanted to wring his fucking neck, squeeze his life away, make him squeal like a fucking . . .

'Joey, don't,' she begged, her tears welling again.

I froze. What was I doing? This wasn't about me – this wasn't about what I felt. This was about Alice, beautiful, precious Alice. I opened my arms and she fell into them instantly. In my mind I still saw red, but for now, I just had to hold her. How had this happened? How could anyone do that? What kind of sick bastard was he? And all this time . . . and I'd seen him around and never noticed . . . and how had *she* felt seeing him? No wonder she hadn't come to Hall or to the bar or to any of the bops since . . . my mind screeched to a halt. Had it been that night? I remembered that night. She had looked incredible. And then we were back in Henry's room, and Robbie had been trying it on but then Alice had left and then . . . my stomach lurched. I swallowed deeply. I remembered so clearly how he had stood up to leave, and told Danny to stay, and had sauntered out of the room like the dickhead he was. And then what? He had just gone upstairs and . . . my tears began. Angry, disgusted tears. But I wasn't just disgusted with him, I was disgusted with myself. Had I really been sitting downstairs in Henry's, drinking and laughing and acting the twat, while upstairs he . . . she . . .

'Alice, I'm so sorry,' I tried, but the words would barely form.

I felt pathetic as I held her to me; pathetic that I had thought I was protecting her from the world. Because it was too late, the damage was already done.

★

We sat there hugging for almost an hour. There was so much to say, but none of it seemed to matter. All that mattered was that we were here, in each others' arms, reunited friends. And I would never *ever* let go again.

A piercing sound ripped through the moment. It was my phone.

'Shit, I'm so sorry,' I fumbled, trying to get it out of my pocket. I stared at the screen. 'It's Millie.'

Alice didn't say anything, but just held out her hand. I gave her the phone.

'Mills, it's Alice. We're in my room. Can you come round?' Her voice was calmer than I'd expected, but still very soft.

I looked at her, wondering what was coming next.

'I have to tell her too,' she explained, wiping her eyes and her nose. 'I owe her that at least.'

'Ally, you don't owe anyone anything,' I corrected, hating for her to think like that.

But she didn't say anything, just sniffled, crossing her legs once more. The scar on her foot looked more silver than before. We waited.

Millie arrived within the minute, flustered and loud as she bundled into the room. But as soon as she saw us, she stopped.

'Oh my God, what's happened?' she asked, throwing herself to her knees in front of us, instantly taking Alice's hand in hers, squeezing it tight.

There was a long pause and then Alice told her news. Millie burst into tears. Alice cried again and I cried again and yet part of me was strangely happy – or perhaps just relieved that even as the three of us sat there crying, at least we were friends once more. We were a part of Alice's life again – her broken life – and we would be the ones to help build it up again. And from now on nothing else mattered.

19

The next few days were a blur. It didn't feel like Cambridge at all. I barely felt like Millie. I didn't open a single book and I didn't go to a single lecture, or to Hall, or to the bar; I just stayed with Alice. I even slept in her room. Naturally Henry was a bit peeved, and by peeved, of course I mean horny.

'Babe, come on, how the hell can I concentrate in the library if I just keep getting boners every time my phone vibrates in my pocket? The girl who sits across from me keeps practically getting her eye poked out every time I stand up!'

But then Alice had told me to tell him. And of course, he was amazing about it. But then he kept trying to look after me because he knew how upset I was about it all, but he had exams. And I didn't need looking after. And anyway, I definitely deserved a bit of torment after the way I'd acted. I kept hearing my own hideous words in my head: 'You've got no bloody friends – you've got bloody nothing. You've *become* nothing.'

How had I said that? It made me sick. I mean, how could I have been so bloody cruel on top of everything else she must have been going through? And I know I didn't know the truth back then, but I *had* known that *something* was up. But I had just given up on Alice. And then went on to bitch about how *she* was a bad friend? God, I was such a hypocrite. It made me furious. I spent my life worrying about my image and going to the gym and watching what I ate – I didn't even swallow my own boyfriend's cum because it had too many calories, for God's sake! And for what? So that I looked good on the outside? But inside, what had I become? I had just tried to compartmentalise my entire life in Cambridge and when Alice wouldn't fit into the box I wanted her to – the happy-go-lucky maternal figure – I just threw her away? Disposable friendship? Phased out in the spring clean of my life? And yet, without question, now she was letting me back into her life, at her most vulnerable time. I didn't deserve that. But she was giving it. And now, I had to give her my all.

I knew Joey was feeling guilty too. I watched him with her, giving her hugs and telling her jokes, keeping her spirits high but letting her break down when she needed to. The way he looked at her was like nothing I'd ever seen before. He must be in love with her; surely he must. I knew there had always been rumours, but now as the days passed by, I realised that maybe the rumours were based on something real. And I felt so guilty for tormenting Joey for the feelings to which he felt unable to confess. Of course, he could have at the start of last term when Alice had come back to Cambridge single. But then things had changed. And now we knew why. But I knew it also meant that now he would have to hide his feelings more than ever; I knew he thought that the last thing Alice needed was to think about something like that. Because her world had already fallen apart, and if her best friend, her rock, suddenly told her that he was in love with her, it would be awful. Nothing would be how she thought it was. And plus she would think that every single member of the male race had another agenda, and it was up to us to make her see that Robbie wasn't like other men.

Robbie was sick. My blood boiled when I thought of him; I wanted to wring his bloody neck. When I did talk to Henry about it, I would just rant and rave about what a vile, despicable creature Robbie was and how perverts like him should be castrated. I even used the 'c' word about him a couple of times – truly out of character for me. But then one night, once Henry had finally calmed me down and promised me that he would look into buying a home-castration kit off eBay as part of my next anniversary present, I began to cry.

'Baby, don't let him get to you too. That's the last thing Alice would want,' he consoled, kissing my streaming eyes.

But I wasn't crying because of him – I was crying because of me.

'Henry, I've got something to tell you.'

He looked confused, but I needed to be honest with him about what was eating me up inside. 'Henry, I was jealous,' I confessed.

'What . . . what do you mean?'

'That night . . . that bop . . .' I began, my tears flowing freely now, 'I remember when we were going back to yours, and Robbie put his arm around Alice . . . oh, it just seems so sick thinking about it now . . . but I remember feeling jealous. I mean, obviously I didn't want to get with him – I was already trying to decide between you and Danny . . .'

'What is commonly known as a "no brainer"!'

I smiled briefly – I really did love him. 'But I just thought "why the hell is someone as hot as him interested in her and not me?" Isn't that disgusting?'

I knew the answer – and I hated it.

'Baby, it's not your fault you're vain. You just . . .'

'And then when we were in your room and they were talking and I like "passed out" on your bed. Well I actually wasn't that drunk – I just wanted some attention, because I felt like all eyes were on her, especially when she like, spat that drink on him and stuff . . .' The tears poured. 'And then she said she was going to bed and I remember being glad because I was pissed off with her and then she tried to help me and I just pretended to be really wasted because I didn't want to have to talk to her and I wanted to stay after she left because I was so jealous that everyone . . . I was so jealous that *he* had been giving her so much attention . . .'

My sobs made me stop. Surely Henry would hate me. I hated me. How could I have felt that and then right after, Robbie . . .

'Babe, you weren't to know,' Henry assured, rubbing my back. 'None of us were.'

I knew he was right and it helped a little. But not much. It all just felt so unjust. And I knew it was a sick and twisted thing to say, but every night as I lay in bed, I couldn't help but think why did it happen to her? She didn't deserve it. If anyone did, I did. *I'm* the bad person, *I'm* the one who craves attention, *I'm* the slut. Not her. So why the hell did it have to happen to her? None of it made sense. But I had to be strong. I owed her that at least.

*

Summer arrived in full regalia, dancing through the streets, commanding us to smile, wear shorts, and above all, drink Pimm's! Some students had already finished their exams, so the hum of life was finally starting to return to the Cambridge air. Of course this hum, together with the radiant sunshine which left no gargoyle unadorned in burnished brilliance, left all those still stuck in the library feeling more trapped and more resentful than ever. And us first-year History and English students didn't have it easy either – people may have been jealous of our lack of exams, but we still had lectures, and those who were now finished with exams were spending every hour of every drunken day navigating punts along the Cam, indulging in a staple diet of strawberries and champagne and basically living the dream from dawn until firefly dusk. On top of lectures, we also had our weekly essays for two more weeks. Though as our tutors began to receive more and more of the older years' exam scripts to correct, it became evident that freshers had descended to the lower end of the priority list, and frankly, we weren't complaining.

It was a week since I had told Millie and Joey, and while a great weight had lifted from me, I made sure not to smile too hard. Because this time I knew not to just expect an instant fix – one act of confession did not mean it would just go away. But I certainly felt different. It was as if the fist that had been scrunching up my insides was finally starting to loosen its grip. I still felt sad and hurt by it all, but I felt as if I could finally relax into those emotions and admit to them, not just to myself or Flo, but to my real friends – the people who inhabited my everyday world. And though that made it all the more real, it made the hope all the more real too, so real I could almost taste it.

The weather helped too. Summer's arrival was so sweet and as I sat with my friends on the lawn I inhaled it all – liquid happiness – and exhaled pure relief.

'We should go out for dinner tonight,' Millie piped up from where she lay, top rolled up, hoping that her ridiculously toned stomach might tan.

It was already much browner than mine ever went – in fact, lying beside each other we almost looked like an ad for Benetton, the contrast in skin tones so extreme.

'Yeah, let's go somewhere really nice. Treat ourselves,' the heap beside me agreed enthusiastically.

It was Joey. My little star.

'Do you fancy it, Ally?' Millie inquired brightly.

'Yeah, definitely,' I replied.

We had been to Hall a couple of times since I'd told them. He had been there only once, but I had made them promise they wouldn't say anything or do anything because the last thing I wanted was for this to get out. As much as I hated to admit it, his 'our little secret' text did have some advantages to it, because while part of me did want everyone to be aware what a poisonous wretch he was, I couldn't bear for it to be public knowledge. I was more than happy with my nationality being my distinguishing characteristic amongst the masses, but I didn't need a tag like this: a Crisisline's 'survivor' or one of the legal system's 'witnesses'. I just needed to be Alice.

'Where do you fancy then? It's Sunday night – it shouldn't be too busy,' Joey pointed out.

'Ally, you choose,' Millie chirped.

They were being so good. They were striking the perfect balance between concerned and just fun. A big posh dinner was a great idea to celebrate a reunion.

'Ooh, can we go to D'Arrys?' I suggested, picking my favourite eatery in the whole of the town.

'Ooh yeah, and I can have those incredible mushroom thingies to start,' Joey added, licking his lips.

'Sweet, I'll book it,' Millie said, picking a time and then deciding what she was going to wear, ever the image-slave!

I closed my eyes, letting the summer rays shine down upon my pale Irish skin. I knew that in the morning I would wake up with my nose covered in freckles: 'kisses from heaven', as my granny used to call them. But I didn't care; any addition of colour to my face was better than none! But then I thought of that face without any freckles, that flaw-less porcelain perfection that glowed untarnished, untouched. She had flickered into my mind a couple of times during the week, starting to fill me with guilt for the awful things I had said. I had pushed the thoughts away; this week was about something else. But now the week was up, and I was up on my feet, slipping on my flip flops again.

'Listen, guys, I just have a quick errand to run, but I'll pop in when I'm back and we can get ready for dinner and stuff together, OK?'

'Sure you don't want some company?' Joey offered, using

all his energy to lift his head and squint in my direction.

'No, thank you,' I replied.

I appreciated the offer, but where I was going, I would have company. I hoped. Then again, there was always the possibility that she wouldn't show up. I prayed that that wouldn't be the case. Though I had said some pretty terrible stuff, I was upset and I didn't really mean it; surely she knew that? I debated with myself all the way there, until the long grass tickled my ankles, guiding me to her. She had come.

'Hi,' I greeted tentatively, wondering how exactly to go about this.

She looked even paler than usual – pale and pure. It wasn't entirely bizarre for me to view her as my guardian angel. I wondered where she hid her wings.

'You look great,' she remarked, the emeralds examining me from head to toe.

'Thanks.'

'No, really, you look . . . better!' she continued, her eyes smiling at me.

I was so glad she'd noticed, because then it must be true.

'I'm on my way,' I admitted, eyes smiling back.

'So what's brought this on, then?'

I made to tell her, but then stopped myself just before the words were born. What if she was upset? What if me telling her that I had told Joey and Millie made her sad? What if she thought that now that I'd shared that truth with the others, things would change between us? I didn't want to offend her. I didn't want her to think I didn't want to be her friend anymore; of course I did. I was just trying to show her that finally, thanks to her, I felt better. Scared, but getting better.

'I told Joey and Millie,' I announced.

The words lingered. I dared not breathe.

'Alice, that's amazing!' she said, the emeralds so sincere, twinkling in the sun. 'I'm so proud of you.'

And that pride meant the world. The whole, real world.

'But Flo, you should be proud too,' I corrected. 'It's because of you that—'

'Alice, don't be silly. I did nothing,' she interrupted.

I stopped, puzzled.

'Flo, you did everything.' We reunited as our eyes met. 'I'm so sorry about last week,' I began, wanting to erase the shame which still lurked.

'Don't be silly.'

'No, really, I am. I was awful.'

'You were upset.'

'But after all you've done,' I pointed out, the scale of my crime hitting me all over again, wiping my smile.

'Alice, I'm serious – I didn't do anything. You underestimate yourself.'

The emeralds were squinting, smiling, yet always looking like they were hiding something, like they knew something more, something good.

'And have you thought about talking to someone when you get home?' she asked encouragingly.

'You mean my friends?'

'No ... well, that too ... but I mean someone professional.'

The word scared me and comforted me all at the same time.

'Yes, yes I think I will,' I replied, building up strength with every word.

'And does that mean you're going to tell your parents?'

The strength sapped.

'Ah, Flo, it would be so weird talking to my dad about it, and you know I'm not that close with my mum, so . . .'

'So now's your chance,' she interrupted.

'What?'

'Well, you've let Mille and Joey back into your life, why not let your mother in too?' she advised. 'She's your mum, Alice – she really should know.'

I looked at the ground, giving my brain a quick respite to ponder these words. Surely it would just feel weird after all this time, opening up to Mum and telling her something so intensely private. There was no way . . .

'Alice, I heard what you said. That day when we fought – as I was walking away, you told me I was just like her.'

She paused, letting the memory replay between us. I heard the words echo through our air. I breathed them in. I didn't understand.

'What did you mean?' she asked. My insides twitched, as if something dead was coming back to life. 'Alice, I think you need to talk to your mum,' Flo continued, feeding the wrangling of this reborn tick. 'Maybe this is your chance to fill in the gaps.'

'But Flo . . .'

'Alice, if you don't tell her, the gap between you will only get bigger. You need to change that before it's too late,' she pressed, urgency creeping into her gentle tones.

'But . . . but . . . how could I?' I wondered, genuinely at a loss as to how such an idea could ever come about. 'How could I tell her? She'd be so upset,' I mumbled, more to myself than to Flo.

'But the fact that she would be a part of that – to share your pain – might mean the world,' she said.

Still I stared downwards, the scar on my foot suddenly pulsing. But the truth was I wasn't scared about making her upset, not compared to how scared I was about actually telling her, building up that courage to admit the sorry truth. I didn't know if I was strong enough. My friends were one thing, but my mother . . . I smiled, the irony creeping in. All my life I'd told myself to keep my worries to myself and stay strong. Yet giving my worries away required the most strength of all. But something had to give; maybe I had to give Mum a chance to be a mother. And not only to look after me, but to know me, all of me. After all this time.

'But listen, it's time for me to go,' Flo finally spoke, breaking my trance.

'Oh . . . oh, OK,' I mumbled, snapping back to reality, my eyes rising from their patch of earth.

I looked at her, her words taking a moment to process as I heard them all over again, suddenly registering their strangeness; she never left me, I always left her.

'But Alice?'

'Yeah?'

'I won't be here next week.'

We were standing now, so close we were almost touching. But we never touched.

'Well, what about the week after?'

'No, I won't be here then either.'

Her words were gentle as always; gentle and clear. And yet they made no sense. Maybe it was just with the exams and everything, she was busy.

'So when am I going to see you again?' I asked, my voice losing strength. What if she was leaving me? For good? My mind whirred in confused circles, replaying our conversation over and over, trying to work out how we'd got there. This had all happened too quickly – surely I'd missed something?

'Alice, you don't need me anymore,' she said, her voice like a song, her eyes tracing around my face, smiling at every inch of it.

'Of course I do,' I assured her in disbelief, tears starting to form, still trying to catch up with the moment.

I felt like a child. I hated goodbyes. And I didn't understand.

'You need to . . .' she tried.

'But I don't just hang out with you because I *need* you. I *like* you, Flo. You're my . . . my . . . you're my best friend.'

Even as I said the words, I knew they were wrong. And yet how could they be? She had been there for me from day one, literally the morning after, that cold morning when everything had been turned upside down. And yet she had been here every Sunday ever since, helping me grow and stumble through the past few months. She had seen me in ways no one had ever seen me before. She saw the truth.

'You can't go,' I added, my voice cracking. The first tear dropped. I didn't care if we weren't friends in the usual sense; I didn't care if we never talked about normal stuff or

never went to the movies together or to the pub, or whatever. I didn't care. I just cared for her so much; that was all
that mattered.

'Alice, you have to focus now on spending time with
Millie and Joey, your real friends. And then in a few weeks
you'll be off back to Ireland for the summer and you're going
to have to decide whether to tell your home friends, and
your parents, and whether to see a counsellor or what. Because
as you said last week – I'm not a professional. You're going
to have a lot on your plate. You don't need me.'

'But I need you even more because I have to do all that,'
I interjected, my sadness pouring out now.

'No you don't, Alice. You've proven that you don't. You
have Millie and Joey, and I mean look at you – you're so
much happier in yourself already,' she remarked, her voice
full of love.

I didn't know what to say. I couldn't believe this was actually happening, that this was the end.

'I'm sure we'll meet again,' she whispered.

Another tear fell; I needed more than that to make them
stop.

'Promise?'

'Promise,' she matched.

And I believed her implicitly. I took one last look at that
face, into those perfect eyes, before she turned away. From
the back she still looked like a child, moving through the
lush green with grace and ease, practically hovering along
the ground. Her course began to veer right, leading her
into a patch of trees in full blossom. Through the trunks I
could still make out her movement, a glow of white amidst

the dark ranks. But eventually she was gone.

I waited a minute, to see if she'd emerge again. She never even said goodbye; not really. But I knew she wouldn't be back. I knew this was it. I strolled home in a daze, as if I too was hovering along the ground, making my way back towards my new world. I would go there next Sunday, just to be sure, but I knew in my heart that she wouldn't be there. Only in my heart. Always.

★

'To being friends. Always.'

Millie, Joey and I knocked our glasses together and let the sparkle of friendship ring out. The noise shivered through me, but I wasn't cold, not in the slightest.

'Clinky clinky . . .' Millie declared, introducing the phrase she had taught me on consuming our first ever bottle of wine together.

'. . . drinky, drinky!' I finished, taking a swig from my glass and swallowing the tangy wave.

'So easily amused,' Joey taunted, rolling his eyes as he too enjoyed the Sauvignon Blanc.

'This coming from a man who nearly came in his pants when ordering his starter,' Millie retorted with a wicked grin.

'I've told you – the mushrooms are amazing here, they're honestly the best thing I've ever . . .'

Joey stopped himself, noting Millie and my cocked eyebrows. He had proven her point. His cheeks hummed rouge. He slugged his wine, I followed suit.

'God, can you believe we've nearly finished first year?' I

pondered, the single gulp already making me feel contemplative.

They both shook their heads, but smiled. The candles that sat in the wine bottles all along the walls illuminated the faces of the two I loved so much. I was still sad after saying goodbye to Flo, confused too, but right now I had to focus on the positives; focus on everything that I had gained, not lost, to ensure that the newfound possibility of happiness reigned above all, glowed the brightest.

'Let's make another toast,' Joey announced, his eyes glistening.

'To another amazing two years together in Cambridge, and most importantly, to an amazing future together after that, no matter what.'

Our glasses clinked again. But suddenly I was somewhere else entirely, somewhere I hadn't been in a very long time.

*

'A toast,' Paddy had announced last September, raising his glass of champagne to mine as we sat in the bar of the Shelbourne Hotel, 'to my stunning girlfriend.'

I blushed; he could be so cheesy. But I loved it.

'And to being in love,' he continued, the last word thick with layers of importance, 'and most importantly, to an amazing future together, no matter what.'

'I'll drink to that,' I replied, clinking glasses and sipping on the sweet bubbles. I had seen how much these two drinks had cost, and while I had told Paddy that it was far too expensive and that we could just as easily go to one of the pubs round the corner, he had insisted.

'Ally, you're off to Cambridge in three days, where they practically drink champagne instead of water. I'm just trying to introduce you to your new lifestyle,' he teased.

But I knew there was a part of him that wasn't joking. I knew that there was a part of him that wanted to treat me, to wine me and dine me one last time, as if to prove that he, and Dublin, could be just as lavish and amazing as my new university. I had tried repeatedly to tell him that it wasn't going to be all fancy smancy, and that even if it was, there was no need for him to try and compete with that – I loved him, not champagne (although these bubbles were tickling my tongue just perfectly). But this was just his way of dealing with it – his way of congratulating me, and sending me off on my exciting adventure, even if it meant letting me go.

'We'll be fine,' I reassured him countless times, 'I'll be home in eight weeks for Christmas, and everything will be better than ever. Like I said, baby, if it's meant to be, it will be.'

'And we are,' he promised.

'I know,' I replied. And I'm pretty sure I really did believe it.

*

And fate may have had other ideas, but I didn't know if I believed in fate anymore. And maybe that was better; maybe that was more real. I couldn't tell yet; things were still all over the place. But in a few weeks I would be leaving this place, this magical place, and going somewhere else, to that place I called home. And though I had made my peace with Millie and Joey, now there was someone back there, back home, who was thinking of me, thinking of me and thinking that I hated him. Although I wasn't certain what it was that I felt, it was time to set the story straight, to start all over again.

Hey Paddy. Im so soz I havnt bn in touch. Luk, im home on d 22nd + id realy like 2 c u asap 2 apologise 4 + explain why I actd so weirdly last tym I saw u. Drinks in d Sholbourne? My treat? I tink, at last, im finally ready. xx

20

Term played itself out, day melting into balmy day. The Backs – the fields behind the River Cam – were a blur of picnic blankets and bikinis, Frisbees and frolicking students. Eventually I handed in my final essay and had my final supervision, despite being sorely tempted not to show up. But Alice had protested: 'Joey, don't be such a lazy fecker', so in the end I endured that hour-long ramble on the Industrial Revolution and then sprinted out of there faster than you could say 'screw industrial development, it's all about my liver development, mate' and cracking open my first cool, crisp beer of freedom.

'Pimm's me up, buttercup,' Millie chirped as Alice and she fannied about with their girlie drinks, both dressed in scanty summer dresses.

Alice looked amazing, the single red ribbon in her hair so sweet, yet her deep blue eyes keeping it interesting. I closed my eyes. I was so interested. But that wasn't for me to say; not aloud anyway. Why would I risk spoiling the bond we'd only just managed to repair? I was being greedy.

'Hey greedy guts, quit hogging all the strawberries,' Millie shrieked.

'What?' Alice asked, wide-eyed and innocent. But the smudges of red juice around her mouth gave her away.

We all burst out laughing.

'Imagine if Cambridge was always like this,' Millie suggested, rubbing sun cream on her shoulders. We'd been here for almost two hours.

'I think we'd get bored,' I speculated.

'You loser!' Millie teased, flicking some cream in my face. Judging by the heat of my nose, I think I probably needed it.

'No, but seriously,' I continued, rubbing it in, 'the reason we can appreciate being out here and doing sweet fuck all is because we've had a year of working our asses off. It's why everyone says May Week is so amazing, because the balls just feel like the ultimate reward for such an intense build-up,' I surmised. It made sense.

'Oh my God, I cannot wait till our ball,' Millie squealed, 'my dress is absolutely to die for. Although I'm seriously going to have to eat nothing but watermelon between now and Tuesday if I've any hope of fitting into it.'

'Oh yeah, because you're so obese and all,' I teased, rolling my eyes as far as they would go. 'Alice, why do you let her . . .'

'Guys, I think I'm going to write him a letter.'

The Irish accent rang out for the first time in a while. It was now obvious where her head had been. It took us a minute to process what she was talking about, to switch away from our frivolous slagging, but we were here now, on the same page.

'Just a couple of pages or something. I just . . . I just feel like there's so much I want to say, but I don't think I could bear actually, you know, talking to him,' she explained, sounding more pensive than anxious.

We had spoken to her a few times about confronting him; more often than not, Henry and I would beg her to let us beat him up. Millie too had been surprisingly keen on the violence. But Alice had told us no. And besides, I knew it needed more than that – I knew this wasn't just a problem you could solve by giving him a black eye. But I hated that he was strolling around scot-free. And although I had understood when Alice explained why she hadn't been able to complete her statement to the police, it still felt like justice remained very much undone.

'I think it's a really good idea,' Millie encouraged. 'You know it won't be easy, but . . .'

'Yeah, but it would be good for you to,' I added. 'Really cathartic, you know?'

Alice nodded, still deep in thought.

'I mean, chances are you'll never see him again after the ball,' Millie pointed out. Robbie would be graduating in a couple of weeks and then, as far as I was concerned, hopefully disappearing off the face of the earth.

I still couldn't look at him. Every time I saw him around college I exploded with rage. I wanted to grab him and punch the shit out of him and make him hurt and bleed and suffer in a million ways. It took every ounce of strength I had to just walk away. I was furious; I hated him so fucking much.

'Joey, are you OK?' Alice's voice pushed through the anger. 'You've suddenly gone all red.'

I looked at her. I wanted to tell her everything; she had told me her truth, now I longed to tell her mine.

'Pasty twat's been in the sun too long, haven't you?' Millie joshed, spoiling the moment. 'They don't really go outdoors much in Newcastle – afraid they'll get shot!'

'Oi!' I objected. 'Just because we don't have butlers to hold sun umbrellas over us and feed us grapes the whole time . . .'

'*Peeled* grapes,' Millie corrected, winking playfully.

The three of us laughed again, letter and love forgotten. As the latter should be; had to be. Until it was meant to be.

*

As the afternoon blazed on, I knew I was meant to be enjoying myself, but I couldn't focus on the now. My mind grew slowly more and more intoxicated with the idea of this letter, this chance to communicate with *him*. The various things I could say warred within my head. But not like the old voices, thank God. I wouldn't type it, I would let him see my scrawl, know that it had been penned by flesh and blood, penned by that same hand which had touched his . . . I closed my eyes. It was still fresh. I wasn't naïve enough anymore to expect it not to be. But that knowledge alone was a help. And I knew by now, finally, that I needed help. Professional help. And I knew that when I went back to Ireland I would have to seek this help out. I'd seen the Rape Crisis Centre before, on Leeson Street – passed it on so many nights out – just another building. But now it was more significant than any other Georgian doorway on that road. It would be the threshold I would have to cross into the next phase of this seemingly endless process. Above all, I was exhausted. But while I still basked in the Cambridge sunshine, I knew it was my last chance to write this letter and put it in his pigeon hole. Because in a few weeks' time he would be off to the real world, probably some highly paid job in a big firm. It was now or never, and I knew that if I let that chance pass me by, no matter if I was ready to scrawl these words or not, I would never forget it.

Dear Robbie

My mouth was dry. I'd been sitting here for almost half an hour wondering what to write next. This was harder than I'd expected. I wrapped my college scarf around my neck, for comfort, despite the hot weather. I remembered opening the parcel last term, wondering how my mum and dad had got it since as far as I knew they were only sold in Cambridge itself, and they hadn't yet visited me over here. I had told them that for my first term I just wanted space to find my feet. And then after that, well, after that everything changed; my world over here just felt tainted, and I didn't want them to be a part of that – didn't want them to see. But maybe next year they'd come. I could take them punting, show them around the colleges . . . oh why was I thinking about all this? Why was I staring out my window, to where the bright white moon was a hole punched in the sky? But she urged me onwards. knowing what had to be done.

I wanted to write to you . . .

No, that wasn't right – I didn't *want* to per se. I needed to. Or did I?

I felt compelled to write to you . . .

There, that was better.

. . . to tell you some things I think you need to hear.

It wasn't the most eloquent, but it said what I wanted it to – I didn't want him to think that this was about me needing to write this letter, but rather *him* needing to read it, him needing to be put face to face with everything he'd done, every awful thing.

When you did those awful things to me . . .

But no, I had to tell it like it was – I had to leave him in no doubt as to what exactly his crime was – to give it its full, proper name. I took a sip of my tea, but it had gone cold. The silence swallowed me.

When you raped me, and you did rape me, you ruined everything. Your act of violence meant that I lost my friends, I lost my ability to work, I lost the will to live.

What scared me most was that I wasn't even being over the top; it was the truth.

And I thought that I was never going to be able to get over that. And then I had to see you around the place, looking as if nothing had happened, like 'our little secret' didn't bother you in the slightest. And that ruined me even more.

I began to cry. But I couldn't – I couldn't let the tears smudge the page because I wouldn't give him the satisfaction. These weren't tears for now, these were old tears, the remains of that awful time when nothing had seemed possible, when, as Millie had so hideously declared, I had become nothing.

But now at last, I have finally started to move on. With the help of the most amazing friends in the world, I am coming to terms with everything you did, and starting, slowly but surely, to put my world back together.

The tears eased and I began to feel stronger.

But before I could even think about moving on, I had to make sure you knew what an incomprehensibly revolting thing you did, what an incomprehensibly foul person you are. I still have nightmares. I still have to see you when I go to sleep, and how you can sleep soundly I will never know.

I paused. Maybe he didn't sleep soundly; maybe he *did* have nightmares. Maybe I was being too . . . but no, Alice, he doesn't deserve the benefit of the doubt. He deserves to doubt himself in every single way, to know how hideous he is.

I went to the police . . .

Yeah, that would scare him – get him worried.

But I decided that I would rather get on with my life
than have to keep reliving and thinking about the past,
to keep thinking about you.

I paused, the pen shaking in my hand almost as quickly as my left leg; shaking furiously. But it was almost over. I was almost there.

So this is goodbye. Because after today you will not be
in my dreams and you will not be in my soul.

I wondered if such convictions were true, but I had to believe that they were, to believe in myself.

And I only hope that you will experience even a fraction
of the pain that has consumed my life, has stabbed me
day and night over the past six months, over half of my
time in this wonderful university so far.

I hated him so fucking much. But it was time to pass my hatred back to him and then hopefully be more at peace. Sure, it would leave a scar, a cold, silver scar, but that was OK. I would be OK.

So goodbye, Robbie.
From,
Alice

It was done. I wept once more, and then no more. I put it in his pigeon hole and walked away, forward, always forward. I was exhausted but I knew that when I slept he would not be there. He was gone. And that was the sweetest dream of all.

★

'Come in, come in, Alice, take a seat,' my Director of Studies invited, his lisp more generous with saliva than usual.

I sat in the usual armchair, the one I'd sat in as a nervous interviewee not a year ago, then as a triumphant first-term success story, then as failed, disillusioned second-term wreck and, now, as just myself.

'Well, Alice, it seems things have finally started to look up for you,' he began brightly. I knew our conversation referred purely to academic matters, but I couldn't help but feel he was speaking more widely.

'A bit shaky at the start of term, but things really picked up, and according to the feedback from your supervisors, the past few weeks have been your best yet.'

My heart lifted. My ears drank up the news. I was so relieved.

'Thank God for that,' I remarked with a grin.

'Alice, there was no need to be nervous. Everyone has a bad patch in Cambridge, particularly in first year. Takes a lot of adjustment to get used to this place.'

I nodded. There was so much he didn't know. But I appreciated his reassurance nonetheless.

'And let's just hope that some work over the summer will keep your improvement on track and you'll come back next year stronger than ever.'

My eyes were transfixed by the grate where the low coals had glowed in winter. It was empty now, but the words which flickered past my ears were full of meaning. If only he knew. I was sure he'd said the same thing to everyone else at this stage, but the significance was intense. I brimmed with hope.

'Well, enjoy May Week and have a lovely summer. Are you off back to Dublin?' he asked, standing up, bidding me farewell.

'Yes, yes I am.'

'Lots of catching up with the pals at home then?'

I nodded and said goodbye, grinning like a fool. I stepped outside, into the welcoming warmth. I could almost feel my smile echoing from all four sides of the courtyard's reverberating beauty. The sun burned brightly. I burned brightly, my fire returned. I turned left and strolled towards my room where I had left Millie waiting while I went to see my tutor, to receive that vote of confidence. And now the vote had been cast, and cast aside my worry, replacing it with those kind words which had added fuel to my fire.

*

The flame licked the pages. Light. Heat. Burn. I held the bottom corner, but the heat was still intense on my fingers, edging ever closer. It ate through the A4, the charred outline crackling inwards while sparks and fragments spat to the floor. I was surprised by how quickly the fire spread as the paper crumbled beneath it. Bells rang. It must have been an o'clock. This letter had consumed me for hours, and now it was being consumed. Only a few inches left. My fingers began to hurt. Just the final corner now. I saw her name go up in smoke, curling into itself, but it meant nothing. My fingers felt raw, but there was still some left. Eat it, eat it, just fucking do it, make it fucking go away . . .

I ran to the sink and rammed my hand under the cold water. The skin raged. 'Fuck,' I cursed. I was sure to get a blister. Or a scar. Fucking stupid.

The water gushed in methodical gulps, matching my pulse. But the cold didn't dim the pain, but rather it intensified it. I moved my gaze from the wound up to the face which watched. It was time to focus on it instead, to look into those eyes, to try and figure them out.

'FUCK!' I yelled, punching the glass, breaking those fucking eyes and that fucking face I couldn't bear to look at.

Now my hand really throbbed. The tap still ran, but it ran red now, my blood flowing over the shards of mirror. What a fucking mess. I was such a fucking mess. And she . . . I clamped my fingers tight against the wound to stop the bleeding. But my strength was gone. It sapped from me with the spilling of every drop of dirty blood. I closed my eyes. There was only darkness.

Only nothing.

*

I stood in front of the mirror, examining every inch.

'You look gorgeous,' Millie assured me.

'Now in fairness, I look more silly than gorgeous,' I corrected with a grin, adjusting my green hat just a bit to the left.

Tonight was the night of the final bop of the year, and the theme was 'My Summer Destination'. Lack of imagination together with much bullying from Joey had led me to embrace the stereotypes and go as a leprechaun. If only my friends from home could see me now . . .

'Well at least yours is funny, mine's just a bit shit, really,' she complained, painting her skin with pink neon body paint, just as she would be in a few weeks' time at the Full Moon Party in Thailand where she and Henry were destined for the next two months.

'I think you look cool!' I insisted, and she really did. The pink glowed along her golden skin, the most beautiful of canvases. 'But if you get any of it on me I will fecking kill you – I have worked on this colour scheme *way* too hard!' I giggled, examining the flawless green, white and orange attire which I had donned for maximum effect.

Part of me was excited about tonight; it was set to be a good one. But I was still nervous. It was still my last bop since . . . and I couldn't help but get that significance out of my mind. And I knew that I shouldn't. This was the way it was, and had to be.

'He probably won't even come. If he got your letter, he's not going to come,' Millie and Joey had insisted repeatedly in an effort to calm my nerves.

And I hoped they were right. I hoped he had read it. I

hoped it had hurt. Because I didn't want him to show up. I wanted him to be forced to miss his last ever bop in Cambridge – a tiny price to pay for everything he'd done. But at least I would know my words had had an effect on him; at least I would know that this tiny, seemingly insignificant victory would be mine. And any victory was better than none.

A knock at the door. Millie opened it to reveal her boyfriend, wrapped head to toe like a mummy in various coloured patterns.

'Since when are we going to Egypt?' she questioned, frowning at his efforts.

'They're ties, you moron – get it? Tie-land – Thailand? Eh, hello!'

I laughed. It was pretty impressive, you had to admit. Although I'd learned well enough by now that English people were very into their fancy dress – every event had a theme, every night out, every birthday party – and everyone seemed to have an endless supply of costume pieces and good ideas, going all out every time. I could just imagine if my guy friends at home were told something was fancy dress. I reckon a measly eye patch would be about as far as their lazy asses would stretch, whether it was pirate themed or not!

Joey waddled in, completely covered in cereal boxes, sweet wrappers, egg cartons and various other foodstuff containers. We all stared, completely confused.

'OK, OK, let me explain,' he began, obviously excited to put us out of our misery and relish in our compliments for his exceptional lateral thinking. I didn't hold my breath. 'So, if you don't eat all this food, you're . . .'

'Skinny,' Henry shouted.

'Millie,' I added.

She spun around in mock shock. 'Wait, does this mean you think you're coming on holiday with me and Henry? Because if you think I'm getting on an elephant with the two of—'

'No, shut up!' Joey stopped her, wanting us to continue guessing. 'Come on, if you don't eat this food, but you want to, you're . . .'

'An idiot?'

'Anorexic?'

'Hungry?'

'Bam! The prize goes to the leprechaun at the back,' he declared, grinning wildly.

But we were still at a loss.

'Guys, for God's sake, I told you I was going to Budapest with some lads from school.'

All three pennies dropped at once.

*

'So you took the plunge then?' Joey asked me as he poured us some drinks.

'Yeah, I finally decided to give in to peer pressure – it's a terrible thing, you know.' I teased.

'You look fucking hilarious!'

'Coming from the man who looks like he covered himself in Prit Stick and rolled around in a rubbish bin for a bit? Wait, is that where my Special K went?' I shrieked, the box stuck to his elbow making sense of the mystery of the missing box from my kitchen that morning.

'Sorry!' His cheeky smile belied his words.

'You could have at least left me the cereal!'

'Yeah, but I was going to try and stick the flakes to my face like a sort of beard, but then I decided I might get a rash!'

'Ew, I can just picture you getting all sweaty.'

'But maybe girls would nibble them off my face.'

'And that turns you on, does it?'

'Well, I'd better get used to it if I'm going to deal with the chicks out in Hungary, eh?'

We let the laughter take over, despite his terrible joke. My heart surged; he really was wonderful. I wondered if he knew how much I appreciated everything he'd done for me these past few weeks. But what had made it even better was that it had really proven that we could just be friends, best friends, without there being another agenda. All the rumours went up in smoke. He was my older brother, my protector. Someone to watch over me with an abundance of love and care, but not like a boyfriend. No strings attached, just simple, uncomplicated friendship in its purest form, and that filled me with nothing but pure joy.

'Right, let's get this party started,' Henry announced as he opened the door to five more of our friends, each decked out in their strange attire, my personal favourite being a guy who had covered himself with stock cubes and a sign saying 'There's No Place Like Home' because he was off to do an internship in the Swedish capital. As I sat, drinking my gin and tonic and posing for photos like the big leprechaun I was, I couldn't help but admit that there really was no place like Cambridge. And while Ireland would always be home, as the elegance with which I wore my beautiful top hat demonstrated, for me, Cambridge wasn't far behind. Because with this bunch of people behind me, I felt safe. I felt I could be me, the new me; the fragile new me.

'Irish, you're looking very . . . Irish!' Danny teased as I strolled into the bop two hours later, feeling much more sober than he looked. I hadn't been drinking, fearing that I wasn't stable enough yet to challenge my emotions with copious amounts of booze, and anyway, right now I was trying to take control of my life, not to lose it to an excess of alcohol. Particularly tonight, I needed to be completely switched on, to take it step by baby step to stop the memories from seeping in.

'So, what is the meaning of your costume then?' I asked Danny, who was dressed, quite simply, as a six-foot penis. This boy never failed to amaze me.

'Well, Robbie and I were supposed to go as Bangkok, but he's done a runner.'

My thoughts froze. So he wasn't here?

'What do you mean?' I asked, trying to sound casual, but the weakness of my voice betrayed me. Thankfully Danny was too drunk to notice anything amiss.

'He's left,' he explained, swaying from side to side, looking more comical with every movement. 'No one knows where, but he's just packed up and gone. His room's completely empty, his phone's switched off – no one has a clue what's going on. We don't even know if he's coming to the ball on Tuesday.'

His face was forlorn – Tweedledum without his Tweedledee. I had to try to disguise my reaction, bending down to fix my shoe. As I crouched, torrents of relief poured over me.

If he was gone physically, then surely soon he would go from me in every way. Soon. And though the bop and the ball may only have been two nights, I was here, and he was not. I had won. And he was lost; no one knew where he was. And the tiny victory felt much bigger than I'd anticipated. Bigger and better.

*

The next morning, as twenty-five sore heads wandered into the Senior Parlour – a beautiful room above the bar which students could only use for special occasions – the radiant sky spread almost flawlessly, kissed only by a smattering of wispy white against the blue. The Red Breasts, however, looked less than radiant, moving like zombies around the great dining table, piling their plates with breakfast in the hope of soaking up just some of the alcohol from last night, before they started all over again today. For today was Suicide Sunday, so named because it fell just before May Week, and consisted of numerous garden parties and copious drinking which left you destroyed before the real festivities – the balls – even began. And thanks to the bop, everyone in the room was already on the back foot.

'But you all have to have at least one glass of champagne with your breakfast,' Tina reminded, bossy as ever, wearing a crown on her head, the crown that in only a matter of minutes she would be handing over to next year's president.

I sat beside Millie, her pathetic plate of fruit looking far less appetising than my greasy feast, and she was the one feeling the pain.

'I want to die,' she groaned.

'It's Suicide Sunday – I think that's kind of the point!' I joked, taking a large bite of bacon.

The room was pale green, with two large chandeliers twinkling down on us, adding little but effect to the cascades of natural light coming in through the big bay windows. In the back right corner, a baby grand piano stood, and I could imagine the fellows up here drinking port and conversing sensibly while some old chap played a healthy dose of Mozart in the background, all very civilised and proper. I had a feeling today's antics would not be so inclined.

'So what's the plan for the day?' I asked.

'Well, after this I think we're going to the Willows' garden party and then to the Spires' garden party,' Millie said. Despite her aching head she remained thoroughly up to speed with all things drinking society.

'And then there's stuff on tonight in Live, Resolution and Sandy's, but I think we're going to Sandy's.'

'God, any drinking society that calls themselves the Spires are definitely compensating for something,' I remarked.

Millie actually laughed. She was waking up.

'And did you hear at the Willows they get girls to, like, jelly wrestle in paddling pools?' she said, eyes faintly illuminated. 'But please don't let me do it, OK? Because Henry said he'd totally break up with me if I—'

Her rant was cut short by a waiter filling her glass to the brim with bubbly.

I grabbed my glass and turned to face her. She looked as if she was about to throw up.

'Clinky clinky . . .' I offered.

'Piss off,' she spat, her head obviously not cured enough yet for such enthusiasm. I grinned, watching as she struggled to peel an orange, ever persistent. 'How much more effort is this pissing thing going to take?' she cursed, thrusting the orange in my direction. I smirked. Some things never changed, and I liked that a lot.

Once Tina had handed over her crown to a second-year girl in a rather emotional ceremony that made me want to fall about laughing, it was time to head to the Willows' garden party for a few drinks. And, apparently, some jelly. But there was still something I needed to do. I knew this would be a pointless errand, but I felt like I at least owed it to myself, and to my journey, to go.

I told Millie I'd see her at the Willows and thankfully she was too hungover to ask questions, so I left her with the rest of the girls and headed away. The pigeons nodded as I passed, and I nodded at each college: King's, St Catharine's, Peterhouse. And then the grass and then the long grass, everything just as I remembered it. I could probably do this walk blindfolded. But now I could see clearer than before, as the bench came into focus, spotlit by the sun. My expectations were confirmed; it was empty. No Flo.

I sat down and thought of my other bench – mine and Paddy's bench – which our scratches had claimed. Was every period of my life going to be marked by various wooden seats? I smiled. I wondered if I could get a plaque put on this bench. But what would I write? 'Here sat Alice and Flo, trying to make sense of it all'? Or 'Alice and Flo = best friends'? But yet again I wondered, had we really been best friends? And *that* didn't make sense, because yes, of course we had been. I had felt a stronger bond with her in that short time than I had ever felt with anyone. But could I really say that? Could I really compare? Because the bond I had with Millie or with Joey is so different to that which I had with Flo. Or should I say, *have* with Flo? I didn't know. Because if it had been so strong, and still was, then where was she? Why had she left me? And yet, why did her absence not leave me feeling devastated? I supposed it was because she had promised we would meet again. And yet, how could she promise something like that? We didn't have each other's number, I'd never seen her around town before. And I wasn't going to come back here every Sunday for the rest of my time in Cambridge, hoping that she might turn up. Yet I still sensed that her promise was real.

'Alice. You don't have to be perfect,' Flo's voice flowed through my memory. 'Just because you've spent your life looking after your brothers and your friends and everyone else doesn't mean you have to be perfect. Nobody is.'

I remembered frowning, resenting the implication that I thought I was.

'Flo,' I had replied, desperate to make her see, 'it's not about being perfect – God knows I'm not. But you have to understand – this was my big adventure. I've told you how my friends felt about me leaving Dublin; they were scared and sad and I think deep down they resented me a bit for abandoning them. So what, now I'm supposed to come back and say, actually, no – I've failed my big adventure . . .'

The memory stopped, becoming another.

'Honey, not everything can heal on its own, you know? I

know it might hurt, but sometimes you need someone else to make it better, OK?'

But I was no longer eight. And my foot no longer hurt. And though something much bigger, much more painful than some broken glass, had tried to break me since, the hurt was easing. The wound was raw; not yet a scar, a cold, silver scar, but it was getting there with every day that passed. I hadn't failed. Flo was right: something had happened, something terrible, but I now had to accept that there was nothing I could do about it, that bad things happen and as much as I had tried, I couldn't fix it by myself. Because not everything can heal on its own. It might hurt, but sometimes you need someone else to make it better. I had needed someone else.

And although now that someone else was Joey and Millie, and soon to be Paddy, and Róisín, and my mother, and a counsellor . . . my mouth went dry, my head spinning at what was to come. But I could never let myself forget about Flo, who had come and listened to me week in, week out without fail. She was my white rabbit, which led me down the hole to this haven, this strange place which had shown me things and taught me things I now clung onto with all my might. And she had given me the strength, without so much as the blink of an eye. I thought of her, gazing into the distance, without even blinking; those emeralds staring, always staring, at something I couldn't quite see. I looked straight ahead into the greenery which had so captivated her, trying to see if I could spot it. The leaves danced, teasing me. But then a sudden strange feeling surged through me. I was so close to fixing my eyes on that elusive thing – on the truth. But it was just out of sight. I squinted, blocking out the blinding sunlight, and I could see clearer. But not perfectly. It was OK, maybe I couldn't know all the answers. I took one last look into the distance – into Flo's distance – and knew that it was time to go. I could come back some day if I needed to. And who knew, maybe her promise would come good. But I didn't need to know when that was, I didn't need all the answers. Just the hope. And that, I finally had.

＊

I made my way to the Willows' garden party, following the noise and the stench of alcohol. I tried to spot a familiar face in the crowd amidst the chaos, but was stopped by a young gentleman asking me if I wanted to take part in the jelly wrestling competition later that afternoon. I politely declined, and then out of the blur came Millie's glowing chestnut mane. I called her name and she spun round, eyes glittering, hangover nowhere to be found. 'Alice, this is Brian,' she announced, introducing me to the tall blond with whom she was chatting. 'Ooh, hold on, there's Henry. I'll be back in a minute.'

And suddenly she was gone, leaving two strangers to talk.

'Nice to meet you,' I said shaking his hand. He had a great smile, his teeth a dazzling white. 'So what college are you at?'

'Homerton,' he replied.

'Oh my God, you're the first person I've ever met from there!' I announced.

'Yeah, we get that a lot what with being so far out and

all. We did a swap a while ago with the Red Breasts, which is where I met Millie, but I don't think you . . .'

But I had stopped listening, because I realised that my last statement had not been entirely true. How could I have forgotten? Especially after where I'd just been.

'Do you know a girl called Flo?' I interrupted him, excitement running through me.

'Eh, I'm not sure.'

'What year are you in?' I quizzed, my delight mounting.

'First.'

Bingo.

'And what subject?'

'Medicine.'

I grinned – what were the odds?

'So then you must know her – her name's Flo, she's a first-year Medic too,' I garbled, my pitch higher than usual.

But Brian looked blank.

'No, I think you're confused. There's no one called Flo doing Medicine in Homerton,' he informed me slowly, looking at me like I was slightly demented.

'No really, there is. She's my best friend,' I persisted.

'Well, what's her surname?'

I paused. Shit. This was embarrassing. Maybe I'd just been confused – maybe she didn't go to Homerton – maybe I'd heard her wrong. But I was so sure . . . unless she'd told me the wrong college. But why would she?

'Listen, I think you've got your wires a bit crossed,' Brian suggested tentatively, clearly wondering why I was getting so worked up about it. 'But anyway, I think I'm going to go get another . . .'

'Sorry about that, guys,' Millie's voice burst in. 'Jesus, I wish I'd brought my sunglasses with me. That sun is literally blinding. I can't see a thing, can you?'

I didn't know if she was talking to me or not, but the answer was too clear not to reply. 'I can see perfectly.'

★

My mum still loved to tease me about the imaginary friend I'd had when I was younger – I used to call her Florence, after Florence Nightingale. Turns out I had been quite enamoured with the concept of this lady with the lamp, so much so that I converted her into my very own best friend whom no one else could see. 'Alice and Florence = best friends!' I used to write as soon as I could. Then I went to school, and my teachers used to ask me who Florence was and I would reply 'not telling' with firm, indignant pride. She was my secret. My best secret.

And then one day she just went away. Mum always jokes that that was the day I officially grew up, but she makes it sound as if I left Florence. But I didn't. She left me. She didn't even say goodbye; not really. And I'll never quite know why.

★

I smiled. She had returned. And now I knew that she would again; she had promised.

But my smile vanished. The light grew dark. Because maybe no one had ever really come.

21

It was less than a week before Alice would be home. I couldn't believe it was nearly two months since we had seen each other. I sighed. I had played that last night over and over in my head so many times by now that it had run raw. At least once a week I had gone to bed, exhausted from college, and just when I thought sleep was going to carry me away from my complicated world, there it was, that look of hatred in her eyes, me on top of her, inside of her, invading her . . .

I would awake with a start, shaking, sweat pouring over me. I dreaded nodding off again. But in those bad dreams, it was like there was someone else there too – another figure hovering just over my shoulder, as Alice looked up at me or it and froze in terror.

And then Alice had texted me a few days ago, saying that she wanted to meet up and explain. And while part of me was so relieved to get that message, I couldn't believe that after two months of torture, of troubled thoughts and that constant question of whether I should contact her, she could just send me a quick text, and suddenly everything was supposed to be OK?

'Paddy, your work just gave the impression of being very

distracted, or preoccupied with something else,' my tutor had commented when my grade had come in much lower than expected.

But what did I expect? I *had* been preoccupied. And I just hoped that when I saw Alice and got some explanation, that it would be enough.

*

It was May Week. An air of magic permeated Cambridge's ancient streets, shadow and light waltzing in time. It felt like here, anything was possible. We spent Monday on the Backs, drinking and sunbathing as all around us we watched the marquees and Ferris wheels being erected for the coming celebrations. Trinity was having its ball tonight, and while we weren't going, we were going to embark on a journey so many others did along the Cam, in a punt, to watch the famous fireworks.

'I still think we should break into the ball,' Henry declared as we wandered through Sainsbury's, stocking up for the evening's voyage. 'Danny said that one year he just dressed up and said he was a bongo player in the reggae band that was performing, and they let him straight in.'

'A reggae band?'

'Yeah.'

'I'm trying to decide which of you looks the least Jamaican, but honestly, I just can't choose,' I remarked, finding it hard to believe that such a tale was true.

'Whatever, Irish, you can ask him yourself. And Robbie . . .'

He stopped, but it was too late. 'Sorry,' he mumbled.

I smiled. It was OK. I couldn't ban people from saying his name, for God's sake. There were still no signs of him reappearing in Cambridge and hopefully it would stay that way. I couldn't deny how much better it felt to just step out of my door, down the stairs and into the radiant court-yard and know that there was no chance of him being there. No, he was nowhere to be seen now, not even in my dreams.

But I promised myself that even if he did show up tomorrow night at our ball, I would stay – and have the time of my life and that was that. He may have spoiled my rela-tionships, my self-esteem and the past six months of my life, but tomorrow night belonged to me and my friends, a night of hard-earned extravagance before we went our separate ways for the summer. I swallowed. I was not looking forward to saying goodbye. It was so frustrating that as soon as we'd put things right, it was time to split.

'Oi, loser, stop daydreaming and go get some plastic cups.'

I moved into the next aisle to do as I was told. Only there was someone in the way of my desired shelf – a confused figure clasping what I could vaguely make out as two different varieties of paper plates. One was a Barbie pattern, the other Cinderella. His face stared downwards, scrunched up with tension so the features contorted, struggling with this mammoth task. I didn't want to rush what was clearly a crucial decision, as his beady eyes flashed from left to right – from pink to pink – completely at a loss. I decided to put him out of his misery.

'I think Barbie's probably the safest bet – the Cinderella

ones might turn into pumpkins if the party goes on too late, you know.'

But my wit trickled away as his eyes met mine, the same kind eyes that had watched as I fled from the police station.

'Alice.'

He remembered.

I smiled, not knowing what to say. I wanted so much to tell him that despite the fact that our brief encounter had all come to nothing, he really had helped me – had started the forward motion of my revelation of the horrible facts. Strange and all as the circumstances were, I was glad I'd seen him again. Glad it had ended like this.

'I hope she likes them, Marty,' I said, glancing at his potential purchases.

'Eh . . . thanks,' he replied, face now a mix of confusion and shock.

I smiled one last time and walked away, paying for the plastic cups and heading out into the evening's glow to rejoin my friends. Clare Bridge loomed over our heads as we rammed our way through the chaos of wooden vessels which filled the river from bank to pristine bank. We huddled under blankets and sipped our cider, Trinity's vast columns illuminated by spotlights, while trails of fairy lights led black-tied ball-goers over the bridge to where more marquees awaited, crammed no doubt with all the indulgences one could ever imagine. On the far side of Trinity, St John's looked dull for the first time ever, fading into the darkness while its neighbour flaunted its excess.

We watched on, jealous, but every lavish image was a

mere tease for what was to come this time tomorrow, when it would be our turn.

'Ooh, that girl's dress is gorgeous.'

'Oh my God, there's the oyster tent.'

'Fuck oysters, how much fun do those bumper cars look?'

'Jesus, is that a real hot air balloon?'

We were like kids in a candy store, only the candy was up on the manicured banks, protected by patrolling guards, while we were nestled in the safety of our boats, rocking against the other plebs. I thought of Marty – of his ginger hair and his pink paper plates. I was glad he knew I was OK – that things were finally starting to go my way – that the hurt was starting to go away.

The fireworks took my breath away. But I made sure not to lose it completely, for this was only a practice – tomorrow was it, the grand finale, the night to remember. And most of all, the night to help me forget.

★

'Oh my God, Millie, these are so much better than Trinity's,' Henry shouted over the noise of the fireworks.

We were all enthralled by the event, with its concoction of scents which filled our nostrils at every turn, its sweeping marquees and hidden rooms.

'I love you,' I whispered into Henry's ear.

'I love you too,' he replied, kissing me so that just for a second I was a million miles away from the dazzling display.

But I came hurtling back with a bang, Sinatra's 'New York

New York' echoing out as the sparks flew up, perfectly in time to every beat.

'Is it working?' I asked Joey beside me, who was trying to figure out the video mode on his phone.

'I think so,' he screeched over a thunderous boom, holding his Nokia in the air, trying to capture the magic.

One particularly dazzling explosion made the air suddenly like day, brighter than bright, before warm, velvety darkness. But in the light, I had seen something I hadn't noticed before.

'Joey, what happened your hand?' I quizzed, spotting more than one nasty looking red mark on his knuckles. They looked fresh.

'Nothing,' he replied, switching the phone into his other hand and shoving the one in question straight into his pocket.

'When did you get that?' I persisted, trying to work out where he could have obtained such an injury.

'Ah, I think I got it the other night at the bop when I was drunk. Wow, that was a massive one,' he exclaimed, switching the focus back to the fireworks.

But as they glinted in his eyes, I could have sworn I saw just the flicker of something else, but what, I didn't know. I turned back round to watch, clutching Henry's arm and squeezing it tight. On his other side I could hear the distinct lilt of Irish 'oohs' and 'ahs' floating through the night. I hoped Alice was happy. I hoped we had done enough. And even though I knew she wanted to tell as few people as possible, she still needed someone back home who would share her secret too.

'Well like I said, I think I'm going to go to the Rape Crisis Centre to arrange a counsellor. And I'm meeting up with

Paddy as soon as I get back, so I think I'll tell him,' she had told me as we got ready tonight.

'And what's the story there? Do you think something might happen with you guys?' I didn't know whether that was an appropriate question or not, but I just wanted her to think about things properly. If she did tell Paddy, and then during the summer they got back together, where would she be if it went wrong again? I wasn't sure mixing romance with this was a good idea. I had never encouraged Joey to speak out about how he felt, despite the fact that I could tell it was chewing him up inside.

'I'm not sure what's going to happen, to be honest,' Alice had replied. 'My head isn't in the right place to think about any of that. But I am going to tell him. After what happened . . .'

'Just be careful,' I said.

I looked at her, her long black dress slinking to the floor. 'You look amazing,' I told her.

She stared at me, hesitant, as if about to say something but not sure how. But she didn't speak, just walked towards me and hugged me tight. It took me a second to respond, caught slightly off guard, but then I willingly returned the hug. She clenched me with such an intensity that I didn't know what to think. Was this her way of saying thank you? Or was she scared of leaving Cambridge, of letting go? I knew we'd keep in touch while I was in Thailand, and then, when I was back, there was talk of her coming over to London to stay for a bit. Either way, it would be a while before we could do this again. I prayed she'd be OK.

'OK, so what does anyone want to do next?' Alice asked

when the fireworks had finished, bright trails lingering across the jet-black sky.

'Let's go up to Hall for the buffet,' Henry said.

'But then we'll have no room for the chocolate fountains,' I pointed out.

'Eh, hello – it's a ball – we can have everything!' Henry replied.

'Eh, hello, you try squeezing into a size six!' I retorted at my greedy boyfriend.

'I think I need more champagne,' Joey said.

'Well, according to the map, there's Bellinis in the room beside Hall,' Alice said.

'What time's the band on?' I asked.

'Ooh, and we have to go to the casino,' Joey insisted.

'Not until I've rammed you up the ass with a bumper car,' Alice replied menacingly.

'Irish, I didn't think you were into that sort of thing.'

A new voice had joined our mix as we spun around to see the infamous Danny saunter up to where we stood. I could feel Alice stiffen. I took her hand.

'Having a good night?' I asked brightly, knowing the question which was on all our lips, but needing to put in some spadework before it could be asked.

Ever since we'd arrived, all of us had been quietly on the lookout for that one face we hoped we wouldn't find – it was like *Where's Wally*, only we didn't want to see the stripes. But now Wally's friend was here, and it was make or break – we needed to know the answer.

'Yeah, it's awesome. Have you found the hog roast yet?' Danny slurred, clearly pissed.

'No. That's beside the Martini tent, isn't it?' Joey said, flicking through his guidebook for the evening.

'I can't remember, but it's awesome . . . anyway, you ladies are looking lovely. Though Irish, I still think you should have come as a leprechaun again – that was bloody brilliant.'

'So did you manage to find Robbie then?'

Henry's question was so direct that it made me jump. Alice's hand squeezed mine. But I supposed it was only a significant question if you knew the truth, and our lips were completely sealed.

'Nope – 'fraid not, mate. Seems like he's just disappeared off the face of the earth. Wanker,' Danny replied, seeming less than impressed by his friend's antics. 'No one's heard . . .'

But we had all stopped listening, and the fingers which locked with mine could relax again.

'Right, well let's go get some grub then,' Henry announced, knowing we'd all heard what we wanted to or, in Alice's case, needed to.

But she didn't need to worry anymore. The only thing that needed to trouble her mind this evening was what luxury to indulge in next.

*

'Imagine we were playing for real money,' Alice teased my boyfriend later as she whooped his cocky ass at blackjack in the casino room.

'Ah, but you forget sometimes, Irish – I'm only after your lucky charms.'

The two of them giggled, while Joey and I watched on, having been less than successful with our faux gambling. The room was dark and smouldering, a live jazz band buzzing out. But I couldn't survey the surroundings too intently without surveying something else. I was trying to figure out whether Joey seemed distant or not, so I took the plunge and asked him if he was OK.

'Yeah, I'm fine,' he lied.

'Joey, I'm not an idiot,' I continued, lowering my voice and taking a step back to let some others join the table, separating us from where Alice and Henry stood.

'Look, I just . . . I just find it hard, OK?' he sighed, his eyes struggling to keep out sadness.

I didn't know what to say. Although her ways may have been rubbing off on me, I still knew that Alice would be much better at dealing with this. But I also knew she couldn't, because she was the problem, or at least, the matter.

'Have you thought about telling her how you feel?' I asked tentatively. He looked shocked, having never actually admitted his feelings to me, but I gave him a look that told him I knew. He sighed, too weary to object, his shoulders sinking as I knew his heart already had. Still I waited for his answer, hoping that he would say no. I mean, obviously he'd thought about telling her – judging by his demeanour he'd thought of very little else all night. But I still hoped he had the good sense to think better of it. It was better for all concerned.

'I wrote her a letter,' he admitted, not meeting my eyes.

My stomach lurched. What did that mean? Had he given it to her? Was he going to? I knew we had encouraged Alice to write to Robbie to tell him all the things she was feeling, but this was a different situation entirely. This was . . .

'Millie, relax. I'm not going to give it to her,' he said dejectedly, and I felt guilty for the massive relief which consumed me. 'I got rid of it.'

There was something in those eyes that didn't quite sit right with me. He was agitated, clutching his guidebook tightly in his hand, his wounded hand. Was it a cut? Or was it a burn? And how . . . but there had been enough questions already. And we'd all been through enough to even consider dealing with this as well. No, he would just have to suck it up and keep his lips sealed, and then over the summer he would find some nice Newcastle lass and all would be well. Because harsh as it may have sounded, his broken heart was nothing compared to our broken Alice.

*

The sun awoke just as I was getting sleepy. Millie and Henry had disappeared somewhere, but Joey and I still wandered from court to court, where morning bathed the fading guests in pale light and the smell of breakfast wafted in. We got a bacon roll and a Bloody Mary each. The night had been worth every penny. The past eight hours had been like nothing I'd ever experienced. But the fairytale was soon to end – there was only one hour left of the ball, and then on Friday I would be up in the clouds, heading back to Dublin, leaving it all behind. And though I was on cloud nine now, I prayed that these photos and these memories would help me from landing with a crash, and ease me through the transition of worlds that awaited me.

'Come on, there's no queue,' I pointed out, grabbing Joey's hand and running to the Ferris wheel, its neon lights much weaker in the dawn, but beautiful nonetheless.

We sat down as the old man in charge lifted his cap and told us to hold on tight. His wrinkled face looked unappreciative of the sun's growing strength, scrunching inwards with leathery creases as his hands pulled a lever.

'Did I mention I was afraid of heights?' Joey winked as we began to move.

I smiled. He had seemed a bit strange tonight, as if not everything was quite right. But I was sure that for him, like me, though the ball had been amazing, it still signified the beginning of the end. We rose higher and higher, flying upwards, the wind billowing up my dress as I shrieked with delight. It was an end, but it wasn't *the* end. In fact, it was a new beginning. We finally reached the top, gazing over the luscious trees and back into Cambridge town. I felt like a child in Disneyland, up in the sky, staring out at a fantasy kingdom. Only Cambridge was real. Not so long ago, it had been hell. It was strange how quickly things had changed. And yet, I was still wary. I had been here before, told myself that I was cured and that everything was fixed. But then it had all fallen apart. And a part of me wasn't entirely convinced that that couldn't happen again. My stomach lurched. The Ferris wheel jolted once more, hurtling us back to the ground, bidding the clear air goodbye. I wasn't cured, or fixed. I still felt weak, still dreaded having to go home and open up to Paddy, and a counsellor, my mother, maybe Róisín . . . my head spun at the very thought of going through it all again and again. I wasn't sure if I could do it. We had reached the bottom. Was that it? Surely not. But it was all or nothing. And I had *done* nothing. I had *had* nothing, I had *become* nothing. The Ferris wheel jerked, it had life in it yet. Its aged spokes began to spin, climbing again towards the squinting sky. I wasn't nothing anymore, I was something. And I had all summer to keep working on that something. The turrets whooshed by. When I looked back at my journey, on the past year of my life, I knew that I had gone into it and come out of it as two very different people, two very different Alices. I had been growing and shrinking and growing and shrinking, but finally, I was able to fit through that wooden door, to cross over into the next phase. Because as the wind buffered my hair and stung my eyes, I knew that this Alice was better. This Alice was real.

We were at the top again, staring out across my wonder-land at the most beautiful skyline I'd ever seen. Etched by time, this had taken years, decades, centuries to complete, and though it was time for me to go, in a few months I would be back, and this would all be here waiting for me patiently. I took Joey's hand in mine, but I didn't look at him. I looked at those other eyes, the eyes which had watched me come and go, the eyes which had seen me rise and fall. But now I was higher then ever, and I smiled out, praying it would last. The gargoyles smiled back, telling me it would. They promised. It was history.

★

She held my hand in hers, squeezing the knuckles; my stinging knuckles. I squeezed back, despite the pain. And it was enough, nearly enough. I closed my eyes. Almost.

And that's when I fell.

ACKNOWLEDGEMENTS

As always, this book would never ever have happened without Mum and Dad – from taking me to hot places so I could at least tan while on the laptop, or just generally putting up with a whole new stress level courtesy of the third-novel/university finals combo, your support will never fail to see me through.

To David, Julie-Ann, Sophie and Niamh – the girls, for making my brother's dreams come true, and David, for still being the very best of role models.

To the rest of my family, close and extended, near and far, alive or remembered, for keeping me sane, but not too sane, and backing me all the way.

To my almost-family: Debbie – 'the rock/upon which I stand'. There can never be a replacement (American or otherwise).

To all the Cambridge crew – my English buddies, the Cupids, Hattie and Heather, Luke and Luke, and of course, my rock in Gaul, Fitzy – for making the past three years beyond compare.

To all the gang at home – three years apart and still smiling – JP for life, Jay's Green Devil, and all my lovely ladies. Not to mention Campo and the many much-appreciated visits.

Wherever the next step takes us all, we still began together, and that's what really matters.

To Sheila – agent, friend, dinner-party hostess and fellow rugby fanatic – for taking all my dreams seriously.

To Patricia Scanlan – my book mummy – never too busy to give advice, time, brunch or candles.

To Ciara Considine, Breda Purdue and all at Hachette Ireland – for all your hard work and belief in me and Alice and how far we've come.

To Kate Howard and all in Hodder UK – for taking me to the next step, bridging the gap, and broadening my possibilities.

And lastly but most crucially:

To Ellen O'Malley-Dunlop, and all at the Dublin Rape Crisis Centre – for their untold generosity and dedication to such a worthy cause, and for opening my eyes and guiding me all the way – I only hope I have done you justice.